GETTING
Played

New York Times Bestselling Author
EMMA CHASE

Getting Played / Emma Chase – 1st ed.
Library of Congress Cataloging-in-Publication Data
ISBN-13: 9781093368857

CHAPTER
One

Lainey

June

Sometimes life surprises you.

I never really understood that expression. I happen to think life surprises us *all* the time. Every day. In big ways and small ways—awful ways and beautiful ways.

For some—like my Great-Granny Annie—just waking up in the morning was a surprise. *"The old ticker's still tocking. Isn't that nice?"* she would say as she waddled out to breakfast behind her walker.

Until the day she didn't waddle out to breakfast. Because Great-Granny Annie's old ticker had ticked its last toc. And even that was surprising, in its own way.

Sometimes it's the flower we spot growing through the sidewalk crack or the coffee spillage on our white shirt as we drive into work. It's the awesome sunglasses we thought we'd lost that show up in last year's coat pocket—or even better—

1

the twenty bucks we didn't know we had showing up in last week's jeans. It's the car accident, the lottery win, the call from an old friend, the Nickelback song we always secretly loved but haven't heard in forever coming on the radio.

It's all surprising—every moment. Life can be a bitch . . . but she's never boring.

A few weeks ago, I got a big surprise. The chance for my life to take a completely unexpected turn—and today is the day I sealed the deal. Signed the papers. Set my feet walking in a whole new direction.

I'm a lifestyle blogger. I post videos about interior design, fashion, skincare. The title of my blog even has my name in it—*Life with Lainey*. And now my channel has been picked up by Facebook and contracted to do a weekly web series for the next year. It's the biggest trend in social media entertainment and all the platforms are scooping up content providers, like me, and getting on board.

When I started blogging and posting videos a few years ago—it was a hobby—not a career path or anything I'd thought I could make money doing. But then, I started getting subscribers and followers—a lot of them. Next came advertisers and sponsors. And now, here I am, in this great bar down the Jersey shore with my sister and her boyfriend, celebrating this whole new chapter—this new unexpected adventure—in my life.

Surprise, surprise, surprise.

The best things in life always come along when we're not looking for them.

"Oh. My. God. How hot is he?" the woman next to me says to her friend.

Speaking of the best things in life...

"Sooooo hot," her friend sighs back.

They're talking about the drummer on the stage a few feet away. I know they're talking about him, because I'd bet my bottom dollar every woman in the bar—except my sister—is talking about him.

Despite the cheesy cover band name—Amber Sound—they're actually really good. And their drummer is outstanding. He's singing "She Talks to Angels" by the Black Crowes—singing *and* playing, which hardly any drummers do because it's super hard.

But this guy's a unicorn.

With great hands, a gorgeous mouth, sun-kissed hair and sculpted golden-tan arms that contract lusciously with every move he makes. His voice is warm and rough—like heated sand brushing slowly over your skin. And he's got an aura around him—the cocky, vibrant kind—that sucks in every woman within a ten-foot radius, like a hot alien tractor beam.

"He's looking this way!" the woman at the bar whisper-squeals. "He's looking right over here."

He *is* looking over here. Little excited sparks burst in my stomach—because the hot drummer guy has been looking over here a lot.

And I'm not the only one who's noticed.

"All these do-me gazes between Lainey and the drummer are giving me a second-hand boner."

My sister's boyfriend, Jack O'Shay, has picked up on it too.

"You wanna get freaky in the bathroom, Erin? A blow job would be awesome right now."

Jack has a unique, piggish kind of charm—it grows on you.

"Well, when you ask me like that, how can I resist?" The sarcasm is heavy in my sister's voice. "You're so romantic."

"I know." Jack grins, playing along. "But I'm storing up the big guns for after the wedding. You want the full Romantic Jack Experience, you need to let me slap a ring on it."

Erin and Jack have lived together for the last three years. For about half that time, he's been trying to get her to make an honest man of him. But before they hooked up, he was a dog—the man-ho kind—humping any leg that would let him. Although he's been the epitome of domesticated devotion ever since, there's a part of Erin that worries it's the chase that's keeping him around. That once she gives in, he'll lose interest.

Complicating matters more is they work together. Jack is an investment banker at Evans, Reinhart and Fisher, and Erin is the executive assistant to Jack's friend and the firm's golden boy, Drew Evans.

I've met Drew—he's a funny guy. Smart, successful . . . almost pathologically self-interested. He wasn't happy when Jack and Erin's one-night stand in Vegas didn't stay in Vegas, but evolved into an actual relationship. Drew made it abundantly clear that should things between them go south—*he's* getting custody of Erin.

He tried to put that in writing a few months ago.

The sounds of my sister and Jack debating the romance quotient of a bar-bathroom blow job fades into the background.

Because the drummer is looking at me again.

And I'm looking back—watching him, watch me. His gaze moves from the spiral curls of my honey-blond hair to my shoulders, lingering at my cream bo-ho knit tank-top, before dragging down over my light blue ripped jeans.

Then the corner of his mouth hooks into a sexy, suggestive, grin.

And my vaginal muscles clamp down in a needy clench that would make Dr. Kegel stand up and cheer.

I take a long sip of my drink, fanning myself—'cause Nelly knew what he was talking about—it's getting hot in here.

A moment later, the lead singer—a dark-haired guy in a leather jacket—thanks everyone for coming out, wishing us all a good night. I watch as the drummer stands up from his kit, talks to his bandmates for a minute—slapping hands and laughing. And then he's turning, stepping off the stage in loose, easy strides.

Walking straight to me.

And it feels just like an 80s movie—the swoony scene that always comes at the end—when the former plain-Jane-turned-prom-queen finally gets the guy.

"Hi."

He's even better-looking up close—his eyes are cerulean with flecks of green and gold. Ocean-blue eyes.

"I'm Dean."

Dean.

It's a good name. A player's name—a hot guy's name. It fits him.

I feel myself smile, a little giddily, a lot turned on.

"Hi. I'm—"

"Beautiful." He says it intensely. Like he means it. "You're really fucking beautiful."

And just like that I'm a puddle on the floor. Sold. Gone. Done.

His.

It's not that I'm easy—it's that Dean, the ocean-eyed drummer, is just that good.

He glances at the almost empty glass in my hand. "What are you drinking?"

"Vodka and sprite."

"Can I get you another one?"

I forgot about lust. I forgot the power of it—the pulsing, pulling, palpable connection that springs up between two people who are instantly attracted to each other. I forgot the excitement and fun of it. My heart pounds and my palms tingle, and for the first time in a long time, I feel reckless and young.

I feel alive.

"Sure. Another one would be great."

⎯⎯⎯⎯⎯⎯⎯⎯⎯⎯

Introductions are made and the four of us hang out for a while, chatting the way strangers in a bar do.

Then, expectedly, my sister yawns and announces, "We're gonna head home."

I glance at my phone. "You made it until eleven o'clock. That's a new record."

They're not known for their late-night partying, even on a Saturday night.

"I blame myself." Jack rubs the back of his red-haired head wearily. "All those years of ragging on Steven about being a homebody little bitch have come back to bite me on the ass."

I glance up at Dean, and he gazes warmly back with an invitation in his eyes.

"I'll hang here a while," I tell Erin and Jack. "I'll get an

Uber home later."

"Of course you will," Jack says. "It's like blue balls—if you don't get some after all the eye-fucking you two have been doing, you'll give yourself a migraine."

Erin covers her forehead with her hand. "Jack—stop talking about eye-fucking. You're embarrassing my sister."

Jack snorts. "What's embarrassing? Eye-fucking is a tried-and-true hook-up tool. It's how you reeled me in."

"I reeled you in by pretending like I wasn't interested." Erin smirks, lifting her chin and tucking her blond hair behind her ear. "Classic Jedi Mind Trick."

Jack lifts an eyebrow. "Or maybe, I took your Jedi Mind Trick and Inceptionated that shit by pretending I was only interested because you weren't interested—when really . . . I was interested all along."

Erin blinks.

We all blink.

"Did you?" she asks.

He smiles smoothly. "Marry me and I'll tell you on the honeymoon."

Erin shakes her head and laughs. Then she turns toward me.

"Do you have your TigerLady?"

A TigerLady is a self-defense device. It fits in your fist, with sharp little spikes sticking out between the knuckles to do serious damage to any dumbass, would-be assailant who wants to get touchy-feely. Erin bought it for me for my thirty-fourth birthday. She's only eleven months older, but she takes her big-sister role very seriously.

"Of course." I tap the Louis Vuitton backpack that I found at a yard sale last summer and bought for a tiny fraction of the retail price.

Erin looks at Dean. "No offense, you seem nice and all—but Ted Bundy seemed like a nice guy too."

He holds up his hands, his expression laidback and amused.

"None taken. Ted Bundy ruined it for all of us."

Jack steps up closer to Dean, chest out, eyes hard. He points from his forehead to Dean's face. "Photographic memory, dude." He tilts his head toward me. "Anything happens tonight that she's not okay with, I will hunt you down, find you, and literally nail your dick to the wall."

Wow.

Now I'm embarrassed. And I'm never going to get to have sex again.

"That's some vivid visualization you painted there. Nice job." Dean chuckles, shaking his head. "Listen, man, we're going to hang out, have a few drinks, have some fun. She'll be all good with me, I promise."

Jack stares a second longer, then nods.

Erin hugs me, like a blond Koala with separation anxiety—the drinks we had making us both rock a little on our feet.

"Thanks for coming with me today." I say against her hair.

"Of course! And congratulations—I'm so happy for you, Lain."

Then she's waving over her shoulder as Jack takes her hand and they head out.

Dean guides me to the bar with the press of his hand on my lower back. I hop up on the stool and he rests his arm against the shiny dark wood, leaning close enough that we can talk without raising our voices.

"What was the congratulations for, Lainey?" he asks.

I like that—the way he says my name—the way his mouth looks when he forms the word. It makes the sparks come back, but more—they spread out over my shoulders and down my arms to the tips of my fingers.

"A new job. Well, not exactly new—more like an upgrade." I wiggle my drink. "I'm celebrating."

He takes a drag on his beer bottle. "What do you do?"

"A little bit of everything. I'm a blogger and an entertainer—an aesthetician, an interior designer and a life coach. I try to help people live their best lives for less."

Dean takes all that in with a nod. "So you're like . . . a guru?"

"Yeah, I guess am." I smile. "You wanna join my cult?"

"I'd follow you." Dean looks deliberately at the back of my chair—at my ass. "If only to be able to keep watching you go."

He wiggles his eyebrows—because that line was so cheesy it should've come with a box of crackers.

And we laugh. He makes me laugh.

And everything after that is just really, really easy.

"So, Amber Sound—where'd that name come from?"

An hour later, Dean and I are still at the bar—still talking and drinking.

He slams back a shot of vodka before answering, "Okay—sophomore year in high school, me and the guys decide to start the band. And Jimmy, the lead singer, was dating this girl—Amber Berdinski—who he was dying to nail, but she wouldn't let him past second base. Amber tells Jimmy if he's really into her—he has to prove it. By getting a tattoo of her name. So—" Dean shrugs "—he did."

"No!" I gasp.

"True story. On his ass."

I cover my eyes. "Oh, my God."

"But then, Amber still won't bang him. She says if he's really, really double-dog-dare serious about her, he'll name the band after her."

I peek out between my fingers. "And he did."

Dean nods. "And Amber Sound was born."

"So what happened then? Did Amber give up the goods?"

"Nope." Dean laughs. "She dumped his sorry tattooed ass the day after our first show."

"Ouch." I cringe.

"By then, there was no turning back. We already had fliers made up and the name painted on the side of Doyle's—our lead guitarist's—van." He lifts his finger. "But there's a life lesson there. Never get a tattoo of a girl's name on your ass—"

"Or a guy's."

"Or a guy's." He nods, agreeing, "And never name your band after someone just so you can get down their pants."

"Words to live by." I tap his beer bottle with my glass and we drink to that.

The vodka and soda goes down like water now.

"You've been playing together since sophomore year? That's a long time."

"We get together only in the summers now, tour the regular spots that we've been playing for years. It's the breaks in between that have kept us from getting sick of each other."

He toys with the label on the bottle and I notice his

hands—big, strong hands—with clean, neat, nails at the end of long fingers that have just the right amount of girth. And I think about how those hands would feel on me, against my skin—everywhere.

Dean follows my eyes, maybe reads my mind. He takes my hand and opens my palm, lightly tracing my lifeline with the tip of his finger. A little sigh escapes my lips and my eyes close.

Then he taps gently on my hand, on my wrist, in a rhythm—a beat.

"Guess the song," he says softly.

I open my eyes and he's smiling. It's a teasing, playful smile that makes my knees wobbly.

"Guess," he coaxes, still tapping.

I close my eyes again, concentrating for a minute—and then it comes to me.

"'Video Killed the Radio Star'!"

"You got it." He laughs, nodding. "You're good, Lainey."

I don't really have any experiences with one-night stands or meeting guys in a bar. During my prime pick-up years, I was too busy working the night shift at the 24-hour Mini-Mart, and taking care of a boisterous baby boy during the day.

I always imagined a random hook-up would feel sleazy or cheap and awkward. But this—whatever this night is or turns out to be—it feels good. Seamless. Fun.

And for me, that goes down as another wonderful surprise.

I slide my open hand toward him.

"Do it again."

Another hour goes by and the bar is still hopping. The song "Sex and Candy" by Marcy Playground comes from the speakers—and I wonder if there's a "Marcy" out there somewhere that their lead singer wanted to bump uglies with.

The conversation between me and Dean flows easy—we talk about everything and nothing at the same time.

"If you could only listen to one song for the rest of your life, what would it be?"

He frowns—and even his frown is hot. Possibly hotter than his smile.

"Damn, that's hard."

I don't relent.

"Life's most crucial questions usually are."

He tilts his head toward the ceiling, exposing the enticing swell of his Adam's apple. And there's something so deliciously manly about it—I want to lean over and lick it.

But then he dips his chin, blocking my move. "Tom Petty's Greatest Hits."

"That's not a song—that's a whole album."

"That's my answer."

I poke the curve of his bicep—it's like prodding a warm, sexy, rock.

"That's cheating."

"Then I'm a cheater." He shrugs. "Screw it."

Later, we delve into each other's souls . . . kind of.

"Tell me something you hate," Dean asks, before downing his shot.

"I hate commercials where you have no idea what they're trying to sell you until the end."

His head bobs in agreement. "They suck."

"What about you?"

"I hate people who drive in convertibles with the top down and the windows up. Like dude . . . pick a side."

And he says it in such a serious, adorable way, I crack up.

Dean watches me, staring at my mouth, his eyes deepwater blue and enraptured.

"That's a great sound." He leans in. Closer and closer.

"What sound?"

He takes a curl of my hair, brushing it between his fingers thoughtfully. "Your laugh. It's a beautiful laugh, Lainey."

"Thanks," I say softly. "I work really hard on it every day."

His lips stretch into a full, chuckling smile. Then he grabs the bottle of vodka on the bar, tosses down a few bills and tilts his head toward the door.

"You want to get out of here?"

And I don't hesitate. "Yeah."

We shuffle across the back parking lot of the bar—holding hands, taking swigs from the bottle and giggling. Because alcohol is a time machine—it makes you young and silly.

Dean leads me up the steps to an apartment above a detached garage. "This is where we stay when we play at the Beachside Bar. But these days, Jimmy and the guys get hotel rooms with the wives and kids, so it's just you and me tonight."

He flicks on the lights revealing a small living room with a couch and television, and a tiny kitchen. It's sparse, and void of any real personality, but it's clean.

I follow him through the set of French doors that lead out

to a balcony, with two cushioned lounge chairs and a hot tub that overlooks a dark, wooded lot.

I nod, smiling. "Nice."

"I'm going to take a quick shower. You good here?"

I give him two thumbs-up. "I'm good."

Dean takes out his phone, fiddles with the buttons and sets it on the table, leaving Amos Lee to sing "Wait Up For Me," as he goes inside. And I soak it all in—the warm breeze, the way the moonlight shimmers on the trees, the smell of the ocean in the air, and the loose, languid feel of my bones.

Here, now, in this moment—life is really good. And when it's good, it should savored, enjoyed. Celebrated.

A few minutes later, the song changes and "Boardwalk Angel" plays from Dean's phone. I close my eyes, humming along, tilting my head up to the sky and spinning slowly in time to the music.

Until I feel him. I turn around and Dean is leaning against the door-jam, the heat of his eyes following my every move.

He's wearing jeans—shirtless—his hair a damp, dirtier shade of blond. The muscles of his arms and chest are long and taut, all beautiful swells and shadowed ridges. Little water droplets glisten on his shoulders and I'm suddenly very thirsty.

"Hi," I whisper, a little breathless because—*wow*.

His mouth does that sexy quirk thing.

"Hi."

Dean moves forward, eating up the space between us and I step in into his arms like it's the most natural thing in the world. His hands skim up my back, pressing me close, and mine slide down his arms—loving the warm, smooth feel of his skin beneath my palms.

And then we're dancing. Swaying together to this slow

song about the boardwalk and carnival lights and falling in love on a carousel. And there's a sweetness to the moment—a magic and tenderness—that I just might remember for the rest of my life.

"This is a good song. John Cafferty and The Beaver Brown Band."

I feel the chuckle that comes from his chest. "Most people would've said Eddie and the Cruisers."

I shake my head. "Not me. I know my music."

He strokes my hair down my back.

"What kind of music do you like, beautiful?"

"I like songs that tell a story. That make me feel. That make me remember. There's a song for every big moment in my life."

"Me too." He rests his chin on the top of my head. "When I was a kid, music always made sense to me, even if nothing else did."

"Yeah." I nod.

And he smells so good—like sandalwood and spice and a unique, clean man-scent that's just him. I want to run my nose across his skin—smelling up every inch of him.

When the song ends, our eyes lock. And I whisper his name, because I like the taste of it on my tongue. "Dean…"

He swallows harshly, his throat rippling, his eyes tracing my face.

"Lainey… *Jesus.*"

Then his mouth comes down on mine—hard and hot. His hands sink into my hair, angling my head, and a needy, frantic spike of pleasure streaks up my spine with every stroke of his warm, wet tongue.

It's a great kiss, the kind they write songs about. A movie-star kiss—that gets the audience all hot and bothered. The kind of kiss that deserves surging background music—a whole soundtrack—that goes on and on and on.

"I wanted to do this the second I saw you," he tells me between kisses.

I sigh against him, molding my body to his, warm putty in his strong, talented hands.

"I wanted that too."

His fingers dance across my rib cage, pushing my tanktop up and off. And the sensation of our bare stomachs pressing, my breasts rubbing against the hard heat of his chest, is nothing short of heaven.

"It was all I could think about the whole set. Walking off that fucking stage and kissing the hell out of you."

I wrap my arms around his neck—pulling him nearer, wanting him closer.

"Yes."

Dean's arm is an iron band across my lower back, lifting me off my feet, moving us into the apartment. He pushes me against the wall, grinding the unrelenting ridge of his erection against my pelvis. And it's so good—that mindless kind of good that's all instinct and no thought. An effortless intimacy that makes me tremble.

He holds my face in his hands when he kisses me—and I love that. The way his tongue delves deep, his fingers brushing my cheek, like I'm something precious.

His lips slide down to my neck, rasping against my skin.

"Lainey, are you drunk?"

"Yeah." I rub my cheek against the spiky stubble on his jaw, and moan with how damn good it feels. "But not too drunk. I know what I'm doing. I know what I want."

He straightens up and looks into my eyes, both of us breathing hard.

"Tell me." He sweeps his thumb against my lip, like he can't stop touching me. "Tell me what you want and I'll give it to you."

"I want you."

I skim my palm over the ripples of his abs into the front of his pants, cupping him, taking the hot, impossibly hard length of him in my hand and stroking up and down.

"I want this. I want to feel you inside me."

He groans, diving back in. "That's a great answer."

He kisses my breasts over the lace of my bra, sliding to his knees, nibbling my stomach on the way down. My jeans are unbuttoned, tugged down and off my legs.

"What do you want?" I ask, because I want to hear his words.

For a moment, he stares at the pale, pink lace of my panties.

"I want to make you come so many fucking times."

That sentence—and the rough, needy way he says it—almost makes me come all by itself.

Dean pulls me forward by my hips, pushing my panties aside, and puts his mouth on me. And he goes down on me like a guy who really, *really* likes going down on a woman. He takes his time, kissing me open-mouthed—swirling his tongue and sucking gently at my flesh.

Heat surges through my veins and it feels like the floor has left the building—like I'm about to fall, about to fly. My nails scrape the wall beside me for something to hold on to.

Dean's voice is low and husky. "You taste like fucking candy." He skims my panties all the way down and off, then he looks up at me—into my eyes. "Open your legs for me, Lainey."

And it's the sexiest moment of my life.

Until I do.

And Dean spreads me with his fingers, and drags his tongue up and down, slow and deliberate. He slides his fingers inside me, pumping his hand, and his tongue moves to my clit, making tight, hard circles over and over. I've never had an orgasm in this position—standing up—but Dean seems hell-bent and determined to make it happen.

His fingers, tongue and lips work me over in the same rhythm. And that decadent, telltale pressure starts low in my stomach, building and cresting and spreading out through my limbs.

"Oh, God," I whimper. "Oh, God."

My hips rotate all on their own, and I grip Dean's hair—pressing mindlessly against his face. The sensations claw and climb higher and higher, until a deep moan drags out of me that would make a porn star blush. And everything goes tight and pulsing and I'm plummeting with the pleasure—falling so hard, right over the edge.

Before I can come all the way down, Dean skims up my body, and I cling to him on shaky limbs as he lifts me off my feet, kissing me down the hall to the bedroom. He sets me on the bed, the blanket cool and downy against my knees. And I curl my way around him—like a cat worshiping her scratching post. I kiss his shoulders, his chest—everywhere I can reach.

I make a wet trail down his torso, tracing the lines of his abs with my tongue. I kiss the V of his pelvis—that sexy, sculpted indentation that disappears down the waist of his jeans. I rip at the button of his pants and push them down his hips because I've felt the massive bulge between his legs—and now I want to see it.

I want to taste it.

When his jeans are a puddle on the floor beside him, I'm not disappointed.

Dean's cock is beautiful. It seems silly to think of a dick as beautiful—but this one is. The kind that should be sketched in a high-level art class or described in vivid detail in a bestselling romance novel. It's big, thick, velvety smooth and rockhard, with a glistening rounded head that I want to feel between my lips and down my throat.

I wrap my hand around him, pumping, and then take him in my mouth, swirling with my tongue, leaving him nice and wet. I tighten my lips around his shaft, dragging back, then moving down again—all the way—until the head of his dick taps the opening of my throat.

"Fuuuck." His mouth opens on a groan above me. "That's so good." And the hot gravel of his voice turns me on even more.

I suck him hard, bobbing slow, taking him deeper, making it good for both of us. I clench my thighs—feeling the slippery heat between my legs, because he tastes so good.

Then Dean's gripping my upper arms, pulling me up, kissing me hard.

And I mumble out rushed words against his lips.

"I don't do this."

I don't know why I want him to know, but I do. That for me, this is something different. New. Special.

"I never do this, Dean. Ever."

"You should." He touches my cheek, my hair. "You should do this all the time. You're really good at it."

And then we're falling back onto the bed—a tumble of laughing limbs and moans. We roll around, mangling the sheets. Dean's body is a wonderland, and I explore every bit of it. And he plays me like an instrument. He teases and tortures me, strums his slick fingers between my legs, rubbing and petting, while his lips wrap around my nipple, sucking in long, slow drags.

Dean's a multitasker—and it's glorious.

Then he's climbing over me, kneeling between my spread thighs. I watch as he brings a condom wrapper to his mouth and tears it with his teeth.

"That's so hot." I moan, reaching for him.

It's like a whole new porn fetish category—I could watch this man rip open condom wrappers all night long.

He takes himself in his hand, his movements sure and confident, and rolls the latex down his length, pinching the condom at the tip. And he's so hard when he presses against my opening—so big when he pushes inside. We moan, long and low, as our bodies rock together.

All my senses are focused right there—where we're connected—on the surging feel of him filling me where I'm tight and wet around him.

Dean's head rolls back on his shoulders. "Your pussy is heaven." He holds my hip for leverage, thrusting. "Literal heaven."

And I love it. The sound of his voice, the color of his eyes, the taut contraction of his muscles, the relentless breach of his cock, the feel of his solid hips between my thighs. I love how his big hands hold my waist, lifting me, angling me to take all of him. I love how his spine curves and chin dips low, and how he watches himself disappear inside me.

I love it when he rolls us over, so he's flat on his back and I'm straddling him.

"Ride me." His voice is jagged and raw. "Ride me, Lainey."

And I love that too.

I straighten my back, arching, my hair falling long all around. And I swivel my hips and squeeze my muscles hard around him—he's so deep this way, and I want to feel every inch.

Dean grips my ass in his large hands, sliding me back and forth. And I love the way he looks up at me—the heavy-lidded heat in his eyes and the harsh rise and fall of his chest—that makes me feel every bit as beautiful as he said I was.

I love all of it. Every moment. This wild rollercoaster of perfect, aching, pleasure.

Dean lifts up, licking my breast, kissing my neck. Then he cradles the back of my head as he shifts again, taking us down, so he's on top. And he glides back and forth into me—riding me in smooth, steady strokes.

"Christ, you feel—"

He presses me into the bed, going deeper, fucking me faster—pushing the breath from my lungs with every thrust.

"I'm gonna come." His voice is a mirror of mine—urgent and clinging. "I'm gonna come so hard."

It's his words that get me there—those words.

A keening sound comes from the hollow of my throat, and I clasp at his back, wrapping my legs around his waist. It feels like a whirlwind is building inside me, swirling and stretching. *So close, so close…*

And he feels it too—I know it in the way his thrusts go wild, in how he rocks forward and forward, pushing like he can't get close enough, pressing in so deep I feel the liquid heat of him in my womb.

Golden stars burst behind my eyelids as perfect white-hot pleasure tears through my body and pulses in my veins. Dean drives into me one last time, groaning my name into my hair.

I come back to languid awareness with the feel of him nibbling on my lips. A minute later, I open my eyes to see that sexy, dirty-boy smile aimed down at me.

"I'll be right back." He pecks my nose. "Don't fall asleep."

I wiggle a little underneath him.

"After that, I think we've earned it."

"No." He braces up on his elbows, looking down at where we're still connected.

His hips slide forward in a shallow jab of a thrust.

And he gets hard.

Again.

Inside me.

"We'll sleep when we can't move. Right now, we're just getting started."

And it's official—in a past life, I must've been a very, very good girl.

My eyes creak open the next morning, only about a half hour after Dean let me close them. And I want the sleep—I need the sleep—I've earned *all* the sleep.

But my internal clock is an asshole, so once I'm up—I'm up.

I untwist myself from the cream sheet and slip out of bed,

leaving the sleeping hunk of warm sex machine behind me. I scurry around the apartment on a mini scavenger hunt for my clothes, and then I head for the bathroom. In the trashcan beside the sink, I notice the used condoms—a whole box's worth of used condoms—and I grin like the filthy girl I never knew I was, remembering how each one ended up getting gloriously used.

I guess if you're only going to have sex every five years or so, this is the way to do it. Like a camel—fill the hump.

The reflection of the woman who stares back at me from the mirror is wonderfully wrecked—tousled hair from strong, gripping hands, smudged makeup, swollen lips, flushed cheeks . . . shining happy eyes. There's a dark red hickey on my right shoulder—and I remember how that got there too. With my back to Dean's chest, his hand covering my breast, and his mouth latched on to that spot as he came deep inside me.

After cleaning up my face and using my finger and Dean's toothpaste to scrub away the morning breath, I step out of the bathroom. He lays on his back, one arm bent over his head, the other resting on his stomach, his spent cock—still impressive in its sleepy state—resting against his thigh.

And there's a pull—that magnetic connection—that nudges me to crawl my ass right back in that bed with him.

But I fight it. Because I don't know how these morning afters are supposed to work—but I know it always feels better to leave before being left. To get out when the getting's still good—to not overstay your welcome.

So, I sit on the bed and run my fingers through the thick blond hair that's sticking up in adorable angles.

His eyes open with a deep inhale of breath.

"Hey."

"Hey."

He starts to sit up . . . and then lays right back down.

"Shit, I'm still wasted." He covers his eyes with his forearm. "What time is it?"

The words just come out, I don't really think before saying them. "Early. But I have to go. My son has book-club at eight."

Dean drops his arm and blinks, looking up at me like he's not sure he heard right.

"You have a kid?"

"Yeah. Well, a teenager now."

Those ocean-blue eyes widen. "No shit?"

I nod, smiling. "No shit."

Dean clears his throat, but his voice is still scratchy. "Teenagers are cool. Amazing and totally irrational at the same time."

I chuckle. "This is true."

He glances around the room. "You want coffee? I can probably manage some scrambled eggs. Possibly toast if I really dig deep."

A sweet warmth fills me. Maybe I'm setting the bar too low, but the fact that he offered to make me breakfast instead of rushing me out the door like the scenarios my sisters have described, is nice. *He's* nice. More than nice.

And if I didn't already know it before, I do now—I like him so much.

But still, I shake my head.

"I already ordered a car. Stay in bed, go back to sleep. I can't do breakfast."

He nods slowly, his expression hard to read. He runs his fingertip gently up my arm. "Lainey, last night . . . it was intense."

The word comes out soft, tender.

"Yeah."

"And awesome." He meets my eyes, his mouth beautiful and earnest. "Last night was really fucking awesome."

I run my tongue over my lip, remembering the taste of him.

"It really was."

In the pause that comes after, I wait for him to ask for my number, if he can see me again. If I want to grab a coffee sometime or dinner—at this point, an invite to some vague future brunch would make me ecstatic.

But he doesn't.

And I guess that connection I felt was a one-way street.

Though disappointment creeps in, I refuse to let it take hold. Because last night was amazing and hot and perfect—and I don't want to taint it by hoping for more.

My phone dings with the notification that my car is here.

"I gotta go."

Dean leans up on his elbow. His other hand slides under my hair, gripping the back of my neck—and I love that too—the feel of his hand on me.

He brings me down close to him and he kisses me, slow and gentle, one last time.

His forehead rests against mine and he whispers, "Bye, Lainey."

I give him a smile. "Bye, Dean."

I grab my bag and head out the door, and don't tempt myself by looking back.

My Uber driver is a fan of Bob Dylan. I close my eyes and rest my head against the window as "It Ain't Me Babe" plays on repeat during the drive home to my parents' house in Bayonne.

The house is silent as I ease open the front door, knowing just where to stop before it creaks. I walk up the mauve carpeted stairs to my son's room—to check on him.

Rationally, I know Jason's fine and sleeping—and any time you open a fourteen-year-old boy's bedroom door without knocking, you're risking seeing things that can never be unseen. But it's a habit, a mom-compulsion I can't seem to shake.

He's on his side, wrapped in a cylinder cocoon of blankets with just his head sticking out, the way he's slept since he was two. He's got my honey-blond hair and delicate features. He's long and lanky right now, but he'll fill out.

I named him Jason after my dad. Because his father is an idiot, and a jackass, and not one of my better choices. He didn't want anything to do with us—when Jay was born or in any of the years since. But it's for the best—I don't want someone so stupid around my kid anyway.

I close the door softly and go to my room, changing into an oversized sweatshirt and worn yoga pants. Then I pad down to the kitchen.

A few years ago, my mom went through a cock phase.

She redecorated the kitchen in barnyard-red and white with rooster accents. It's not my taste, but that's a big part of my excitement about doing *Life with Lainey*. The hook of the web series is I'll be living in a house—an old house—while decorating it on a low budget, room by room, with my unique style and sparkling personality.

Jason and I will be moving at the end of the summer. It's

an amazing perk—the first time I'll have my own place, even if only just for the year.

I lift the tail of the cookie-jar rooster that I found at a yard sale in Hunterdon County, and take out a tea bag. Then Erin walks into the kitchen in gray polka dot pajamas and fuzzy purple slippers.

"What are you doing here?" I yawn.

"There was an accident in the tunnel and Jack didn't want to deal with the traffic. Plus, he gets a cheap thrill out of doing it in my old bedroom with my cheerleading trophies watching us from the shelves."

"That's one twisted puppy you've got there. You should definitely marry him."

"Is he paying you to say that?"

I nod. "Five bucks for every mention."

Erin looks me up and down as she sits at the table. "Someone looks like she got some last night. Did you just get home?"

I sigh in blissful satisfaction, the orgasmic endorphins still flooding my brain.

"I didn't just get *some*—I got it all. I had *all the sex*. The sweaty quick kind, the dirty rough kind, the slow lazy kind. It was ah-maz-ing."

"Good for you. Are you going to see him again?"

"Nah." I shake my head. "I didn't offer and he didn't ask."

And for just a second, I let myself feel the sadness of that. The regret and disappointment. Then I shake it off, breathe it out, banish it away.

"I've got too much going on anyway—with the move and the show and all."

"That's true."

Erin goes to the counter and starts to make her own cup of tea. "Hey—where's the house you and Jay are moving to again?"

Like I said before, life can be bitchy and she's never boring. Every once in a while—she also has a wicked sense of humor.

"It's a small town, south of here." I blow on the steam wafting from my teacup. "It's called Lakeside."

CHAPTER
Two

Dean

August

Most high school kids are good at one thing—sports, art, academics, being a smartass, getting high, the smooth-talking baby-politics bullshit of student government. They figure out whatever their "thing" is and congregate with other students who have the same talent. And then you have a clique.

"Dig, Rockstetter! Tuck your chin—move your feet!"

When I was a student here at Lakeside High School, I was good at a lot of things. I moved through cliques as easily as that X-Men mutant guy passes through walls.

"Why the hell are you looking behind you?! Keep your eyes on your target! That safety is gonna be right on your ass, you don't have to look back to check!"

I played the drums, taught myself when I was seven, so I was cool with the grunge crowd, the druggies, the band geeks and theater freaks.

"Left, Jackowitz! Your other left! The play is Blue 22—you go left! Run it again."

I had a good face, an athletic build. I'd discovered early that sex was awesome, so not only had God gifted me with an above-average sized dick—I knew what to do with it. That put me in good with the pretties, the popular kids, and especially the cheerleaders.

"Where's my offensive line? That's not a line—you're like Swiss cheese!"

I had great hands and quick feet—I could catch anything. That fact didn't just make me a football player, a wide receiver—around here, it made me a star. Anyone who tells you growing up a football God in a small town isn't fuck-all awesome is either clueless or lying to you. It's like that expression "money can't buy happiness"—it's entirely possible that it can't—but it sure as shit makes being happy a hell of a lot easier.

"Nice, that's how it's done, Lucas. Good job." Garrett Daniels—head coach of the Lakeside Lions, and my best friend, claps his hands. Then he calls downfield to the rest of the team. "All right, let's go! Bring it in!"

Garrett got sucked in by the teaching tick after his NFL quarterback prospects were shattered in a college game—along with his knee. He mourned the loss, then brushed himself off and came up with a new life plan. In addition to being able to coach the best sport ever, he gets a real kick out of teaching—from making history come alive for his students. His words, not mine.

"Twenty-minute break," Daniels tells the sweating gaggle of teenage boys that huddle around us. "Hydrate, get some shade, then we'll run drills for another hour and call it a day."

It was different for me. I had no illusions about being a *Stand and Deliver, Dead Poets Society*-esque, Mr. Keating shaper of young minds—that's not my style. But the pay is decent, the benefits are good, and the hours are a cakewalk. The summers off allow me to tour with the band I've been playing drums in since I was a kid, and being the football team's offensive coordinator lets me enjoy the smell of the grass and the feel of the pigskin in my hands. There's no downside.

Teaching lets me live life exactly how I want— uncomplicated, easy.

I like easy. Sue me.

"You just get back today?" Jerry Dorfman, former jar-head, current guidance counselor and defensive assistant coach asks me, as the players stream off toward the water cooler.

"Last night."

I tour the Jersey shore with Amber Sound from June til August, slipping back into town just in time for preseason practice.

"So . . . how was it?" Jerry nudges me with his elbow.

"Good. It was a good summer."

"Don't give me *good*—give me details. I'm married now. I have to get laid vicariously through you."

Don't let him fool you—Jerry wasn't getting laid before he was married, either.

Last spring he tied the knot with Donna Merkle, Lakeside's megafeminist art teacher. And, I'm saying this as a guy—when he's not on the clock or dealing with a kid— Jerry's a pig. The whole faculty and student body are still pondering the mystery of how the two of them happened.

"What's the matter—Merkle holding out on you?" I ask.

"Hell no." He runs his hand down his "Dad-bod". "My wife can't resist this fine piece of male specimen. But . . . there's no harm in hearing about your adventures in punani-land."

Punani-land? And the guy wonders why he's not getting any.

"Yeah, Coach." Mark Adams, the fresh-faced team trainer and newbie gym teacher, agrees. "When I went here, we all knew you got more ass than a toilet seat." He makes the *Wayne's World* "we're not worthy" gesture. "Teach me your mighty player ways."

I'm not *that* much of a player. Not anymore.

Back in high school, in my twenties—sure—that was another story.

These days, I'm all about keeping it straightforward, casual, good. I think friends with benefits is the greatest invention of the twenty-first century. I don't lie or do headgames, and I don't do relationships—there's nothing easy about them.

But that's the thing about small towns—who you used to be sticks forever—even if you're not really that person anymore. Although there are worse things to be than the town player. And, I don't want to disappoint the fans.

So, I smirk. "Well, there was this one girl."

Jerry rubs his hands together and Adams pumps his fist. Garrett's there too, but he stopped giving a damn about my sex life decades ago.

"Was she hot?"

My eyes roll closed in awe.

"Smokin' hot."

With endless legs that felt incredible squeezing my waist,

a pussy that tasted as sweet as cotton-fucking-candy, silky honey-gold hair that looked real pretty wrapped around my hand, and these big, innocent, sparkling hazel eyes that could rip your heart out.

And her laugh . . . it was long and light—the kind of sound that pulls you in, makes you want to laugh with her.

Lainey.

Last name—unknown. Number—unknown.

With that thought comes the sharp kick of frustration that nails me right in the gut. Because if I'd been more than half awake, or sober, I would've asked for her number.

Goddamn it.

Typically, in the summers one bite of the apple is enough for me—there's a lot of fruit on the trees. But I definitely would've gone back for another taste of her.

"Was she a freak in the sheets?" Adams asks.

"I bet she was a deep-throater," Jerry adds. "Nothing's more glorious than a woman without a gag reflex."

And it's weird. Normally I don't have a problem with Jerry and Adams talking like two pervy asshats, but hearing them direct this shit at Lainey seems all kinds of wrong.

There was something about her—a sweetness, a charm

. . .

"I never do this, Dean. Ever."

. . . that makes me feel protective. Proprietary.

"We had a good time." I shrug, blowing it off. "Like I said—it was a good summer."

Jerry and Adams open their mouths to argue, but I swiftly cut them off with a stern, "Enough."

Just then, the dark-haired captain of the cheerleading squad—Ashley Something—jogs up to Garrett, who's been ignoring the whole exchange.

"Coach D, can we use the field to practice our half-time routine while the team's on break?"

"Sure." Garrett checks his stopwatch. "We've got about ten minutes left."

"Thanks!"

Ashley bounces away and a few seconds later, a flock of cheerleaders take the field in a square formation, decked out in blue-and-gold uniforms.

Teenagers today have a thing for the 80s aesthetic. The style, the music—thank God, not the hair. My theory is they subconsciously long for the old-fashioned days they've heard their parents talk about—before electronics and social media ruled the world.

"Mickey" by Toni Basil pounds out of the field speakers.

And the cheerleading squad starts to dance.

But . . . there's nothing old-fashioned about it.

There's some hip shaking, a little skirt flipping . . . then things get weird. When they start sucking their fingers into their mouths, turning around and smacking their own asses—then smacking each other's asses—swirling their hips and kicking their legs like they had a high-paid pole dancer for a choreographer.

"I'm uncomfortable with this," Jerry says in a stunned voice. "Is anyone else uncomfortable with this?"

I raise my hand.

Garrett—whose wife's fifteen-year-old niece is one of the cheerleaders shaking their shit out on the field—raises his hand higher.

Young Adams looks conflicted.

Because when male teachers have reached a certain age

you look at your female students sort of like you'd look at your sister. On a basic level, you recognize that they're hot—young, pretty, perky in all the right places—but they don't turn you on. You're not attracted to them.

Because they're *kids*.

It doesn't matter if they're technically eighteen, or if they pass around nudes like goddamn baseball cards . . . they're still naïve, clueless *kids*. All of them.

In some ways, these kids are more kids than we ever were.

In one synchronized move—the cheerleaders strip off their sweaters—leaving them only in tiny skirts and gold bikini tops, with the word "Score" written across their chests in big blue letters.

"Whoa!"

"Jesus!"

"Where the hell is McCarthy?" Garrett looks around. "No way she's gonna let this slide."

No sooner does he say her name than she does appear—like the devil.

Michelle McCarthy has been the principal at Lakeside High School for forever. She hates me—I'm pretty sure she hates all of us. When I was a student I thought her high-strung frustration was entertaining—but now, as an adult—I think she's a goddamn riot.

Miss McCarthy marches out onto the field, waving her arms, her pudgy cheeks ripe tomato-red, and her meek, hunched assistant, Mrs. Cockaburrow, following behind her like a docile indentured servant.

"No—no—shut it down! Shut. It. Down!"

The music cuts off and the cheerleaders look crestfallen.

"There is no stripping on the football field!" McCarthy declares. "Where's Ms. Simmons?"

Kelly Simmons is the special-ed teacher and cheerleading advisor. Back in high school, she and I used to bang each other's brains out—in-between relationships with other people, and sometimes during those relationships. She was the hottest girl in school and kind of a bitch. Now she's the hottest teacher in school, and still kind of a bitch.

"She's in the parking lot with her husband," one of the cheerleaders volunteers. "I think they're having, like, marital issues."

McCarthy's finger swings like an axe in the air. "Regardless—you're not doing that routine on the field. Clothes stay on. You're students, not strippers!"

Ashley stomps her foot. "Strippers are people too, Miss McCarthy."

"Not in high school, they're not!"

Lucas Bowing, our starting quarterback walks up next to me. "I don't see what the problem is. I think they looked good."

Beside him, sophomore defensive end Noah Long stares hypnotized at the bikini-topped girls. "Yeah. Mickey is F-I-N-E, fiiine."

Then they both start dancing, and grunting, and swinging their hands as if their tapping imaginary asses.

"For God's sake, stop twerking," I order. "Badly—I might add. You're supposed to be hydrating, go drink some frigging Gatorade."

As he moves to go, Long lifts his chin in the direction over my shoulder. "Hey Coach—Dork Squad's looking for you."

I turn around and spot three of my students standing at the fence.

I teach Honors and Advanced Placement Calculus around here. I have a genius level IQ—some guys will say that just to get in your pants—but for me it's actually true.

Math was another thing I was good at in high school. I loved it, I still do—the symmetry and balance, the patterns I could see so easily. There's a beauty to a solved equation— like a symphony for the eyes. It's another reason teaching ticks all the boxes for me.

"Lay off the Dork Squad." I stare hard at Long. "Any of you screw with them, I will drill you into oblivion. If you guys act like dumbasses, trust me, I will run you like dumbasses."

My students are considered the easy kids by other teachers. They're invested in their grades and they're smart—but they're also fragile. Because they're different. At a place and time in their lives when different isn't an easy thing to be.

So I make it my mission to look out for them.

Long shows me his palms.

"Nah, Coach—the Dork Squad's cool. The Mathletes are the only reason I passed algebra last year."

The Mathletes is an academic club I supervise. They tutor other students free of charge and travel from school to school to do battle in mathematics competitions. Sometimes, the math games are just as brutal as the football games—sometimes more.

"Good. Make sure you spread the word."

I turn and trot over to the fence.

"Hey, Coach Walker."

"Yo, Coach W!"

It's Louis, Min Joon and Keydon—juniors—I had them

all last year and they'll be in my class again this year.

"Students." I nod. "How's it going? You guys still have a few days of summer left, what are you doing here?"

"We wanted to check out the renovations to the private study rooms in the library. They're dank—Miss McCarthy didn't scrimp." Keydon answers.

"How was your summer?" Min Joon asks. "Did you play with the band?"

"I did. And it was awesome as always. How about you guys—did you do anything cool?"

Most teachers have to ride their students' asses to make sure they do their schoolwork. I have to ride mine to make sure they do something—anything—*besides* schoolwork. So they have fuller, fleshed-out lives—and so they don't consider offing themselves if they don't make valedictorian.

I joke around, but . . . that's a genuine concern for my kids. One I take serious as fuck.

"I took a couple summer classes at Princeton," Louis says. "Just to keep myself fresh."

"O-kay. Did you meet anyone interesting?"

"The professor was nice. On the last day I gave him a list of strategies that I thought would make him a more effective instructor."

"I'm sure he appreciated that."

Right before he set the list on fire.

"I did the YouTube Up All Night challenge," Min Joon offers. "I was awake for forty-nine hours, thirty-seven minutes. It's a record."

"You gotta sleep, Min. At your age, you grow when you sleep—that's why you're so damn short. Sleep, dude, it's not hard."

I look to Keydon. "What about you?"

"I did a physics program in London with a hologram of Stephen Hawking."

"You spent your summer in a basement in England with a computer-generated image of Stephen Hawking for company and you're happy about it?" I ask.

He smiles broadly. "It was righteous."

I press my thumbs into my eye sockets.

"I have failed you. Utterly and completely failed you."

They laugh—they think I'm being funny.

"But it's okay." I clap my hands, regrouping. "We'll work on it this year."

"Are we gonna go over the summer packet on the first day?" Louis asks excitedly. "It was way hard—I loved it."

"Yes." I breathe out heavily. "We'll go over the packet on the first day."

Louis holds up his hand with his pinky and pointy finger extended and his tongue sticking out—the nerd version of the heavy-metal horns gesture.

I shake my head. "Don't do that."

Garrett blows the whistle behind me and the team takes the field.

"I gotta go—get out of here."

"Okay—bye, Coach!"

"Go play a game that's not Fortnite," I call after them. "Swim in the lake, talk to a girl—not about school."

They wave, nodding—most likely not listening to a damn word I just said.

"Rockstetter's worried about his grades—and Jerry agrees. The kid's not the brightest bulb in the box. We need to get him a tutor for his real classes and some easy-A electives to build up his confidence. He needs to keep his GPA up so he can play the full season."

After practice me, Garrett and Garrett's wife—Callie formerly known as Carpenter—are hanging out in his office.

Garrett and Callie were the "it" couple back in high school. If the dictionary had a word for first-love that ended up being true-love, Garrett and Callie's picture would be right next to it.

They broke up when she went away to college, then picked up right where they left off when she blew back to town a few years ago. They're married now and didn't waste any time on the procreation front. They have an awesome eighteen-month-old son, Will, who thinks I'm the shit and Baby D number two is already on the way.

Garrett looks up from the papers on his desk. "What do you think, Cal? Can you fit Rockstetter into one of your classes?"

Callie worked for a theater company in the years she lived in San Diego—and now she's the theater teacher at Lakeside.

"What are you saying? That theater isn't a real class?" She crosses her arms—a classic female warning sign. The equivalent of a dog showing its teeth, right before it bites you on the ass.

"That's not what I meant."

"You think it's an easy A?"

Garrett hesitates. Like any guy who doesn't want to lie to his wife, but knows if he tells the truth it could be days before he gets another blow job. Possibly weeks.

"Maaaaybe?"

"My class is demanding. It pushes emotional and intellectual boundaries. It gets the kids out of their comfort zone."

"Of course it does." Garrett nods. "But . . ."

It's the "but" that gets us in trouble. Every fucking time.

". . . they're just singing and jumping around on a stage. It's not rocket science."

"Tossing a ball around on a field isn't rocket science either."

"Wait, wait, hold up—what do you mean, 'tossing a ball'?" He puts his hand over his heart, like he's trying to keep it from breaking. "Is that what you think I do?"

Callie rolls her eyes. "No, Garrett. I think you are master of gravity and propulsion."

"Thank you."

"And your arm is a lethal, precise weapon of victory."

"Okay, then." Garrett grins. "Glad we got that straightened out. You had me worried, babe."

Callie hops off the desk. "I'll talk to McCarthy. We can put Rockstetter in my fourth period theater class—but he's got to do the plays. I always need more guys on stage."

I lift my hand. "And I'll set him up with some nice, patient, tutors."

Callie nods, then says to Garrett, "I'm going to head out, pick up Will from your parents and stop at Whole Foods to grab something for dinner."

"You shop at Whole Foods?" I ask, grinning.

"Yeah, all the time."

You can tell a lot about a person from where they do their grocery shopping. You got your basic, no-nonsense, working-class grocery-shoppers—teachers, cops, anyone who comes home from work dirtier than when they left. They stick with ShopRite, Krogers, Acme, maybe a Foodtown. Then you got your Wegmenites and Trader Joe-goers—housewives, yoga-class takers, nannies and their whiney charges. And finally, there's the Whole Foodies. We're talking hard-core high-maintenance—the vegans, the gluten-frees, artists, people with life coaches and personal trainers, and apparently . . . the Callies.

Garrett pinches the bridge of his nose, 'cause he knows he's about to get ragged on.

"Do you guys, like, make goo-goo eyes at each other over an organic quinoa avocado salad at the café?" I ask.

Callie's brow furrows. "Sometimes. Why?"

I look down at my best friend. "That's adorable, D. Why didn't you tell me you were a Kombucha-man? Now I know what to get you for your birthday."

Garrett flips me off.

"You guys are so weird." Callie kisses her husband, then sweeps out the door.

I shake my head at Daniels. "You married a Whole Foodie, dude."

"Yeah, I know." Garrett tilts his head, looking out his office door, staring at his wife's ass retreating down the hall—wearing the same goofy smile that's been stuck on his face since the day Callie Carpenter came back into town. "Best damn thing I ever did."

After checking out my classroom to make sure it's good to go for the first day, I hop in my car and head home—giving a beep to Oliver Munson when I pass him on Main Street. Ollie's a fixture around Lakeside. He suffered a brain injury as a kid and now spends his days hanging out on his front lawn, waving to cars and passersby. It's not as sad as it sounds—Ollie's happy and he's cool—and the whole town thinks so.

I pull into the driveway of the Depression-era colonial on 2nd Street that I've called home my whole life. It's old, almost all the houses in Lakeside are old—but I make sure I keep it up—the grass is cut, the roof is solid, and the white paint is clean and unchipped. I walk through the door, toss my keys on the front table—and go completely still.

Waiting. Listening.

For the sound of my prowling archnemesis.

I spot her head peeking around the living room wall—her eyes glowing like two yellow embers, her fur as black as a monster's soul.

Lucy—or Lucifer for short—is the only pussy I've ever met that didn't like me.

Grams found her a couple Octobers ago, and got duped by her meek meows and pitiful purrs. It's been a War of the Roses between us ever since—with me doing everything I can to keep her away from my shit and her finding new and creative ways to get into my room so she can shred my pillows and piss in my shoes. And any time Grams isn't looking, she tries to scratch a chunk out of my ass. The only thing she hasn't messed with yet is the drum set downstairs in the basement I soundproofed myself. She knows that's a red line for me—she lays one claw on those drums and it's a one-way ticket straight to the dog park.

Lucy hisses, baring the double-barrel needles she's got for teeth.

And I give her the finger—with both hands.

"Is that you, Dean?" a papery voice calls from upstairs.

"Yeah, Grams, I'm home.

I live with my grandmother—or more, these days, Grams lives with me. She raised me, which wasn't always an easy thing to do, so I make sure she has it easy now. She's shrunken and wrinkly—but as feisty as ever.

I keep one eye on Lucy and head into the kitchen, pouring myself a glass of orange juice.

"I was just on my way out," Grams says, shuffling into the kitchen.

"Where are you headed?"

"To the senior center to work out."

That's when I notice her black leggings, T-shirt, the Jane Fonda-era leg warmers covering her calves and the tiny, half-pound, hot pink weights clenched in her aged hands.

"Work out?"

"Yes. That nice girl from Workout World is coming to show us how to lift some steel."

I run my hand across my mouth—because Grams doesn't appreciate being laughed at. And she may be pushing eighty, but she can still tug on a smartass's ear like nobody's business. And that shit hurts.

"You mean pump iron?"

"That too." Her voice changes to a Hanz and Franz accent from the old *Saturday Night Live* skit, and she strikes a body-builder pose. "She's gonna pump us up!"

Gram slowly leans over to tie her sneaker, but when it becomes a struggle for her to reach, I crouch down and do it for her.

"I have to keep my girlish figure," she explains. "The

GETTING *Played* | 45

Widower Anderson has been giving Delilah Peabody the eye."

Lakeside has a very active senior center community—there's drama, cliques, studs, mean-girls—it's just like high school. But with pacemakers.

I straighten up. "You tell the Widower Anderson if he breaks your heart, I'll kick his ass."

The Widower Anderson is, like, a hundred years old.

"Or . . . steal his cane."

Gram pats my cheek. "I will, Deany."

A horn honks outside.

"Ooh! That's the bus." Gram picks up her weights and hobbles toward the door.

"I'm going to the store," I call after her. "Do you need anything?"

"The list is on the fridge."

I move to the fridge to grab the list, and as soon as the sound of the front door closing reaches the kitchen—Lucy comes out of nowhere—launching herself at my leg with a piercing screech I'll hear in my nightmares.

But, like I said—I'm quick—so I hop away from the flesh-tearing claws before they can sink into my skin.

"Not today, Lucifer," I taunt her from the back door. "Not today."

The Stop & Shop at Lakeside can sometimes feel like a high school reunion. Or an impromptu back to school night. You run into students, parents of students, old classmates.

Tonight's pretty quiet though, and I don't see anyone, until I'm in the checkout line. When a familiar voice comes from behind me.

"Hey, Jackass."

Debbie Christianson and I dated for a month our junior year of high school. She was super into me—until she caught me screwing around at the house party she threw while her parents were out of town. With her best friend. In her room. In her bed.

Did I say I was a player in high school? There were times when "prick" would be a more accurate description.

But, you live and learn and grow the hell up.

And it all worked out—after graduation, Debbie went to Rutgers, the same as me, and we ended up being really good friends. The kind without the benefits.

"Debs! How's it going?" We hug, and I wiggle my finger at the blond toddler in Debbie's arms. "Hey, pretty lady."

"Good—we're good. Wayne got a new job in the city, so I switched to part-time at Gunderson's so I can have more time home with this one." She bounces her daughter on her hip. "How about you? You ready for another year at Lakeside? I hear the football team is looking stellar."

"Yeah." I nod. "It's gonna be a good . . ."

My voice trails off. Because something catches my eye at the customer service counter.

Someone.

It's a woman, one I haven't seen around town before. Nice legs, great ass, with long, golden spirals that cascade down her back—calling to me—like the ghost of summer's past.

My hand literally twitches with the remembered feel of those satiny strands sliding through my fingers. And I take a step toward her—this weird, surging feeling filling up my chest.

But then she turns to the side. And I see her profile.

And the surging feeling freezes, cracks, and drops in pieces to the floor.

Because she's not who I thought she was. Not who some crazy, ridiculous part of me that I don't even recognize—was *hoping* she was.

Debs looks from me to the chick at the counter and back again.

"You okay, Dean?"

"Yeah." I shake it off. "Yeah, it was just . . . it was a weird summer. But I'm all good—you know me."

"Yeah." Debbie nods slowly. "I do."

In college, Debs used to joke that if I ever fell hard for a girl, it was going to be epic. Like watching one of those giant Redwoods in Washington State getting chopped down at the base. *Timber!* And she'd hoped she had a front-row seat when it happened.

The checkout girl gives me the total for the groceries, and I pay and put the bags in my cart. Then I turn back and give Debbie's shoulder a squeeze.

"It was good seeing you. Take it easy, okay?"

"You too, Dean." She waves her daughter's hand at me, and the cute little girl grins. "We'll see you around."

I walk out the automatic sliding door, mentally bitch-slapping myself.

I gotta get this girl out of my head. It was *one* night. And sure it was a great night, mindblowing—screwing Lainey was like sunshine, and rainbows, and scoring an 80-yard game-winning touchdown—everything fucking is supposed to be.

But it's not like I'm going to see her again.

I need to let it go. I need to get laid. Everybody knows the best way to get the big head straightened out is to get the little head some action—Confucius said something very similar.

I'll swing by Chubby's this weekend—it's always a lock for a sure thing. Or, I can text Kelly. If her and her husband really are splitting up, hanging out could be just what the doctor ordered for both of us. Just like old times.

CHAPTER
Three

Lainey

August

E ven though it's taken the contractors two months to make the house suitable for human occupancy, moving day creeps up and arrives fast. Early in the morning, when the sun is just peeking over the horizon, Jason and I drive down the long winding road of Miller Street to the end, and pull into the driveway of what will be our home for the next year.

The place is about three hundred years old and was boarded up for a few dozen decades. It's a three-story colonial with a full wraparound porch. The aged red bricks are now covered with cheerful, butter-yellow siding, and the trim and shutters that frame the floor to ceiling windows have been painted in fresh, pristine white. I'm going for a warm and inviting nautical look, to complement the house's lakeside location.

We step out of the pickup truck and Jay and I stand beside each other—taking it all in. There's an early morning mist drifting off the lake, surrounding the house. The air is silent and a lonely goose drops down from the sky, making a soft ripple on the still water as it touches down.

"So? What do you think?"

Jason glances around, his hazel eyes surveying. "I think it looks like the set of a horror movie."

In retrospect, letting Jay watch the *Friday the 13*th slasher film marathon when he was nine was not the wisest mom-call I've ever made.

And now that he's said it—I admit, there is a bit of a Camp Crystal Lake vibe to the property. Plus the dock in the back, as well as the round window on the top attic floor are straight out of *Amityville Horror*.

"There's a lot of trees," Jaybird notices.

Bayonne has an urban landscape, more city than town—and while Lakeside is only a two-hour drive away, it could be a whole other, countrified world.

"Trees are good. You'll get used to it." I jiggle the house keys. "Let's check out the inside and bring this stuff in. I want to set up and record before everyone else gets here."

When I duck back in to grab a box from the backseat, a wave of nausea washes through me.

I've been drinking too much coffee lately and my stomach isn't happy about it. I take a bottle of ginger oil from the center console and sniff it, then sprinkle a drop on my tongue to settle my stomach. Essential oils are a gift from the gods.

Jason and I plop our boxes in the foyer and give ourselves the tour. It's a stunning home, with gleaming refinished hardwood floors, an open floor plan and tons of beautiful, natural light. Except for the top-of-the-line appliances in the kitchen, the space is devoid of any furniture—that was the deal. I'll be designing each room, adding every perfect piece myself. Some will be donated by advertisers in return for product placement—but to make the looks realistically attainable for my viewers, I plan on finding most of the furniture on my yard sale excursions, off Craiglist, or building them from the ground up.

The molding in the house is original, and the sheet-rocked walls new, bare and eggshell-white—totally blank canvases just waiting for me to bring them to life.

I'm Dr. Frankenstein—but prettier—and this house is going to be my monster.

On our way up the curved oak staircase to the second floor, Jason says, "Oh—I balanced the checkbook last night."

"I told you, you don't have to do that."

"I know." He shrugs. "I just like doing it."

Jason is like an old man in a fourteen-year-old's body. I used to worry it was because my parents had such a big hand in raising him—but now I understand, he's just an old soul.

"The first payment came in from Facebook," he adds. "It's a nice chunk of change. We should put it into a money market fund, diversify our portfolio—maybe open a 529 for me for college? I'll do some research."

And he's smart—really smart. I don't know where he gets it from. I did okay in school, but for Jason, academics are his thing. His innate talent.

In Bayonne, he wasn't bullied—I would've been cracking skulls if he had been—but he was…isolated. The other kids didn't get him. He didn't have a crew or a tribe. That's why he was okay with moving to a new town at the beginning of his junior year.

And it's why I think this is going to be good for him—that here, in Lakeside, maybe he'll find his people.

"Wow—can I have this room?"

There are five bedrooms in the house—we're in the back, left corner one, on the opposite side from the master suite. It has its own connecting bathroom, but more importantly to my Jaybird—there's a built-in window seat that overlooks the lake. Jason's a reader, a studier, and I can already picture him sitting there with his e-reader and online textbooks for hours.

I nod, seeing the decorating future in my head.

"What do you think of colonial-blue for the paint color? And a couple wide oars for shelves, in distressed cream, maybe a rustic ship wheel for there on the wall? There's a carpenter in town, I was going to swing by his shop to see if he has scrap pieces we can take off his hands to build your headboard, and maybe a desk."

Growing up, I was my father's sidekick. His little helper. And, because money was always short, he's a handy, resourceful guy. He taught me the ways of power tools, house repair, automotive maintenance . . . and now, I'm handy too.

My son smiles brightly—and right then and there, my whole day is made.

"Cool."

It takes me a little over an hour to get the tables and chairs and decorations set up in the backyard. I take several pictures to post later to the *Life with Lainey* Instagram and Twitter accounts, then I adjust my tripod and set up my phone to film the show's first live broadcast.

Some of my videos are prerecorded and edited—but this one, I wanted to do live. So the Lifers can experience this moment with me, feel the authenticity through the camera. That's what my viewers are looking for—a connection. They want to feel like they're part of the action, part of the experience, a part of my life. And in a very real way, they are.

I tuck a blond curl behind my ear, look into the camera, and hit record.

"Hi, Lifers! The big day has finally arrived! Moving day is here! I'm going to show you the property in a second, but first I wanted to talk about the logistics of moving. Anyone who's done it knows it's a nightmare and the cost of a good moving company can be extreme. So, because I'm always looking out for your bottom line, I'm going to show you how to move for less. The key to that is . . . a moving party! You get every friend and family member with a car to get on board and help you move—and label your boxes ahead of time with who's taking what—to be sure that what everyone is moving will fit in their car. If you promise them a party afterwards, they'll be more excited to help you out. If you make it fun, they will come."

I stand behind the camera and pan the shot across the party area I've created on the back patio—and I also keep my eye on the number of viewers watching the post live. I've done a pre-launch marketing campaign online, so the viewers watching and liking the live video are already over one hundred thousand and climbing. My advertisers will be pleased.

I zoom the camera in—focusing on the folding chair and table settings—and talk behind the shot in a voice-over.

"Remember what I always told you—the only difference

between shabby and shabby-chic is looking like you meant to do it. I chose teal-blue and yellow for my color scheme, because these padded folding chairs I found at that garage sale last month are teal-blue. I coordinated them with this fabulous set of mismatched cream dishware, and the yellow from our lemons—" I focus in on the clear glass bowls of lemons strategically placed in the center of the folding table. "—add the perfect pop of color."

I swing the camera back to my seat and sit down, picking up the pre-filled glass pitcher of hazy lemonade.

"I'm a big fan of decorating with fruit. It's affordable, the colors are great and it's practical. My refreshments for my moving helpers today are lemonade for the kids, and for the adults—" I gesture to the bottle of vodka on the table, like a showcase showdown girl from *The Price is Right* "—vodka and lemonade cocktails! Grey Goose generously donated the vodka we'll be enjoying today, and it's one of my favorites. Vodka and Sprite, with a squeeze of lime is an amazing drink too."

For a split-second I'm distracted by the remembered taste of vodka on my lips. Of where I was and who I was with the last time I drank it.

It's like orgasm-PSTD.

It's not the first time I've thought of Dean—he's been popping up in my thoughts a lot these last months. But like every time before, I sweep the memories away and push on.

I smile into the camera. "Another way to set the stage for a successful moving party is ambiance. Decorations. These don't have to be time-consuming or pricey."

I take the camera over to the overgrown bushes and trees that surround the patio. They're strewn with glittering star or-

GETTING *Played* | 55

naments and twinkling lights.

"These are solar string lights from Kendall for just $2.99 a box, and I'll post the coupon code for you in the comments after this video. And then, we have these little beauties."

I zoom in on the golden stars.

"I picked these up from the dollar store at 75% off—but, if your local store doesn't carry them, they're a piece of cake to make."

I move back to a tray table in the corner, where my supplies are waiting.

"You start with a simple star cut out of plain cardboard. And remember—Lifers never pay for cardboard. Your local grocery stores and shops will have some they're willing to let you take off their hands, if you're willing to ask. Then, because you guys already know I'm a glitter girl—" I hold up a bottle of golden glitter and a paintbrush "—you paint on your glue and sprinkle your glitter. Make sure you let one side fully dry before working on the other. Then, all you need is a string to tie at the top, and voila!" I hold up the finished shining star ornament. "Instant moving party ambience. These can also be used again for holiday decorations."

I put the star on the table and brush off my hands. Then I stand up and hold the camera at face level.

"And now . . . do you guys want to see the lake?"

The flurry of hearts and smiley faces that slide up the screen tells me they do.

I tap a button on my computer on the chair, because mood music is important. And a moment later, the song "Learning to Fly" by Tom Petty fills the air. It's a great song—uplifting, upbeat.

And once again, Dean's gorgeous smile slides into my

head.

"Tom Petty's Greatest Hits . . . That's my answer."

A little shiver ripples through me at the memory of his rough, beautiful voice, and a longing, yearning ache echoes hollowly in my chest.

But I shake it off and refocus. *Refocus, refocus, refocus.* That's my word of the day—the month—possibly the rest of my life.

I pan the camera across the lake, capturing the glittering diamonds of the sun on the water's surface and the group of geese that glide peacefully by in a perfect triangle formation.

It's beautiful. Serene. It already feels like a home—one that would be so damn easy to fall in love with. The awe that shadows my next whispered words comes straight from my heart.

"Can you guys believe I get to live here?"

I shake my head, laughing, and spinning in a circle as the breeze blows my hair back. Then I wink into the camera.

"Me neither."

I turn my head back toward the water.

"It's going to be a great year. We're going to build a fire-pit and refinish the dock and turn this place into a dream house."

From the corner of my eye, I spot Jason at the back door, waving his arm, then giving me the thumbs-up.

"Okay, Lifers, Jaybird just gave me the signal that the gang's all here and it's time to kick moving day into high gear."

I talk about Jason in my videos, but I've never shown his face. I figure being a teenager is hard enough without having your picture strewn across social media by your mom.

I pan the camera across the party setup one last time—with the lake in the background. Then I lean over into the shot. "The coupon code and products from this video will be waiting for you in the comments. Otherwise, I'll see you guys for another live video on Wednesday night when we'll start working on the kitchen—because that's the heart of every house. Also, Wednesday is Lifer Self-Care Night—so I'm gonna show you how to mix a homemade honey and sugar foot scrub that'll knock your socks off. Leave any questions for me in the comments—sharing this video with your friends isn't expected, but it's always appreciated. Bye, Lifers."

With a wave and a smile, I stop recording. And now it's time to get my move on.

I love my family. They're nosy and noisy and feel like a hurricane of crazy when they're all in the same room—but I love them.

My sisters and I could be a case study in nature vs. nurture. Five girls, with the same parents, same DNA makeup, born on average about two years apart, raised in the same house . . . who couldn't be more different if we tried.

"Valentina, Ines—put your galoshes on if you're going near the water! And don't get your pants dirty!"

First, there's my oldest sister, Brooke. She's married to a perfect, handsome husband, Ronaldo, with two perfect girls. They live in a four-bedroom house, in an upper class neighborhood, where Brooke presides over school PTA meetings, drinking Chardonnay with the other moms in their tailored slacks, pearls and perfectly matching cardigan sweater sets.

Things go downhill from her.

"Where's the alcohol? I had too much caffeine this morning—I need a shot of something to bring me down."

Judith is my next oldest sister. She's the shortest among us, but what she lacks in height, she makes up for in personality. Jude's a workaholic CPA, who's married to Michael—another workaholic CPA. Michael only shows up to the big-holiday family gatherings where he generally gets sloshed before dinnertime and when leaving, tries to kiss everyone good-bye . . . on the mouth. Judith never goes anywhere without her phone, her hair is in a perpetually messy bun and a perfume of freshly brewed coffee surrounds her, like it's seeping from her pores.

"Already on it, Jude. The alcohol's outside. I'll get you a glass as soon as I finish writing this line down."

"It's nine o'clock in the morning," Brooke clucks.

My third oldest sister, Linda-the-middle-child, shrugs. "It's five o'clock somewhere. Let's make believe we're wherever that is."

Linda is a bestselling sci-fi author who walks around with a purse full of scribble-filled sticky notes and a pencil stuck in her hair—sometimes several pencils. Linda shares custody of her son, Javen, with her recently exed ex-wife, and the only clothes I've ever seen her wear are pajamas, sweatpants and—if she's feeling fancy—jeans.

Next is Erin—we've covered her pretty thoroughly already.

And last, there's me.

My dad's a retired sanitation worker, a union guy, and my mom is a retired florist. They're great parents—affectionate, supportive—and tired. They've been tired for as long as I can remember. I guess raising five girls successfully to woman-hood will do that to you.

Two years ago we all pitched in to send Mom and Dad on a cruise through Alaska. When they got home, they showed us the pictures from the trip and they were almost all photos of their stateroom. Because they slept—the whole week.

For the next few hours, my family unpacks their cars, stacking everything in the den and the garage where my designated work area will be. Because Snow White was right, and whistling—or bopping out to music—while you work is always better, I hook my phone to the Bluetooth speakers installed throughout the house and pull up my moving-day playlist. Songs by Smashmouth, and Tina Turner, "New Fav Thing" by the Danger Twins. It makes the time go faster and it's funny to see my mom and dad shaking their booties at one another as they carry stuff in.

Most of the items are raw materials—paints, tools, brushes, fabrics and faux furs I'll eventually make into curtains, accent pillows and rugs. There are some larger, used furniture items that I'll refinish and refurbish into new, unique pieces. This is a big house—it's not going to be easy filling it on a tight budget

"Did you pull this out of a flood zone?" Judith looks down at the warped, worn side-cabinet she and Linda just dragged in.

"No—I scooped it up from Mrs. Kumar's curb on the last heavy pickup day."

"What the hell is this for?" Jack, Erin's boyfriend, gestures towards the rusty, patina coated, penny-farthing, high-wheel bicycle I found at a flea market in Pennsylvania.

I gaze at the bicycle warmly—like the treasure it is—

because I love what I do.

"I'm either going to use the big wheel as the base for an accent table—or just hang the whole thing on the wall. I haven't decided yet."

I've always been a picker, a dumpster diver, a saver-for-laterer, a recycler. It makes me sad to think of something that was once loved being discarded without a second thought.

When I was a preteen and outgrew my immense collection of stuffed animals, instead of tossing them like my mother wanted—I sliced them open and gutted them. I used their stuffing to make new pillows and sewed their fuzzy pelts together to make a one-of-a-kind rug for my bedroom floor.

Morbid? Possibly.

But it gave a new purpose to the furry companions that had seen me through thunder storms and scary movies and tummy aches.

I was a lifestyle blogger at heart before the words even existed.

After everything's been moved in, and the den resembles the overstocked junk yard of an owner with fabulous taste, the family enjoys pizza and cocktails on the back patio. I'm with Jack and Erin in the kitchen making more lemonade, both the adult and kid-friendly kind.

I bend over slightly at the waist, rubbing my breasts covertly with my forearm, wanting to just full-out massage the poor girls. Because they're aching—a cold, excruciating, throbbing sort of pain—like my nipples have frostbite.

"You okay?" Erin asks.

"Yeah—it's just my boobs are killing me." I glance at Jack, leaning against the white marble counter. "Sorry."

"Don't apologize. Boobs are my second favorite thing to talk about."

"What's the first thing?"

He wiggles his eyebrows. "You're sister's boobs."

Erin laughs, then she turns to me, still smiling.

"Oh, my God—do you know what I just thought of? Remember, when you were preggers with Jay—but you were still hiding it from Mom and Dad? And we were all home from school in the car going to get the Christmas tree, and your boobs were hurting so bad, that you had them pressed up against the heating vents in the back of the car? You said it felt like they were frozen—two boobsicles."

"As if I could ever forget." I snort out a chuckle. "That sucked."

But then I stop chuckling.

And everything inside me freezes—going as stone-cold as my poor chilly nipples. Because I *did* forget—what it felt like to be pregnant. The early signs.

It's like God gives women amnesia about the really shitty parts of child-bearing, so we won't mind doing it again and again. But now, in this kitchen—it's like a horrible lightning bolt of epiphany has struck me. Like the blinders have fallen away.

And I remember all the early symptoms. The soul-deep exhaustion, the heavy, sluggish, bloated feeling, the nausea . . . the painful, aching breasts.

Everything I've been experiencing *for the last three weeks.*

I chalked it up to the excitement and stress of starting the show, the move—but there's something else. Something else I totally forgot.

"Oh, no."

I start counting backward in my head. The days, the weeks, not retracing my steps . . . but my menstrual cycle. And I feel the color drain from my face.

"Oh no, oh no, oh no, oh no."

"Are you gonna puke?" Jack takes a few steps back—out of the potential splash-zone. "Is she gonna puke, Er?"

A—yes, I'm definitely gonna puke.

And B—

"Lainey, what is it?"

I look into Erin's eyes, the "B" spilling from my lips in hushed, shocked words.

"I need to take a pregnancy test."

CHAPTER
Four

Lainey

"**W**hy does this keep happening to me?!"

Three positive pregnancy tests later—we're all in the kitchen, with all of my sisters fully updated on the latest unexpected, development. My parents are still clueless and supervising the grandchildren down on the dock.

I'm pregnant. Knocked up. In the family way. Unplanned. *Again.*

No matter how many times or how many different ways I say it to myself—I still can't make it make sense. When I first found out I was pregnant with Jason, the overwhelming feeling was fear—fear of what I was going to do, what my parents would say, fear of the unknown.

This time around I'm older—though wiser is still up for debate.

And I'm just utterly . . . flabbergasted. Flabbergasted is a really good word.

"We used condoms! We used *a whole box* of condoms!"

"Wow." Judith smirks. "The drummer-boy really brought it, huh?"

Brooke twists her pearls. "Not the time, Judith."

Jason's father was my first—my first serious boyfriend, my first everything. We used condoms too, though a bit fumblingly. And by the third or fourth time we'd had sex—*boom*, I was pregnant.

"Was there any P and V slip and slide action going on?" Erin asks me.

"No! There was no P and V contact without latex, at all."

I stare at my laptop screen, searching for an answer that will make this make sense. Because that's what you do when you're flabbergasted—you Google.

"Are my vaginal secretions acidic or something? Do they just eat through the condom?"

"That would be cool." Linda grins. "Like a Sigourney Weaver kind of *Aliens* vagina. I'm gonna use that." She writes it down on a sticky note.

And I think I might be hyperventilating.

"Do you think it was a stealthing?" my brother-in-law Ronaldo asks.

"What's stealthing?" Brooke asks.

"It's when a guy slips off the condom for the big finish without the girl knowing."

"Ew. That's a thing?" Brooke asks.

"Unfortunately, yeah."

"Jesus, what the fuck is wrong with men?" Judith asks.

"That's why I'm a lesbian," Linda announces. "You should all try it. No offense to the penises in the room, but pussy is where it's at."

Jack points at Linda. "I couldn't agree more."

Brooke gapes at Linda. "Your wife had an affair with your marriage counselor."

"Well, Genevieve happens to be lesbian who's also an asshole," Linda explains. "We're gay, not perfect."

I shake my head. "He didn't stealth. He wasn't like that. I watched him take the condoms off. And put them on for that matter—the way he ripped open the foil package with his teeth was one of the sexiest things I've ever seen in my life."

"Well, there you go!" Judith throws up her hands. "Opening condoms with your teeth makes them, on average, 30% less effective."

This seems to be new information to everyone one in the room.

"Really?" Brooke asks.

"Oh, boy," Erin groans.

"Maybe you should take one of those pregnancy tests," Jack says hopefully. "If I put a bun in your oven—you'll have to marry me."

Erin smacks his arm. "Focus, Jack. We're in the middle of a Defcon 1 level Burrows-breakdown here."

That's when my mother walks into the kitchen. And we all go still and silent—it's a reflex.

She smiles sweetly. "What's going on?"

In benign, synchronized voices that can only be achieved through years of practice, we all respond, "Nothing."

She aims that probing Mom-gaze at each of us. Erin steps forward, acting as the shield.

"We're talking about Christmas presents, Mom. For you and Dad."

"Hmm." She nods, reaching for the child-friendly lemonade. "All right."

She turns toward the door, still suspicious—but at this point, I think my mom has learned sometimes it's better not to know.

Once she's out the door, Brooke shakes her head. "Dad's gonna lose it. This time he's gonna stroke out—definitely."

My dad's old-school. A believer in getting an education, getting married and having kids—in that order. Still, when I dropped out of college to have Jason, he handled it well—even though I could tell at the time he was disappointed in me. And he loves Jason with his whole heart—he couldn't be prouder that he's his grandson.

But now, I'm worried about letting him down all over again. That he'll view this as a mistake, a failure—his failure as a dad.

"Hold the cell-phone, everyone," Judith says. "Don't you think you're jumping the panic gun a little bit here? I mean, it's not like you have to *stay* pregnant. They make a pill for that now, you know."

Brooke makes the sign of the cross. She teaches CCD at their local church. Like I said—couldn't be more different if we tried.

But Judith does have point. I'm a free-thinking, independent woman—and now really is not a good time for me to have another child. It's pretty much the worst time ever.

But then . . .

I hear a laugh from outside. And it's the best laugh—the best sound in the whole world. I move to the window and look out, watching him—my son, my heart, my little bird, my sweet boy. It wasn't easy when I had him—but it was still the most amazing thing I've ever done. I've never regretted it—him—

not for a second. And however difficult it will be now at thirty-four—it'll have to be easier than it was at nineteen.

How can I . . . how can I know that and not have this baby too?

It's just that simple, and just that hard.

I don't have to analyze it—in those few, quick seconds my mind is made up.

I'm having this baby.

I feel my sisters' eyes on me. And I know they see it on my face—the decision is already made.

Linda blows out a big breath. "Who's gonna tell Dad?"

Brooke holds up her hand. "I told him last time. Judith—you're up."

"Great." Judith moves to the adult vodka and lemonade and takes a big gulp—straight from the pitcher.

"Easy, cowgirl," Linda says.

Judith wipes her sleeve across her mouth.

"I'm drinking for two—for me and Lainey."

Yeah. She's got a point there.

The next morning, I push back the work I'd planned to do on the house and make an emergency appointment with Dr. Werner, my OBGYN in Bayonne. After an exam and a pee-in-a-cup test, she confirms that I am, indeed, preggers—about eight weeks along. Then she has me lay back on the table for an abdominal ultrasound.

I watch the screen, the familiar gray blobby shadows—but then I see it—right before the doctor points it out. That steady, rapid, rhythmic fluttering, like visual Morse Code that says, *Hi—how are you? Here I am.*

It's the baby's heartbeat. Seeing it blows my mind.

Makes it real.

And the first bud of excitement—of joy—blooms inside me.

It's crazy how quickly twenty-four hours can change your perspective. It's a miracle I don't have whiplash. Of course I'm still excited about the show, the house—but this is different. More. Bigger. Huge. A life-changing kind of surprise.

And not just for me.

After leaving the doctor's I stop at a Starbucks in town, plant myself at a table and whip open my laptop. Then I search for Dean—in every way I can think of. I don't have a last name or an address. He told me about high school but not where he went or the year he graduated. So I start with what I know—the band.

Amber Sound doesn't have a website or contact information. In an image search, just a few nondescript, grainy pictures appear. I zoom in close on one in particular. I can't see Dean's face . . . but I'd know those hands anywhere. Next I try the number for the Beachside Bar, but it goes straight to voicemail, saying they're closed for the season.

I stare at the screen, nibbling on the tip of my fingernail, wracking my brain for another way to reach Dean, and coming up with zilch, nothing, nada.

Shit.

"Hey sexy—how's it going?"

Chet Deluca grew up in the house next door to my parents'. He's a body builder, kind of the neighborhood Casanova, and a total ass. He's always had a thing for me. Which he showed in multiple gross ways through the years—from peeping into my bedroom window with his telescope, to telling the whole school I had a threesome with him and his brother, Vic, when I turned him down for senior prom.

I close my laptop as I answer with a brisk nod.

"Chet."

He tugs at the wide brim of my brown fedora. "This is cute. I saw your show online, Lains—you're looking good enough to eat out. We should hang."

Chet also doesn't know how to take a hint—or a straight-up "fuck no," for that matter.

I stand, smoothing down the hips of my indigo peasant skirt and adjusting my hat back into place. "No, thanks. I'm not interested."

"Another time then—you must be real busy." His eyes drag up and down over me, and my stomach flops like a fish on a dock.

I wonder if I barf all over him, if he'll get the message then.

Instead, I pick the path that requires less clean-up, and grab my bag, heading for the door. "I have to go."

Chet's voice follows me. "You change your mind, Lains—you know where I live."

That I do—and another perk to living in Lakeside is I can totally avoid him.

I walk in the door, toss my bag on the kitchen counter, and rest my hat on Myrtle—the mannequin head I got free from Chevy's department store when they were redesigning their woman's section. Her featureless face is a little freaky, but as long as you have her turned to look out the window, she makes a great hat-rest.

After Judith breaks the initial baby news to my parents, I'll put on my big girl panties and follow-up with them this weekend—over a hot cup of herbal tea that will go down nicely with all the uncomfortable awkwardness.

But for now, I have bigger fish to fry and more of a doozy of a conversation to have.

I head up to Jason's room and tap on the half-open door.

"Come in."

He's on his mattress on the floor, his back against the wall and his laptop in front of him.

"Hey, Mom."

"Hey."

I plop down next to him on the mattress, watching on the screen as Jason plays online Soduko.

"School starts on Monday."

His lightning-fast fingers tap at the keyboard, filling in the rows and columns of little boxes with numbers.

"Yeah."

"Are you okay with clothes? We could hit the mall later if you need anything."

"I'm okay with clothes. Last year's backpack is still in good condition, so I'm all set."

My recycling quirks have rubbed off on Jay.

And maybe it's because I had him young or I'm a single mom, but Jason and I have always had a good, open dialogue. We talk about things my parents never discussed with me. Drugs, sex, alcohol, vaping, porn—I want him to know he can come to me if he has problems or questions, and I believe the most dangerous threat to a teenager is curiosity. If we don't talk to them about the things that could hurt them, they're going to investigate for themselves.

That being said, telling your fourteen-year-old you got knocked up by a one-night stand—by a guy's whose last name you don't even know—is not going to be fun.

"I have to talk to you about something, Jay. A big-talk."

He doesn't take his eyes off the screen. "Is this gonna be like the "big-talk" about the clitoris? And you told me I should research all I could about it and that I'd thank you one day? 'Cause . . . that was awkward."

"Nope." I shake my head. "This one is gonna be so much worse."

"Wow." He puts the game on pause, closes his laptop, and sets it aside. "Okay."

I swallow roughly, my mouth suddenly dry.

"So, a few months ago, when I signed the papers for the webshow, I went out with Aunt Erin and Jack to celebrate. And that night . . . I met a man."

When I pause, Jason looks at me—waiting—his expression a nudging, wordless, *"Okay, and . . . ?"*

"And he was a really great guy—funny, sweet, talented. I liked him a lot, right away, and he liked me too. He treated me well, and we . . ."

Jason picks up on where I'm headed. His features pinch with a hint of hesitance and a slight tinge of disgust. "You hooked up?"

I nod. "We did. We hooked up."

We hooked up *a lot.*

"Sometimes, adults can spend the night together, and connect in a moment, enjoy each other, and make a wonderful memory. And that's all it's supposed to be—it doesn't always have to lead to a relationship."

"O-kay . . . why are you telling me this?"

Here we go. Time to drop the baby-bomb.

"I'm telling you because we used protection—it's really important to me that you understand we used protection. But . . . protection doesn't always work. That's why you shouldn't have sex until you're prepared for all the emotional and physical consequences that may result. Because, even though we used protection . . . it didn't work. And I'm pregnant."

My son's eyes widen, and bulge.

"You're pregnant? Like—with a *baby*?"

"Yeah." I nod. "With a baby. That's usually how it works."

"Holy shit."

"Pretty much."

"So . . . you're having a baby? For real? I'm going to be a big brother?"

I put my hand over his. "Yes, I am. And yes, you are."

"Wow." Jason scratches his head behind his ear. "Is this guy—is he going to help you? Am I going to meet him? Is he going to be around to help with the baby?"

"Well . . . that's the thing . . . he doesn't know. I'm working on finding him but I haven't been able to do that yet."

"Oh."

God, this must be weird for him. It's weird for me.

"Are you . . . feeling okay?" He glances down at my flat stomach. "Is the baby okay?"

"I'm tired, a little nauseous. I went to the doctor today and she said the baby and I are both healthy as horses. Then she prescribed me prenatal vitamins which are the size of horse pills—so it all makes sense now. But yeah, I'm good. I'm good with the whole situation. It's not going to change anything with the show. We're still going to be living here for the next year, now there'll just be a little extra content."

I've already taken notes on future videos I can do on a healthy diet during pregnancy, preventing stretch marks, designing the nursery.

Jason's quiet for several moments, then he looks at me with the adaptability and agility that only children possess.

"Okay. Cool."

I lean toward him. "Are you all right with this? You can tell me if you're not. If you have questions or feelings—you can talk to me."

He nods. "I know. And I'm fine. I mean, that's life, right? It happens and we roll with it. That's what we do."

And it seems my recycling quirks aren't the only part of me that's rubbed off on Jason.

"I think it'll be fun to have a baby around. A little brother or sister that I can show things to. It's going to be great, Mom. Don't worry," he adds.

The smile that stretches across my face is big and relieved—and so, so grateful. My throat clogs and my eyes go damp, because my son is amazing.

I lean my head against his shoulder, my voice soft. "You know you're, like, the best kid ever, right?"

He shrugs. "I do okay."

Late that night, in my pajamas, I climb onto my own mattress, with my computer on my lap and "Ophelia" by the Lumineers playing low on my phone. The walls are bare in the master bedroom, my boxes and suitcases of clothes line the walls, but still—the house feels warm and safe around me. It already feels like home.

I look for Dean online again. I even try searching "Dean, the sexy drummer in New Jersey" but it just sends me to a bunch of "singles in your area now" websites. So, I open up the video camera on my computer—focusing on my makeup free face, the freckles across my nose bare for all to see. I press record and talk in low, hushed tones.

"Hey Lifers. I don't know when I'll be ready to post this. It feels more real than it did yesterday, but still . . . surreal. I'm having a baby. It wasn't planned, it's totally unexpected, but with every passing minute, I'm happier about it."

In my mind I imagine a little boy or girl, a toddler, with sun-kissed hair and ocean-blue eyes, and a great smile—with a talent for music. And it's so bizarre that those could be the only things I know for sure they got from their father. But that may have to be enough.

I look into the camera. "You guys wanted to experience life with Lainey? Well strap in—it's gonna get nuts."

CHAPTER
Five

Dean

I admit, I get a kick out of the first day of school—I always did. Maybe it's the nerd in me, but there's something exciting about a fresh box of #2 pencils, a clean notebook, a new, unblemished folder.

Okay . . . it's definitely the nerd in me.

But that doesn't change the fact that the first day of school is like New Year's in September—the start of a whole new year—endless possibilities.

I have a personal dress code I stick to for work—it helps me compartmentalize, get into teacher mode and separate myself from the wilder, free-wheeling summer nights with the band. No T-shirts, sweats or hoodies allowed—it's all button-downs, sweaters, jeans, suits and ties on game day Fridays, and . . . glasses.

I'm notoriously nearsighted. Woman are into the glasses—but generally not on a drummer. Contacts are for the summer, my dark, square frames are for the rest of the time.

They make me look smart—most people subconsciously associate glasses with intelligence. They make me look like a teacher. And when it comes to teenagers—perception is half the battle.

The first period final bell is still ringing as I close my classroom door, because my kids are already at their desks.

Standing at the head of the class, I greet my band of brainiacs.

"Ladies and gentlemen, welcome back to school. I'm sure you're as excited as I am to explore the never-ending wonders of AP Calculus. It's going to be a good time, people."

I scan their eager, awkward, acne-cream tinted little faces as I pass out the syllabus and go through my PowerPoint presentation of how grades will be calculated. All the usual suspects are here—Louis, Min Joon, Hailey, Martin, Keydon, Daisy, Quinn and Diego.

Fun fact: Diego has a twin sister in regular math named Dora. His parents are obviously monsters.

There's also one new face in the pack: Jason Burrows.

He's got sandy-colored hair, and a 5 Seconds of Summer-ish, pretty-boy look that girls today really go for. After telling the class to take out their summer packets for review, I lift my chin at Burrows. "I don't expect you to have it completed. You can—"

He pulls the packet from his folder.

"It's already done, Mr. Walker. I found it on the school's website and finished it last night."

Oh yeah, he's gonna fit right in.

I call the kids up at random to post their answers to the problems on the board. Most of the answers are close—but wrong. These kids may be the cream of the smart, but they still have a lot to learn.

Daisy Denton, a shy, bespeckled redhead who's obsessed with butterflies, gets one right on the money.

"Good job, Daisy. You want to ask your question now or later?"

Any student who gets an answer correct in my class gets to ask me a question. Any question, nothing's off-limits, and I'll answer it truthfully, no bullshit. It's a great way to establish rapport and hopefully trust.

"I'll ask now." Daisy blushes, merry and bright. "What's the secret of life, Coach Walker?"

"Starting the year off with an easy one, huh?" I tease.

Her cheeks turn a darker shade of crimson, but she's smiling.

I adjust my glasses. "The secret of life is . . . good friends, good food, and good music. You have those three—everything else falls into place."

"What do you consider good music?" Daisy asks.

Technically that's two questions, but since Daisy is basically a mute most of the time, I don't point that out.

I hear a sweet, spellbinding voice in my head that, despite my best efforts, I haven't been able to forget. *"I like songs that tell a story. That make me feel. That make me remember."*

"Good music tells a story, Daise. It makes you remember exactly where you were and how you felt when you heard it."

Some of the kids nod, most of them looking at me like I'm Gandhi and Buddha and Nostradamus all in one. It's nice to be idolized.

"Okay, summer packet is done." I smack my hands together and sit down behind my desk, leaning back in my chair.

"Hey—new kid." Jason Burrows's eyes go wide and round. I gesture for him to stand. "Do your thing—you know the drill. Tell us about yourself."

He stands up, wetting his lips, looking a bit nervous. But that's okay—because if yolks want to make friends, they gotta crack their shells.

"My name is Jason, I'm a Junior, I'm from Bayonne. I'm fourteen—"

"Fourteen?" Louis asks. "That's young for a junior."

"Yeah." Jason nods, shrugging it off. "I skipped a few grades when I was younger."

That gets their attention.

Because my students may not be football players or track stars—hell, some of them can't even walk straight. But that doesn't mean they're not competitive. Bloodthirsty.

They'd sell their mothers for an extra tenth of a percentage in their GPA. Tonya Harding and Nancy Kerrigan? Pfft—amateurs. My kids wouldn't have wasted time with a crowbar—they would've gone straight for the chainsaw.

Hailey gnaws on the end of her pen. "A few grades? You must think you're pretty hot stuff."

"Not so much." Burrows shakes his head. "I just really like school."

They look him over, judging and weighing, like sniffing wolves deciding if a loner is going to be a new member of the pack—or lunch.

"Where do you live?" Diego asks.

There's only about eight thousand residents in Lakeside.

Where you live in town can say a lot about who you are. Wealthier families live on the North side of the lake or in the newer homes of Watershed Village; the old timers, like Grams, live below 6th Street, and the rest of the working-class families live everywhere in between.

"On Miller Street, at the end, by the lake."

Louis practically jumps out of his chair.

"Wait, wait, wait—I saw them doing work on the old boarded up house on Miller Street. *That's* where you live?"

I see where this is going—and it's nowhere good.

"Yeah, it's not boarded up anymore. My mom does these decorating videos on—"

"Holy shit, have you seen them?" Min Joon asks.

Burrows looks around. "Seen who?"

"The boys in the attic," Martin says excitedly. Then he goes on to explain the legend of the haunted house of Lakeside. The one Burrows currently lives in.

"If you stand in front of the house at midnight on Friday the 13th and look up at the attic window, you'll see the ghosts of the two 18th century boys who haunt the house."

Burrows turns as white as the chalk on the ledge behind me.

"That's not true," Keydon argues.

"It's totally true!" Louis yells. "My uncle saw them—he told me!"

I try to turn it around.

"Okay, guys, let's get back—"

But they're on a roll.

"I heard they committed suicide," Hailey says.

"I heard their mother slit their throats in their beds," Min Joon insists.

Even quiet Daisy gets in on the act. "I heard it was the nanny and then she hung herself from the top stair railing."

"Uh . . . I . . ." Burrows looks like he's going to puke any second now. Not the best way to make a first impression.

"Hey, guys!" I stand up, clapping my hands. "That's enough, all right? Let's bring it in and get back to work."

I glance at my poor, terrified, new student and do the only thing I can.

I lie.

"The house isn't haunted. It's a joke, they're just messing with you."

He swallows so hard, I hear it. "Are you sure?"

I look him right in the eyes.

"I swear to God."

It's a good lie—God will understand.

And Jason almost believes me. Then, Garrett walks into my classroom.

"Sorry to interrupt, Coach Walker." He hands me a manila folder. "Here are the revised plays we talked about, for practice later."

"Thanks."

"Hey, Coach D," Diego calls. "You know the boarded up house at the end of Miller Street?"

"Yeah, I know it." Garrett answers.

"What do you think of it?"

"Haunted as hell."

And the whole classroom explodes.

"I told you!"

"So haunted!"

"I knew it!" says Jason.

Ah shit. I am *so* getting an angry email from this kid's

mother.

"Me and Coach Walker saw the boys in the attic ourselves, when we were twelve."

I try to catch Garrett's eye while running my hand across my neck—the universal sign for, "Dude, shut the hell up." But he doesn't notice. Having Will has dulled his brain a little—he's not as observant as he used to be.

"And Louis—your Uncle Roger was with us." Garrett laughs. "He wet his pants and you can tell him Coach Daniels told you that."

"D!" I finally bring Garrett's attention to me.

"What's up?"

"Burrows here just moved in to the house on Miller Street."

Garrett's face goes blank. He looks at Jason.

"Oh."

He was always good on the recovery.

"It's not that haunted." He waves a hand. "It's an urban legend—like alligators in the sewer. Don't worry."

But Burrows *is* worried.

And Garrett is unconvincing.

Louis doesn't help.

"Dude, you're gonna die in that house."

Jason Burrows looks like he's gonna die right now. On my classroom floor. From a heart attack brought on by hyperventilation and fear.

Wouldn't that be a fuck of a way to kick off the school year.

Quinn Rousey jumps up from her desk. "Wait, wait, wait, listen!"

Quinn is a pretty, jittery kind of girl with pixie-cut black hair and a raging case of ADHD.

"I have an idea, I know what we should do, I have equipment at my house—night vision cameras and audio devices from my cousin before they sent him away to the facility in Branson."

"Breathe, Quinn," I interrupt. "And we've talked about this—you gotta lay off the Red Bulls."

She turns toward Burrows and seems to remember to inhale between sentences. "I could come to your house and we could do a séance. Then we could burn sage and recite lines from the Bible and Torah and the Quran just to be safe, because you don't know what religion the ghosts are, but—Oh! And I'm Quinn, by the way." She holds out her hand. "Hi."

Jason looks at Quinn's hand, then slowly reaches out and shakes it.

"Hey."

"So—what do you think? Do you want to hang out? I can come today, or tomorrow, or tomorrow-tomorrow works too."

Several other students nod, inviting themselves right along with Quinn.

And Burrows has this expression—it's the look of a kid who hasn't been asked to hang out very much in his life. Maybe never. And now he's got a pretty, outgoing, energetic girl and half a class of students wanting to do just that.

His eyes are warm and hopeful when he smiles. "Yeah, cool. Tomorrow is good. Sounds like fun."

For the next half hour, we do a worksheet—mostly a review of old material. Then with five minutes left before the bell, I announce, "That's a wrap for today. As you were, people."

And I pull up "We're Not Gonna Take It" by Twisted Sister on my phone and hit play—loud enough to enjoy the song as it was meant to be heard, but not so loud that one of my fellow educators will go bitching to McCarthy.

My students from last year know the drill. A few talk, Daisy doodles a butterfly on her folder, Diego pulls his cap down and closes his eyes.

Jason Burrows takes out his phone.

"We're not allowed to go on our phones at the end of class," Min Joon tells him.

So Burrows takes a textbook out of his bag.

And I whip a wadded-up ball of paper at his head.

"No studying allowed."

"Well . . . what am I supposed to do?"

I stand up and approach his desk, playing perfect air drums in time to the song.

"Be a kid. Chat amongst yourselves, look out the window, play frigging Seven-Up, I don't care. You just can't study or screw around on your phone."

He still looks confused, so I explain. "Your brain is a muscle . . ."

Louis raises his hand. "Technically the brain . . ."

"Shhh," I put my finger to my lips. "The teacher is talking."

My voice resonates across the room like a better-looking version of the Cobra Kai sensei from *The Karate Kid*.

"How do we build muscle, class?"

I open and close my fist in time to their response.

"Contract, release, contract, release."

"If you don't release will you build muscle?"

"Nooooo," the class answers in unison like a well-trained army of geniuses.

"If you don't rest, will you build muscle?" I ask.

"Nooooo."

"No." I look down at Burrows. "You'll get worn out, injured, burnt out . . . and you're no good to me dead."

I spin around to the class. "Extra credit point on the next quiz for the first person who can tell me who said that!"

I like to keep them on their toes. And these kids eat up extra credit like a puppy scoffs down dog biscuits.

"Boba Fett—*The Empire Strikes Back*!" Hailey calls out.

"Correct!"

I bring my attention back to Jason.

"So you see, young Burrows. You have to rest your brain once in a while in order to keep getting smarter. Which is why we don't study or screw around on our phones at the end of AP Calculus."

I turn around and walk to my desk. But when I sit down, Jason has his hand raised.

"Yes?"

"Boba Fett didn't say that."

"No?"

He shakes his head. "The actual quote is '*He's* no good to me dead.' 'Cause he was, you know, talking about Han Solo."

Slowly I nod. "And now you've got an extra credit point on the next quiz too. Well done."

I like this kid. I don't always like all of them—that's the dirty little secret of teaching. But I like him.

"You a big fan of *Star Wars*, Burrows?"

"Kind of." He shrugs. "My mom's into all those old movies."

Old movies . . . nice.

"She says everyone my age should watch them, because they don't make them like that anymore."

"Your mom sounds like a smart lady." I smile. "And I think you are going to fit in with this class just fine."

CHAPTER
Six

Lainey

Most bloggers, Instagramers, and influencers do their damnedest to project a flawless image to their followers. Perfect lighting, background, makeup, clothes—perfect double mocha latte with an intricate oak tree leaf designed in the foam.

I've never been a flawless person. Or organized. I'm more of a hot mess who happened to be blessed with good skin. But my followers like me that way—so I show them the good, the bad, and the morning sickness ugly.

Which is why when I'm recording in the kitchen and the wave of nausea that's been crashing down on me all day turns into a tsunami, I leave the camera running while I dive into the small hallway bathroom. Later, I'll edit out the sounds of my wrenching heaves that feel like they're emptying my stomach and my soul. But the before and after, that stays in the video.

Because it's real.

I step out of the "barfroom" a few minutes later, dabbing at my face with a damp towel. "Sorry about that, Lifers. This kid is killing me. I never had morning sickness with Jaybird. Is this like an omen of things to come—'cause if it is, I'm screwed."

I posted the pregnancy video announcement last week—the Lifers are all super excited for me. Though I occasionally mention Mr. Hot-Baby-Daddy or Sexy-Drummer-Guy interchangeably, I've kept any other details about Dean and his level of involvement purposely vague.

I grab the pencil and notebook that sits on the shiny marble counter top and record the "vomitous" occasion for posterity. Then I hold the notebook up to the camera.

"Did I tell you guys I started a pregnancy journal? It's for me, mostly, and for the baby when they're an adult, so I can guilt them into taking care of me when I'm old."

I hold up a picture of myself taken in the master bath mirror yesterday—topless and turned to the side with my arm across my breasts, to show the weekly progression of my surprisingly expanding stomach. That's different from Jason too—I'm only about three and a half months and already starting to pop.

"And it's for Mr. Sexy-Baby-Daddy too, so he won't miss out on any big moments." I set the notebook aside. "Anyway, where were we?"

The kitchen is finished. I decorated it in shades of white with wood touches—to go with the overall nautical theme and because it's super easy to change out accent colors. There are white cabinets for storage below the counter, but on the walls above it, it's open thick, butcher-block shelving that hold neat rows of white ceramic dishes and glasses. There's a matching hood above the stainless steel range and an accent wall of distressed horizontal oak planks with a massive five-by-three chalkboard sign hung across the top that reads LAKE.

I installed the two-inch tile backsplash myself—on camera. It was painstaking work—but also meditative. Listening to music helped pass the time as well as romance audiobooks—a suggestion from one of my followers.

Finally, the sculpted glass chandelier that hangs over the shiny, white, marble-topped island gives the whole room a real touch of sophistication.

I pick up the empty spray bottle on the counter and pour each ingredient in. "We mix together one cup of hydrogen peroxide, two teaspoons of baking soda, a drop of dish soap and a squeeze of lemon—and voila! We have an effective, lemony-smelling carpet and fabric cleaner that's safe for babies, pregnant ladies, animals and plants—that you can make yourself for pennies."

It's baking soda day. I've shown them how to make homemade teeth-whitening trays, toothpaste, insect bite cream, heartburn remedies and now carpet cleaner.

Baking soda is a miraculous substance—you can use it for everything.

I spray the bottled solution into the air. "And that's it for now. All our recipes are in the comments below this video and I will see you tomorrow when we'll continue working on decorating the living room. Bye, Lifers!"

I press the end record button and plop my tired self down in a chair—my stomach still feeling moody. Jason walks into the kitchen a little while later. There's an infinitesimal pause before he sets his bag on one of the white wicker island stools—and I know he's noticing my pale cheeks and the pink burst-blood vessels in my eyes.

"Hey, Mom."

"Hey, honey. How was school?"

"It was good."

Jason fills up a glass of water at the sink and passes it to me.

"Thanks, sweetie."

"How are you and the bump doing? Did you get sick again?"

"Yeah, I did. It's probably going to be a regular thing for a while so I don't want you to worry."

"Okay."

And then he looks at me—worrying. With those young old-man eyes.

He slips his phone out of his pocket and sends a text. Then he moves to the garbage can, tying up the bag to take it out, without being asked. His phone pings on the counter with a few incoming texts.

I sip my water. "What's that about?"

My son shrugs. "A few of us were going to go to the football game tonight."

Jason has friends. It started the first day of school and in the six weeks we've lived here, his place in the little band of misfit kids has solidified. They're a nice group—polite, smart, a little hyper, a little odd. They've even taken it upon themselves to decorate the attic with dozens of dangling Blair Witch Project-like talismans, because apparently the house is teeming with ghosts. But they make Jason happy—they make him smile easier and more often than I've ever seen, so unless they start talking animal sacrifice or building an altar to Satan, I don't mind.

"Coach Walker said there's half an extra credit point in it for us if he actually sees us at the game."

Ah, the illustrious Coach Walker.

According to my son, Coach Walker sounds like a combination of Captain America, Eddie Vedder, Chris Hemsworth, and Albert Einstein. The day Jason told me he plays in a band, I almost asked him if the name was Amber Sound, just to torture myself.

"What does football have to do with calculus?" I ask.

Jay smirks in that way kids do when they think adults are being ridiculous.

"He says we need to expand our horizons."

I smile too. "Can't argue with that."

Jay's phone pings again.

"But I'm not gonna go to the game," he says.

"Why not?"

He lifts one shoulder. "I'd rather stay in tonight. Home. With you."

Oh boy. When a fourteen-year-old is canceling plans because he's worried that his pregnant, losing-loser of a mom has zero offline social life and is basically a hermit when she's working on a project—that's some Holy Batman level pathetic, right there.

"Jay—"

"It's fine, Mom. We'll watch a movie, it'll be fun."

My sweet Jaybird can be stubborn—he gets that from me—so there's no point to arguing. Instead, I change tactics.

"I was actually thinking about going to the football game tonight too."

Jason's eyebrows dart hopefully. "Really?"

"Yeah. I mean basically the whole town goes, right? It'll

be good to get out. You'll get your half-point extra credit and the nugget and I will get some fresh air." I put my hand on my stomach. "Why not?"

Football is a big deal around Lakeside. The high school stadium is larger than I expect and immaculate—with rows of fan-packed concrete bleachers, a freshly painted blue and gold snack stand, and a top-of-the-line score board. The October air is damp and crisp but not too cold, so I wear a long-sleeved black thermal top, comfy denim overalls and a knit black beanie with my hair down in curled waves around my shoulders.

Jason and I arrive midway through the first quarter, and as we walk around the outer fence, the whole Lakeside section rises to their feet, cheering, as the band strikes up a soaring victory tune when one of our players dives into the end zone.

Three of Jason's friends catch up to us about halfway around the field.

"Hi, Jason! Hi Miss, Burrows!"

"Hi, kids."

"That's a great hat, Miss Burrows. Did you crochet it yourself?"

Before I can answer, Quinn, a chipper, dark-haired girl, with darting, bright blue eyes, just keeps right on talking.

"I crochet too, especially when I can't sleep and I almost never sleep. It used to drive my Mom crazy hearing me walk around the house at night so she said I had to stay in my room, but now when I can't sleep I just crochet and it works really well. I was going to make us all Christmas sweaters if I have the time and—" she looks at Jason "—do you celebrate

Christmas?"

It's amazing that she can get all that out in one breath.

Jason smiles, because he's used to Quinn's run-on sentences.

"Yeah, Quinn—we celebrate Christmas."

"Oh." She smiles, nodding, and seems to remember to close her mouth. "Cool."

"Come on, Jay," Louis says. "Keydon's on the other side of the field, where he can pick up Wi-Fi, working on this new algorithm that chooses the best plays based on the opposing team's player's stats. It's lit. We're going to show it to Coach Walker after the game."

Jason glances at me hesitantly.

"Go ahead, I'll be fine. I'm going to find a seat and watch the game."

"All right. Thanks, Mom."

As the kids walk away, Louis turns back to me. "There are a few seats left at the top, Miss Burrows!"

I wave a thank you and head in that direction.

The crowd cheers again, standing as I make it to Lakeside's end of the field. The band plays a song and the cheerleaders do a quick track-side routine. The air smells like leaves and wet grass—with a hint of pizza that makes my stomach churn. I'm out of breath by the time I make it to the top of the bleachers, but when I look around, there isn't anywhere to sit.

Just as I turn to head back down the steps, a whirlwind warm little body collides with my leg, holding on tight. He's about two years old with baby soft brown hair, big onyx eyes and a devil of a smile.

"Boo!"

Automatically, I cover my face with my hands and quick-ly peek out—because when an adorable little boy boos you, you boo him back.

"Boo!"

He lets out a delighted belly laugh—until a voice calls out from behind him.

"Will!"

Will's eyes go wide and he bounces up and down like a monkey who wants out of his cage.

"Up, up, up, up, up!"

I scoop up the little runaway—and his warm, solid baby weight feels beautifully familiar to my arms.

Then I make eye contact with the smiling blond woman coming down the row. She's about my age, with soft, pretty features.

"I'm guessing he belongs to you," I tell her.

"Yes, thank you."

I hand the bouncy boy over. "He would've been all the way to the other end if you hadn't grabbed him. Running is his favorite thing to do."

"No problem."

"No!" Will frowns, his little brows squeezing together. "No sit!"

"Yes, sit," his mother tells him, kissing his chubby fist. "We're going to watch the game. You don't want to miss it."

I look toward the steps as everyone in the bleachers stands up again, cheering over something on the field.

"Were you looking for a place to sit?" She cocks her head toward the announcer's box. "There's a spot at the end by us, you're welcome to join us."

"That'd be great, thanks."

I follow her down the row and she sits beside an older couple wearing matching Lakeside High School sweatshirts.

"I'm Callie, by the way. And this," she tickles the toddler's stomach, "is Will."

I press a hand to my chest. "Lainey Burrows."

"It's nice to meet you. Are you new in town, Lainey?"

"Yeah, my son Jason and I moved here a few weeks ago from North Jersey. We're in the old house on Miller Street."

Callie's eyes go wide. "Really? That place is . . ."

"Haunted." I nod. "So I've heard. Haven't seen any 18th century ghosts yet, but I'm keeping my eyes peeled."

She laughs. "It's an old legend around here."

"I'm getting that. You're from Lakeside?"

"Born and raised." Will stands up between her legs, holding her hands and bouncing. "It's a great town—a nice place to grow up, raise kids."

I look down toward the field at the wall of large, padded football players' backs and ask Callie, "Which one is yours?"

She points. "The tall, dark-haired one with Coach Daniels written across the back of his jersey."

I follow her pointed finger to a handsome guy wearing a headset, talking animatedly to two players about to take the field.

"Garrett coaches and teaches history and I teach theater here at the high school."

Next to Garrett Daniels, facing the field, I spot my son's teacher-hero from his jersey—Coach Walker. He's tall, broad-shouldered, wearing his own headset and jeans, which he fills out very nicely. Coach Walker's got a great butt.

A woman in front of me stands, blocking the view.

"Come on defense! Let's go, Lions!"

Will steps away from his mother, braces his hands on my knees and climbs up into my lap. And it's nice—the sweet scent of his hair, his cuddling arms. This time next year, I'll be holding my own little boy or girl, and I relish that thought.

"Boo!" Will says, cracking himself up.

"He's a charmer, huh?" I say to Callie.

"Oh yes. Just like his Dad."

Will holds his arms out toward. the field. "Daddy!"

But the team is too far down for his father to hear him.

"What do you do, Lainey?"

"I'm a lifestyle blogger—interior design, life hacks, that kind of thing. I have a webseries on Facebook called *Life with Lainey* and that's why we moved here—I'm redecorating the house on Miller Street."

"No kidding. That's so interesting!"

"Yeah, it's never boring. I'm lucky."

Callie smiles warmly. "I'm going to check out your videos."

The gray-haired woman beside Callie leans over and says in a gravelly voice, "I'm going to look at your videos too. Callie, you'll have to help me with that internet. I want to redesign our kitchen in the spring."

Callie gestures to the couple. "This is my mom and dad, Anne and Stanley Carpenter. Mom, Dad—this is Lainey Burrows."

Mrs. Carpenter grasps my hand. "Pleasure to meet you, Lainey. We should talk."

I smile, nodding. "I just finished the kitchen in the lake house. I could definitely give you some pointers."

Mrs. Carpenter leans back to her seat, then she takes a cigarette from her purse and lights up.

"Mom, what are you doing?!" Callie snatches the cigarette from her mother's fingers and tosses it in the cup of soda at her side, waving the smoke away. "You can't smoke here."

"We're outside! What kind of world do we live in that a grown woman can't smoke outside? So many rules you kids have today."

"It's not *so* many rules—it's two rules. You can't smoke around your grandson or your pregnant daughter. It's not that difficult."

Mrs. Carpenter waves her hand dismissively and returns her attention to the game.

I glance down at Callie's abdomen beneath her oversized football jersey.

"When are you due?"

"Late March."

I put my hand on my own stomach. "Me too. Well—early April."

Callie puts her hand on my arm. "Congratulations. How's the morning sickness treating you?"

"Oh my God, it's so bad." And it's pretty great to have someone to talk to—someone who understands. "How about you?"

Will shifts back to his mother's lap.

"You know, I was sick as a dog with Will, but this time there's been almost nothing. Garrett thinks we're having a girl because this pregnancy is so different."

"This pregnancy is definitely different for me. But it's been fourteen years since I had Jason, so it could be that I'm just old."

Mrs. Carpenter cackles. "If you're old, honey, I'm an antique. Thirties are the new twenties." She gestures to herself and winks. "And seventy is the new forty. They say a woman's sexual peek is in her forties and I can tell you from experience, they're not lying."

Callie covers her eyes and groans. "Mom, please don't."

And that's how it goes for the next few hours. The Lakeside Lions rack up the touchdowns, but I don't really watch the game. I spend the time talking with Callie and the Carpenters and playing with baby Will.

Jason and his friends find me, just after the final whistle blows.

"Hey, Mrs. Coach D," Jason's friend Louis greets Callie.

"Hey, guys." She smiles, standing up with Will on her hip.

"Mom, we're going to go to Dinky's Diner," Jason tells me. "Quinn will drive me home. Is that okay?"

"Sure. Do you have money?"

He nods. "Yeah, I'm good."

"Okay, I'll see you at home."

After they walk off, Callie nods toward the empty football field. "I'm going to let Will run off some of his energy on the field while I wait for Garrett, so he'll sleep tonight. It was great talking to you, Lainey."

"Same here—this was a lot of fun. I tend to hibernate when I'm working, so this was exactly what I needed."

She waves. "I'll see you around town. And, my email is on the school website—if you ever want to grab lunch and commiserate about the joys of pregnancy, just drop me a message."

"I will, thanks, Callie."

And I really am glad I came out. When you spend so much time communicating online it's easy to not notice how lonely you are. Isolated. That you can go days or even weeks without talking to an actual live human being.

But this—the fresh air, the conversation, the vibe of the town, everyone so warm and friendly—it makes me feel invigorated and refreshed.

It makes Lakeside feel like home.

After the bleachers have mostly emptied out, I make my way down the steps and walk toward the school where my car is parked in the lot outside the gym.

Dean

There's a singular satisfaction in winning a football game. It's better than playing a pounding tune to a charged-up crowd and more satisfying than solving the most impossible math problem. It's the payoff of months of bone-crunching work and mental preparation, and it's every bit of a rush as a coach as it was as a player. Victory and pride and adrenaline floods your blood stream, making you feel invincible, driving you to celebrate—to drink, dance, fuck long and wild and all night long.

After Garrett gives the team the short-form congratulatory speech and warns them not to be idiots at whatever postgame parties they're going to, the players clear out of the locker room, and I walk out to my car with my duffel back slung over my shoulder. It's just starting to drizzle and a cool, misty haze hangs in the air.

"Nice game, Coach," a parent calls.

"Good win tonight, Walker," someone else says.

I nod and lift my hand to the faceless voices. Then, I pop my trunk, put my bag in the back and close it.

And then I see her. A woman, walking alone across the parking lot a few dozen yards away. Her face is shadowed, but the blond locks that spiral down her back shimmer like a beacon under the halo of the street lights. Her limbs are lithe and long and there's something about her—about the way she moves, the swing of her arms and the sway of her hips, that makes my heart punch against my ribs and my cock twitch.

The damp air fogs on my glasses, so I rip them off my face, wiping the lenses on my shirt. When I put them back on, she's already climbing into a pickup truck and closing the driver side door.

And that weird surging feeling—the same one from the grocery store—streaks up my spine and shoves at my shoulders. To move. To sprint the hell over there. To tap on her window and see her face . . . to see if it's her.

Right.

Cause that's not too creepy or anything.

Holy shit, I'm losing it.

I shake my head and watch as the red eyes of the truck's break lights blink, then back out and pull away.

For most guys, any problems we have in life can be traced back to one source—our dicks. Mine's no exception. It's all his fault. The bastard's become finicky. Choosy. Totally pathetic.

Lainey is still the last woman I had sex with.

It's been *months*—the longest drought since the night I lost my virginity to Samantha Perkins in the bathroom the night of her senior prom when I was a freshman. There've been offers—there always are—Pam Smeason when she came home to visit her parents next door, the receptionist at the car wash, the backup bartender at Houlahan's with the pouty lips and fantastic rack.

But my dick wouldn't even raise his head to take a look. Asshole. He's obsessed with a ghost. A memory.

Even when I jerk off—which has been, like, three squares a day—that bolt of desire doesn't strike until I think of Lainey. Imagine her sounds from that night—her scent, the clasp of her snug, wet pussy or how gorgeous she looked with her mouth full of my cock.

That last one does it every time.

Screw this—I'm taking matters into my own hands. Or . . . out of my own hand.

We won the game, I'm feeling the rush of sweet, sweet victory—so tonight my dick better get with the program. We're celebrating. We're going out and picking up a hot-as-hell woman who can't wait to rip my clothes off. If past is prologue, finding her won't take long. Then I'm taking her home and screwing her until I forget my own name.

And more importantly—until I forget Lainey's.

Teachers are a funny breed. We're social creatures—teaching is a social art—but excluding soldiers in the same foxhole, I don't think there's another profession on earth that bonds coworkers together so strongly. Teachers become each other's support systems, their social network, their closest friends—even if they're the type of personalities that wouldn't normally mesh if you didn't work in the same building.

Also—and this is universal—get a few drinks in a teacher, they spill all kinds of hilarious personal shit.

It's how I know Lakeside's creative writing teacher, Alison Bellinger, has a thing for gray-haired dudes. And gym teacher Mark Adams has never done anal. And science teacher Evan Fishler thinks anal was done to him—by aliens. And guidance counselor Jerry Dorfman has hyper-sensitive nipples. And English teacher Peter Duvale has a deeply-rooted fear of the color lime-green.

After the football game, I go home, grab a shower and head to Chubby's—Lakeside's local bar. It's tradition. The students have their beer bashes in the woods or maybe the basement of some upperclassman's house—the faculty has Chubby's.

One night that will forever live in infamy, even our principle, Miss McCarthy, and her assistant, Mrs. Cockaburrow, showed up after a particularly hard-won game. Turns out after a couple boilermakers, Mrs. Cockaburrow's an animal on the karaoke machine—and the woman's got pipes.

By the time I walk in, the gang's all there, gathered around a few pushed-together tables in the back. Jerry's wife, art teacher Donna Merkle, is here along with Kelly Simmons, Alison, Mark and Evan. Garrett was here too—because he's hella superstitious during football season and would never mess with a tradition—but he only stayed for one beer before heading home to Callie and Will.

I grab a drink from the bar and slide into the empty chair next to Kelly as she texts on her phone, her fingers moving quick and pissed off. I never did hit her up for that hookup. My head—and other body parts—just wasn't into it. But from the looks of it, the rumor about her troubles in marital paradise might be true.

She slams her phone down on the table and takes a long drink of whatever dark pink fruity concoction is swirling in her glass.

"Problem?" I ask.

"Richard is working late again. I've been dropping hints that I'm feeling neglected and he's playing it off like he doesn't care."

Kelly enjoys a good head game, she always did. Acting a certain way to get someone else to act the way you want.

"When you marry someone whose nickname is Dick, you can't really be surprised when they act accordingly."

There was a time I was into head games too—when I was young and selfish and an asshole. I'm ashamed to say it was a rush to see how much I could get away with, how much a girl would put up with until she snapped. But I lost interest in games around my third year of college. I guess it was maturity—messing with another person's emotions didn't make me feel cool or smart—it just felt shitty. Now raw honesty is my policy.

I take a drag off my beer and focus on more important matters—scanning the bar for the lucky lady who'll get to ride my face tonight. And I know it when I spot her. Three o'clock, at the bar, long straight dark hair and a sweet bubble ass. Perfect.

I rise from the table and make my move.

This is going to work. I'm going to get off the bench and back on the field. This is going to be awesome.

I lean my arm against the bar beside her. "Can I buy you a drink?"

And then she turns around.

"Coach Walker!"

And my cock keels over like a sad, dying tulip.

Her name is Kasey Brewster. She was a student of mine about ten years ago.

"Hey Kasey, how are you doing?"

Ruby-red lips smile brightly. "I'm great. I'm home visiting my parents. I'm working in the physics department at MIT."

"Good for you."

Kasey was always smart. Bubbly. That doesn't seem to have changed.

"It's so good to see you. God, you look exactly the same!" She leans forward and puts her hand on my arm. "You know, we all had the biggest crush on you back in the day."

It happens. When you're a good-looking, naturally charming teacher, student crushes come with the territory. I typically ignore them, but if things get out of hand I go with the kind but firm, "I'm your teacher and it's never going to happen" speech. Kasey hid her crush well.

"No kidding?"

"Yeah. The more things change, the more they stay the same." She wraps her lips meaningfully around the straw in her glass. "Are you married? Seeing anyone?"

"Nope. Still swinging single."

Her smile grows wider. "You want to get out of here? Go somewhere to get . . . reacquainted? Now that we're both adults?"

Even if my libido wasn't a barren wasteland, since Kasey was once my student, in my mind she'll always be my student—which means she'll never, ever, be hookup material.

I jerk a thumb over my shoulder and let her down gently.

"I'm here with some people. But it was great seeing you, Ka-sey—I wish you the best in everything you do. Take care, sweetheart."

Her eyes dim with a hit of disappointment, but she recovers and the smile bounces back.

"I will. You too, Coach Walker."

As I drag my sorry ass back to the table, Toby Keith is singing from the jukebox about a dream walking one-night stand that he can't forget.

I feel you, Toby.

When I sit down, my coworkers' eyes dissect me like a frog in Bio 101.

We're teachers. This is what we do—read emotions and analyze behavior. If a kid's on the verge of doing something epically stupid, like pulling the fire alarm or releasing snakes in the girl's locker room—which actually happened once, because seniors have way too much time on their hands—a good teacher will feel something off in their gut before it happens.

And every person at this table is a good teacher.

Alison cleans the lenses of her bright, yellow framed glasses then pops the question.

"What's up with you?"

"Nothing."

Merkle leans forward, her wiry red hair spilling over her shoulder. "No, something is definitely up with you—I can smell it. It's the stench of old cheese and desperation."

I lift my beer. "Thanks, Donna."

Kelly points toward the crowded bar. "There are plenty of prospects here tonight. If you're so desperate, get out there and turn on your famous charm."

I scrub a hand down my face.

"I think I'm having an existential crisis. Is that a thing or just an excuse pussies use when they're having a bad day?"

"Definitely a thing." Alison does a little jiggle in her chair. "I love crises—what's yours?"

Ah, what the hell—I might as well tell them—it's not like things could get any worse.

I blow out a breath. "Okay. Over the summer, I hooked up with this girl and she was like . . ."

I search my mind for an adequate way to convey all that Lainey was, in a way they'll understand. My voice goes wispy with awe.

". . . a Hot Dog Johnny's hot dog, with everything on it."

Jerry hums with appreciation, nodding. So does Alison, Kelly, and Mark—they get it.

Donna and Evan don't—they didn't graduate from Lakeside.

"What does that mean?" Evan asks.

"Hot Dog Johnny's is this shabby miracle of a hot dog stand upstate," Jerry tells him.

"In high school, a bunch of us would go camping in the summer," Kelly explains. "We'd stop by Hot Dog Johnny's every time."

"And once you have a Johnny, there's no going back," Mark says.

"They also had great buttermilk," Alison adds.

Kelly rolls her blue eyes. "You're the only one who ever liked the buttermilk, Alison. Cause you're a freak. Who mixes buttermilk with hot dogs?"

Alison is unbothered.

"It was really good buttermilk."

"Anyway," I sigh. "Since her, all other women are just—"

I grimace "—plain old hot dogs. I don't have an appetite for any of them."

Kelly snickers, cause that's her way. "Player Dean has an unrequited crush? We are witnessing karma in action, people."

"I think she ruined me," I lament. "I think I'm broken."

A hushed sympathy falls over the table—a moment of silence for the loss of my sex drive.

Until Merkle's harsh voice shatters the quiet.

"You are such a dick."

"I'm baring my soul over here!"

"Well your soul is a dick then, too. Listen to yourself. You're comparing women to fucking hot dogs, Dean."

"It's a compliment!" I argue. "I'm saying she's the best hot dog I ever tasted."

"Yes—and now all other women are just lips and assholes."

My mouth snaps shut for a moment.

"Okay . . . when you put it like that, it does sound kind of dickish."

"That's why I married her. My baby's smart as hell." Jerry puts his arm around his wife's shoulders. "And she gives great head."

Quick as lightning, Merkle pinches Jerry's nipple until his eyes water. Then she turns back to me.

"Have you considered that maybe a string of random hookups isn't doing it for you anymore? That just maybe you're ready for something a little deeper, a little more meaningful at this stage in your life?"

I drain the rest of my beer, because analyzing this is hard. And boy, do I miss easy.

"I don't know. Maybe."

"We are getting old," Kelly says. "I mean, I could still pass for one of the students, but the rest of you . . . the years have not been kind. Just sayin'."

"I saw Mr. Wendall at the post office the other day," Alison says, shaking her head. "And I realized I'm older now than he was when he taught us. And back then—he seemed really frigging old." She leans forward, whispering like the kid from the *Sixth Sense*, "We're gonna be dead soon."

Jesus Christ. Why do I hang out with these people?

I'm about to slam my head on the table, hoping to knock myself out, when Evan suggests, "Or she could be your prairie vole."

"My what?"

"Prairie voles—a Midwestern rodent that looks like a hamster. The first time they go into heat, there's a frantic rush to copulate with as many different partners as possible, as they search for their mate. When they find them, a sort of biological bonding takes place—and from then on they're monogamous, coupled for life. If something happens to their mate, they're celibate—they never have sex again."

Now I'm picturing bald, horny little hamsters scurrying around in monk's robes.

It's disturbing.

"Thanks, Evan, that makes me feel so much better." I point around the table. "Remind me to cut my tongue out before I share with any of you ever again."

Mark brings a tray of shots to the table. If you can't get laid, you might as well get wasted—it's the next best thing. I pick up a shot and tap everyone's glass for good luck. Because God knows, I need it.

"Bottoms up."

CHAPTER
Seven

Dean

November

Most high school teachers get off easy at November parent-teacher conference night. By the time the average student reaches adolescence, they're basically self-sufficient when it comes to school work, and their parents are healthily disinterested.

This is not the case with my students.

For me, parent-teacher conferences are like a night of bad speed dating. Each parent gets five minutes—I learned my first year of teaching to set a timer. If not, the queue in the hallway devolves into chaos, because every parent, if allowed, will spend the whole damn night telling me about their kid—their allergies, their night-terrors, the spelling bee they dominated in eighth grade. Or, I'll get a lecture on how to better instruct their brilliant future Nobel Prize recipient.

My kids are high-strung about their grades—and those

apples fell close as fuck to the trees.

"I don't understand, Coach Walker. Last year Martin was doing two hours of calculus homework, but this semester he's only been doing one."

Mrs. Smegal—Martin Smegal's mother—is a single mom with a harsh North Jersey accent and a perpetually frowning face.

"He needs to be challenged. He needs to be broken. He needs to be home on the weekends studying because he's terrified of ruining his life by getting anything less than straight A's."

Oh Martin . . . you poor bastard.

I turn on the smile, and the charm.

"I assure you Martin's working very hard. And while we did spend the beginning of the semester reviewing earlier material, the coursework will absolutely be more challenging from here on out." I gesture to Martin's tests and classwork portfolio. "He's the best student in the class, Mrs. Smegal—you should be very proud."

I give "the best student in the class" line to all the parents. In part because it's true—each of my kids rock in their own way—but mostly, it's to get their parents off their asses.

"Oh. Good." Mrs. Smegal nods. Then she wriggles a finger at me. "Let's just make sure he stays the best. No slacking."

"No, ma'am. You can rest easy. I'll keep an eye on Martin."

And finally she smiles—stiff and awkward, like someone who doesn't do it very often—but still it's a smile. It's a win.

The sweet sound of the timer goes off. After Mrs. Smegal's out the door, I check my list to see who's up next.

Burrows. Jason Burrows's mom.

Huh—and she's late. That's new for me.

I start the timer anyway, to stay on schedule, and wonder if I'm going to have my first no-show.

But then a voice comes from the door. It's soft, hesitant . . . and heart-grippingly familiar.

"Coach Walker?"

I spin around.

And it's her. It's Lainey. Standing in my classroom, peering those long-lashed, jeweled eyes at me. It's not a mistake, not my imagination—the woman I've been thinking about for *months,* the woman I've jerked off to more times than I will ever admit out loud, the woman who made me come so hard over the summer, I temporarily went blind—is *right fucking there.*

"Lainey?" I take a slow step toward her, afraid that she'll disappear if I move too fast. *"Lainey?"*

She's as shocked as I am.

Her eyes drift over me—my dark-framed glasses, the collared shirt beneath a light gray sweater—I look a little different than I did over the summer. But then her shiny lips spread into a smile that's so bright and beautiful—I feel it right in my dick.

"Dean? Oh my God, *Dean*?"

This is exactly how Danny Zuko must've felt when he saw Sandy again in *Grease.*

"Holy shit!" I exclaim.

We move forward at the same time, evaporating the space that separates us. And our hug is the easiest, most natural thing in the world. I wrap my arms tight around her lower back and lift her right off her feet.

There's an excellent chance I may never let her go.

I thought my memory had overplayed how good Lainey felt in my arms—that my mind had exaggerated the perfect way her curves fit all snug and soft right against me. But I didn't imagine it—it's every bit as good—better, than I remember.

She looks up at me, shaking her head in disbelief.

"I can't—what are you doing here?"

"I teach here."

"You're a teacher?"

"Yeah."

"I thought you were a drummer?"

"I'm both." I laugh, cause this is nuts. "What are *you* doing here?"

"My son goes here. Jason."

"Jason Burrows is your kid? You're Jason Burrows's mom?"

I knew that—obviously—she just said it. But my short-circuiting brain needs the confirmation.

"Yeah." Lainey laughs too.

Women are complicated creatures. They want you to want them, but—at least in the beginning—they don't want you to want them *too* much. Too much interest, availability, eagerness . . . it's a turnoff. Playing it cool is always the safer move. A little mystery, a little aloofness, keeps them hanging on.

I know this game. I'm *good* at this game. I've been playing it without fail since I was fourteen years old. But in this moment, all those rules go straight out the window, and the God's honest truth spills from my lips.

"I can't believe you're here. I've been thinking about you. Jesus, you have no idea. I haven't stopped—"

My words cut off quick.

Because that's when I feel it—when it registers that Lainey's lower abdomen is pressing against my hip. That it's different from the flat, tiny waist I worshiped with my tongue and hands four months ago.

Very different.

It's distended. Hard. Round.

I look down between us. Lainey's wearing black yoga pants and this tied, layered navy and white shirt number that makes her tits look fantastic, and hugs her tight around the hips—accentuating the unmistakable bulge protruding beneath it.

"I've been thinking a lot about you too, Dean," Lainey confesses in a whisper.

It's . . . a *bump*. That's what I'm looking at. Maybe she's bloated—or decided to eat a small soccer ball for dinner? It could happen.

The downside of being really smart is that it's almost impossible to delude yourself, no matter how much you want to drown in that ignorant bliss. It takes a nanosecond to discard those theories and recognize the obvious conclusion.

And when that happens—my brain becomes a ghost town.

I take a step back. And then I take another one—just in case.

I point at her stomach. "Is that . . . ?"

"Yeah."

"Are you . . . ?"

She nods. "Yeah."

Nope, still can't deal.

"Seriously?"

"Seriously."

I point to myself.

"Is it . . . ?"

And the whole world slants, like the floor of one of those Tilt-A-Whirl carnival rides we used to ride over and over until we threw up.

Lainey looks at me gently, her eyes light, her voice tender.

"Yes . . . it's yours."

When I was seventeen I got slammed by a three-hundred forty pound linemen who got drafted to the NFL the following year. It was a blind hit, I never saw it coming—it knocked my helmet off, knocked the breath out of my lungs, and left me unconscious on the field for four minutes.

This hits harder.

"Are you sure?"

She twists her fingers together in front of the bump.

"You're the only person I've had sex with in five years."

"Damn. That's pretty sure."

"Yeah." She nods.

"But we used condoms. We used a whole . . ."

"A whole box of condoms." Lainey throws up her hands. "I know! That's what I said. The sperm and egg apparently didn't get that message. And there's this whole ripping the condom open with your teeth statistic that's gonna blow your mind, but . . . maybe . . . maybe you should sit down, Dean? You don't look so well."

The pregnant woman is telling me to sit down—this is where we are now.

"That's probably a good idea."

And yet, I don't move an inch. My central nervous system has been frozen by the shock.

"I tried to find you," she explains. "To tell you. But the band doesn't have a website and the bar was closed and . . ."

"We don't advertise." My words are hollow and flat, answering on autopilot. "Since we only play in the summers, we don't take on new gigs."

Lainey licks her lips, nodding.

"That's what I figured."

The timer goes off—and I want to chuck it out the window, smash it with my fists like the Incredible Hulk having a really bad day. A second later, a parent—Louis's dad—sticks his head through the door.

I hold up my hand before he says a word.

"I'm going to need another fucking minute here, Larry."

My words are harsh and totally unprofessional and I don't even care.

Begrudgingly, he closes the door. And I desperately try to pull my shit together.

But Lainey's already a step ahead of me.

"We should talk, Dean, but not here—and obviously not now." She goes to my desk, writing on a scrap of paper and handing it to me. "Here's my number. Text or call me when you're free and we'll meet up to discuss . . . everything."

"Okay, yeah. Sounds like a plan."

She shifts on her feet.

"So . . . how's Jason doing in math?"

And I laugh—sounding a little lunatic even to my own ears. I scrub my hand over my face.

Snap out of it, Walker.

And it's like a default setting. Even with the easy, uncomplicated world as I know it disintegrating before my eyes, I'm able to shift into teacher mode.

"He's . . . he's doing awesome. He's a great kid, Lainey."

"Yeah, he is."

"He's gifted."

"He's always been so smart. Really quick when it comes to school."

"No, I mean—Jason's legitimately gifted. There are some college-level programs you should be looking at for him. For his future. We can talk about that later too."

This seems to come as a surprise to her, but she rolls with it.

"Oh. Wow, okay."

The door opens again, and I've never wanted to knock a parent on their ass as much as I do right this second.

"Goddamn it, Larry—not yet."

When the door is closed again, Lainey moves toward it.

"I'm going to go. This is—we'll talk more soon, Dean."

But when she puts her hand on doorknob—it's like there's a break in the fog—a space of clarity. And I remember there's something I need to tell her.

"Lainey!"

She turns back, her eyebrows lifting and her features supple with curiosity. My feet finally remember how to function and I move closer to her.

"I should've asked for your number—that morning—I wanted to. Later, when I woke up, I was so pissed off at myself for not asking. Because . . . I wanted to see you again." I look into her eyes and I don't hold back. "I've wanted to see you again since the minute you walked out the door."

Lainey blinks those long lashes, taking that in—because she didn't know. When her smile comes, it's soft, a little relieved, and so fucking beautiful it hurts.

"Okay. I'll see you again soon."
Then she walks out the door.

I spend the next three hours is a haze of jumbled thoughts. I nod my way through the rest of my conferences, like a zombie who's just discovered he's spawned a little zombie. McCarthy will probably get some emails about my distraction, and she'll ride my ass, but that's the least of my worries.

After the last conference is finally over, I head straight to Garrett's class, but he and Callie are already gone for the night. So I get in my car and drive to their house—it's only 9:30. And when crazy, monumental stuff happens, guys really aren't so different from chicks—we talk to our friends about that shit.

When Garrett opens the door, he's surprised to see me.

"Hey, man."

I walk in and sit down at the kitchen table before I fall down.

Callie is there, giving baby Will a snack in his highchair.

"Hey, Dean."

Will holds out his hand and squeaks a saliva-slicked version of my name.

"Deeen!"

I smack his palm high-five. "Hey, little man."

Callie puts carrot pieces on Will's tray and looks at me with concerned eyes.

"Are you okay?"

"Yeah." Garrett comes in beside her. "You look like Brian Pataloo at Kimberly Fletchers's Sweet Sixteen, right before he puked all over the cake."

Callie laughs. "That was literally twenty years ago! I can't believe you remember that."

"It was a lot of puke. I still can't believe someone puked that much and lived." Garrett lifts his chin at me. "What's up?"

I don't know how to say it. I literally can't make my mouth form the words. So, I take the long way around.

"Remember the blonde I told you about that I hooked up with in the beginning of the summer? The hot one that I couldn't get out of my head—Lainey?"

"Yeah?"

"It turns out, she's Jason Burrows's mother. We ran into each other when she came to my room, tonight, for conferences."

"I know Lainey Burrows," Callie says. "I met her at the football game last month."

"She was at the game?" I ask in a hollow voice.

The blonde at the truck . . . that was Lainey. She's been right here in town all this time.

"Yeah. She's really nice—and pretty. And about as pregnant as I am."

That trips Garrett up. Because he doesn't get it yet—neither of them do.

"Wait a minute." He looks at me. "You hooked up with a pregnant chick? You didn't tell me that."

"No, babe," Callie says. "She's four and a half months along, the same as me. Which means she didn't get pregnant until . . ."

And we have a winner.

Garrett does the math in his head.

". . . until the beginning of the summer."

Callie pauses crunching on a carrot, mid-chew.

"Ohhh."

Garrett sits down. "Wow."

"Yeah." I nod. "Exactly. Fucking wow."

Will looks at each of us with his big, brown baby eyes and agrees with my take on the situation.

"Ffffuckin' wow."

CHAPTER
Eight

Dean

That night, when I'm not tossing and turning in my bed, or punching my pillow or watching the shadow of Lucifer's padded little paws stalk back and forth outside my bedroom door, I have nightmares. Dark, cloudy dreams about missing gigs with the band because I couldn't remember the start times and being chained to the radiator at the daycare in the high school—even though Lakeside doesn't have a daycare.

My subconscious is a pretty straight shooter, you don't have to be Freud to figure out what they mean.

In the morning, I get up and play the drums. Mindless, pounding songs from bands like Slayer and Metallica, to try and get my head on straight. For the first time in my life, it doesn't help. And when I walk back up the basement steps hours later, I'm just as twisted up inside as when I started.

I text Lainey and we agree to meet up at Boston Market

for lunch, per her request. I get there first and watch as she walks across the parking lot wearing jeans, gray knit boots, a white wife-beater, and this long-sleeved Sherpa jacket that looks like it was made from the wool of a sheared pink sheep. Her long hair is tied up in a high ponytail, with gold aviators covering her eyes.

It's an unusual look—kind of mismatched and thrown together—but it works for her.

Two guys check her out as she comes through the door, and when they turn back for a double-take of her ass, I have the surprising urge to gouge their eyes out with a plastic spork.

Weird.

As I move toward her, I notice the small, unmistakable bump of her lower abdomen. And it hits me all over again that this is actually real. This is my life. This is happening.

Dean Walker is going to be a father.

Holy fuck me sideways.

When you start referring to yourself in the third person in your own mind—that's when you know you're screwed.

"Hi, Dean. It's good to see you. I'm glad you texted me." Lainey rests her sunglasses on the top of her head. Her smile comes quick and easy.

And goddamn, she's pretty.

Flawless, creamy skin, high cheekbones, big round eyes framed with thick, sooty lashes, pouty lips that seem just on the verge of smiling, stupendous tits, long legs, and the kind of ass you want to grab on to and never, ever let go.

I mean—I knew she was pretty, I know what she looks like—but somehow between last night and now, between the summer and now—Lainey's left beautiful behind and moved right into perfect.

There's this throbbing, yearning ache in my chest—and my groin—just from looking at her. It's bizarre and it's never happened to me before and . . . I don't think I'm happy about it.

"Hey. It's good to see you too."

This is good—the exchange of pleasantries—a nice normal conversation, like I'm not freaking the fuck out at all.

Michael Dillinger, a senior, greets me with a "Hey Coach" from behind the counter, and fills our order. I pay for both our meals and Lainey lets me. The place is empty, so we sit at a table in the corner and the song "Even If It Break Your Heart" by the Eli Young Band plays in the background, keeping things from being too silent.

Lainey dives into her mashed potatoes and gravy.

"Mmmm. . ." She sighs with this blissful little whimper of a moan.

And I remember that sound.

It's the exact noise she makes right after she comes. Breathy and sweet.

My shameless dick reacts with a vengeance. And I glance down toward my lap admonishingly. *So not the time, dude.*

"Thanks for agreeing to meet here. I'm like a crack addict lately with their mashed potatoes and mac and cheese. They're the only foods that don't give me heartburn."

Right.

Because pregnant women get heartburn. And Lainey is pregnant.

With. My. Kid.

The inappropriate dick issue isn't an issue anymore. Shock and dread don't mix well with boners.

But . . . even though I feel like I'm about to yak all over

my two-piece meal and biscuit—I can't stop looking at the bump. My eyes keep dragging over it.

It's unreal. Fascinating. Terrifying and surreal—but fascinating.

"Do you want to feel it?" Lainey asks.

"Feel it?"

She nods, dabbing at her lips with the napkin, and standing up.

"It's small but it's there." She lifts her shirt and pushes the top of her jeans down, then she takes my hand and presses it against her stomach. Her skin is taut and warm over the surprisingly firm swell of the bulge.

And there's a fucking baby in there.

I know I'm repeating myself but I can't help it—my mind is so blown there should be pieces of skull all over the goddamn floor right now.

"Wow." My thumb drags back and forth over that petal soft skin.

"Wild, right?"

I shake my head. "It's crazy."

Too crazy not to talk about. To come to a crystal-clear understanding about. To lay down ground rules and expectations. It's not so different from a math problem—I just need to know the parameters so I can solve this mother.

I pull my hand away and Lainey sits down across from me, digging back into the mashed potatoes.

"Okay, so, I don't want to sound like an asshole, but . . . how do you see this working, exactly?" I ask. "What do you expect from me, Lainey?"

She gazes back at me with those hazel eyes—a dozen different emotions swimming in their depths. Hope, determination, joy, worry, attraction and lust—it's all there, swirled together, naked for me to see.

I don't think Lainey has a poker face.

"I don't expect anything from you. Or . . . I expect everything, if that's what you want to give." She puts her fork down, her brow scrunching a bit. "I've had time to process this, to think it through. When I thought I wasn't going to find you, I was prepared to have this baby—to keep it, and raise it and love it. That was my choice, it still is. Now you have a choice to make—you have to decide if being a dad is something you want to do. The rest is just logistics."

"Decide if I want to be a dad?" I lift my chin at the bump. "Kind of late for that, isn't it?"

"It takes more than knocking someone up to be a dad."

My neck goes hot and itchy and my tongue feels swollen, like I'm having an anaphylactic reaction.

"Yeah, I get that."

She goes on to explain about *Life with Lainey*—her blogging, her videos, her deal with Facebook.

"The contract is for one year so Jason and I will be at the lake house until next summer. After that, I was going to get an apartment or rent a house in town so Jay won't have to change schools again." She takes a big breath. "Neither of us planned this, Dean. But, we can get to know each other, we can become friends and we can raise this baby together."

Her gaze moves down to the table. "Or, if you don't want that, then that's okay too."

I hold up my hand. "What does that mean 'that's okay too'?"

"I won't force you to do anything you don't really want to do. Parenting doesn't work that way—not for me. It's too hard and too important. You have to want it, Dean."

"So . . . what?" I try to picture how that would work in my head. "You squeeze out the kid and then afterward, we're strangers? Just two people passing each other at the Bagel Shop on Sunday mornings? *Hey, how's it going, great fucking weather we're having. How about those Giants?*"

Lainey shrugs, her silky ponytail swaying with the movement.

"It'll be what it'll be."

It's kind of eerie how calm she is about all this. It makes me look for the other shoe—a massive, steel-tipped boot— that's bound to be painful when it drops.

"What about child support?"

"If you decide to be a part of this child's life, we can talk about how we'll divide the finances. If not, I don't want your money. I can take care of myself and my kids."

Lainey's got a stubborn streak. It's there in the flash of her amber-green eyes, the twitch of her nose and rise of her chin. It's very, very cute.

And confusing as hell.

Because I've spent more than half my life being chased by women. They always cared more than I did, were always more invested in the relationship than I was. I'm not saying that to be a douche—it's just the truth. They wanted the commitment, the promise, the key to the house, the drawer in the dresser, the ring.

But now, this woman could chain me to her for the rest of our lives. And she's not. Lainey's not just putting the ball in my court, she's laying it at my feet and walking away.

I have no idea what to make of her.

Lainey pushes her empty plate back, and takes a drink of

her water.

"You don't have to decide this minute—we have time. You should think about it, figure out what you want."

She looks up into my face, her big eyes shining, her jaw set.

"The thing is, Dean . . . with kids . . . you have to be sure. Jason's father isn't in his life—he never was and I know that was hard for Jason. But it was a clean break, the hurt was allowed to heal. He has uncles and a grandfather who love him and have filled in that space when I can't. But if his dad had been half in and half out—if he'd let him down, said he'd do things with him then didn't, if he'd messed with his emotions—that would've been like ripping off a scab over and over. It would've . . . ."

"Scarred," I finish softly.

Because I get it. I understand what she's saying. I've seen it in my students, and because of my own screwed-up parentage. Kids know when they're wanted, and when they're not— and it's really fucking important that the people closest to them, want them.

"Exactly." Lainey folds her hands across her stomach, and her pretty mouth purses. "So, if you decide that you're not up for this—I'll understand—no hard feelings, really. But if you decide that you're in, you have to mean it. You have to be sure. You have to be *all in*."

I look back into her eyes and it's like everything inside me is shifting and spinning and upside-down. I don't know what I'm doing—and I have no idea what I want.

I nod slowly. "That makes sense. Totally reasonable."

Lainey gives me a soft smile and stands. "Call me if you want to talk some more or if you have any questions." She tilts her head toward the door. "I'll be over in the haunted house on Miller Street."

I chuckle. Then Lainey leans over and presses a kiss to my cheek, and the scent of her surrounds me. I remember that too—the fragrance of her skin, the taste of her—warm and clean and honey-sweet. The way I craved another taste of her for days . . . weeks, after we hooked up.

She straightens up and turns toward the door.

"Hey," I call softly. "Can I ask you something?"

"Sure."

"Why are you being so cool about this? How are you so . . . not freaked out?"

She thinks a moment before she answers.

"I had Jay when I was nineteen—this is not my first time at the unplanned pregnancy rodeo. And, though my family has helped out, I've raised him on my own. Every instinct I have tells me you're a good guy, Dean. A decent guy. So, while I want to do this with you, if it turns out I have to do it without you . . . I know I'll be okay." She puts her hand on her stomach. "*We'll* be okay."

After Boston Market, I swing by Garrett's house. Two of his brothers, Connor and Tim, are there and the four of us sit out on the deck around the firepit having a few beers while Connor's three boys are down at the dock skipping rocks on the lake.

There are four Daniels boys in total—Connor the doctor, Ryan the cop, Garrett, and the youngest—Timmy the fireman. Being best friends with Garrett gave me a taste of what it was like to be a part of a big family, to have brothers who looked out for you, ragged on you, knocked you around. They always treated me like one of their own. They still do.

"I say run, dude. She gave you an out—take it. You're the genius, right? Don't be stupid."

That heartwarming bit of advice comes from Tim.

Every family has a dick in it. Timmy is the Daniels's dick.

I like the guy, don't get me wrong. But he's got youngest child syndrome and he's got it bad. That means he's selfish, self-centered, with the mentality of a sixteen-year-old. An *immature* sixteen-year-old.

"You'd really ditch your own kid that easily?" Connor gives his brother a judgmental look.

"Depends." Timmy thinks it over. "Does Mom know?"

"Can you not be a dick?" Garrett asks. "For like, two seconds? Is that even possible?"

"Probably not." Tim pats his brother's shoulder. "But, good talk, bro."

Garrett goes to smack him—but through the years Tim's learned to be quick with the block.

"Dude, I'm joking," he says, laughing. "I swear to Christ, Callie's hormones are catching—every time you get her pregnant you get all oversensitive and emotional."

"Shut up, dumbass."

"I'm not going to run," I tell them, steering the conversation back into focus. "I'm paying her child support—obviously. I'm not going to leave her hanging." I shake my head. "But the whole dad thing . . . I don't know about that."

Discipline is not my strong suit. I think you're only young once—and you should make it last as long as possible. I think partying is good for the soul. I think teenagers should learn how to handle their alcohol years before they actually turn twenty-one. I hate green vegetables. I eat them, because they're good for me—but I don't think I could make someone else eat them.

I always saw myself as more of the fun uncle type of guy, who'd send Garrett's kids birthday cards full of cash and who'd eventually retire to Florida with a rotating harem of girlfriends half my age.

As far as life plans go, that was the extent of mine. Children, a wife, a family—they were never part of the picture.

"I mean, really, could you see me raising a kid?"

Garrett looks me dead in the face, his brown eyes dark and serious.

"Definitely."

Connor—who's opinion I've always respected, agrees.

"Absolutely."

"For real?" I ask.

"Hell, yeah," Connor says. "I've seen you with Will—you're good with him."

I jerk my thumb toward Garrett. "Will is *his*. I can give him back."

Garrett shakes his head. "But when they're yours, you don't want to give them back. Everything they do is amazing. They take a shit and it's like a miracle."

Timmy grimaces. "That's gross, Gar."

"And yet, still true." Garrett takes a drink from his beer, looking at me. "You're great with your students."

I wave him off. "They're teenagers."

"Teenagers and babies aren't so different. Most of the time, the babies are easier to reason with."

Connor points at his brother. "This is a fact."

Connor's youngest son, seven-year-old Spencer, calls up to his father to come skip rocks with them. Connor got divorced about two years ago—he only gets the boys every other weekend, so when they're with him—he makes damn sure he's *with* them too. He puts his bottle on the table and heads down the steps to the dock.

"There is the baby-momma perk," Tim throws out thoughtfully. "That shouldn't be discounted."

Garrett shakes his head at his youngest brother. "Please don't frigging help."

Still I ask, "What's the baby-momma perk?"

Tim leans forward. "I'm assuming this Lainey chick is good-looking?"

"Gorgeous." I confirm.

"Well, she's going to need someone to bang her during the next nine months. It's not like pregnant girls are big on trolling for hookups, so that duty will more than likely fall on your dick. We're talking unlimited, easy access booty calls—condom-free—it's not like you can knock her up twice."

That is an excellent point. I'm shocked I didn't think of it myself.

I've been dreaming of getting back inside Lainey for months. And now she's here. Available, eager—I saw the way her eyes roamed over me on conference night and at lunch today—the way her pupils dilated and her nipples hardened. I know when a woman is interested in me, and Lainey is definitely up for a repeat of the summer. Probably several repeats.

I picture how she'll look a few months from now—her breasts fuller, her stomach rounder and heavier—and yep, it feels slightly wrong, but it's even more of a turn on.

Tim's phone rings and he glances at the screen, wiggling his eyebrows. "Speaking of booty calls." He heads up the steps toward the house as he answers, "Hey, baby," leaving Garrett and I alone on the deck.

I look out across the lake and take a long drag on my beer.

"I'm just not sure if I can do this, D," I tell him softly. "What the fuck do I know about being anyone's dad? I don't know if I have it in me, you know?"

Garrett nods slowly.

"Yeah, I get that. I really do."

Even back in high school, Garrett always had his shit together. He was the quarterback—steady, solid, consistent—and I was the risk-taking wide receiver who liked to push the limits and go for the big plays. It's why we made a good team, why we still do. I could kick his ass on an IQ test, but between the two of us—he's the wise one.

"But the question you have to ask yourself, Dean, is a year from now . . . five, ten, fifteen years from now—how are you ever going to look at yourself in the mirror again, if you don't do it?"

The next afternoon, I'm in the living room, pulling old dusty photo albums out of Gram's antique bureau. Looking at pictures I haven't even thought about, let alone seen, in decades.

There's a Polaroid of my mother on the day I was born, propped up on pillows, holding me wrapped in a light blue blanket—looking like the baby-faced, dark-haired, sixteen year old girl she was when she had me.

Afterward she dropped out of high school, got her GED, then left me with Grams and took off when I was three. She bounced around the country for a while—I only saw her a handful of times—before she finally settled in Vegas about ten years ago.

I turn the page and it's the standard toddler fare of messy highchair eating and bare-assed bathtub shots. A few pages after that is a picture of me on my first day of kindergarten. I remember Grams taking this one—next to the tree outside Lakeside Elementary. I grin with a gap-toothed smile, and square glasses and a white button down shirt with a Superman backpack slung across my shoulder.

I was a handsome, nerdy little bastard.

Grams shuffles into the living room, holding Lucy in her arms, rubbing a towel on the beast's damp black fur. On a good day, the cat hates the world, but on bath days she's especially vengeful. Grams sits on the couch beside me, and Lucy does a little shimmy in her lap. Then she turns around, lifts her tail and shows me her asshole before flouncing away.

Subtle.

"Look at you—such a sweet boy." Grams leans over, tracing the kindergarten picture with her shaky hand.

I flip through the rest of the pages and there, at the end, not actually in the album, but stuck in the back is a picture of my father.

It's weird to think of him as my father, because the only image I have of him is this one—when he was younger than most of my students—at the skate park at sunset, smirking into the camera with a sticker-covered skateboard tucked under his arm. Just a boy.

I flick the picture with my finger. "He looks like a punk.

A total smartass."

The kind of kid who'd be parked outside McCarthy's office every other day. Guaranteed.

Grams confirms my suspicions. "From what I remember, he was quite the little shithead." But then her voice softens as she looks up at me. "Though he had a part in making you, so he couldn't have been all bad."

He was tall for sixteen, and broad, with familiar thick blond hair—but that's where the likeness ends. Our features are different, the jawline, the nose. I don't think I look like either of my parents . . . or maybe they just weren't around long enough for me to pick up on the similarities.

"Did he ever see me?"

"No." Grams shakes her head. "He was already a dropout when your mother told him she was pregnant. And he high-tailed it out of town months before you were born. Left in a van with those friends of his, said they were going surfing in Hawaii or some nonsense."

I never resented my mother for leaving, not really. On some level, I knew it was the nicest thing she ever did for me. That she just didn't have it in her to be a real mother. And she knew Grams would take care of me, love me, raise me right.

This dickhead is another story.

"How do you do that? I guess I can understand taking off when he was younger, but when he was an adult—didn't he ever wonder if I was okay? He would've been thirty when I was fourteen." More than old enough to have grown the hell up. Take responsibility. Fucking care, even a little. "What if I needed a kidney or a blood transfusion? How does someone have a kid out there in the world and just not give a shit?"

Grams pats my hand and shrugs.

"It's the way people are built, Deany. When the unexpected happens, some are the type to stick around and some head for the nearest exit. If you're asking that question, you already know which one you are."

Growing up I used to suspect Grams was psychic. She just knew things. If I snuck in after curfew or smoked weed with the band in the woods, even if she didn't actually catch me, she knew. I get that same vibe from her now.

"Where's this coming from, Dean?"

I don't lie—the woman's a gray-haired polygraph. But I don't give her the whole truth, either. Not yet.

"Some stuff has come up that has me thinking, that's all."

Later, I go for a drive around town. Hitting the drums didn't help clear my head, but maybe some aimless driving will be just the ticket.

As I head down Main Street, I spot Old Mrs. Jenkins looking like a hunched ball of brown coat as she walks the bouncy caramel-colored Shih Tzu her great-grandkids got her for her ninety-fourth birthday. Mr. Martinez is cleaning the big picture window in the front of his furniture store with a long black squeegee. A group of boys ride their bikes down the sidewalk—and I instantly flash back to the day I learned to ride when I was six. The day I taught myself, bruised elbows and skinned knees galore, because there wasn't anyone around able and interested enough to do the job.

Then I see Tara Benedict, a girl I went to high school with, pushing her new baby girl in a stroller with one hand and holding her son Joshua's hand with the other. Josh is Tara's son with her ex-husband, but he's not in the picture. He calls her new husband Dad.

All the women I've screwed, all the girlfriends I've had and broken up with—I was never possessive. Not once. I don't think I ever cared enough to put in the effort to be jealous.

And yet, when I picture Lainey in Tara's place, when I think about her raising my soon-to-be kid with some other guy, any other guy—probably a douchebag—one word echoes through me like the screech of an overtightened guitar string that's ready to snap.

Mine, mine, mine.

Lainey was mine that night—every beautiful inch of her. And the baby we made that night is mine. Ours.

And I feel that, right down to the center of my bones.

The sun is just setting on the west side of the lake, reflecting on the water like an orange ball of fire when I drive down Miller Street and pull into Lainey's driveway. The wind gusts when I get out of the car—a flock of crispy brown leaves swirl around my feet as I take long, deliberate steps across the lawn.

The song "Shallow" from that Lady Gaga and Bradley Cooper movie plays loudly from inside. I hear it as I walk up the steps and across the porch, toward the door in the back.

But I stop when I catch the sight of her through the window. And that aching throb in my chest comes back with a vengeance—a steel-fisted punch right to the heart.

Lainey's hair falls around her shoulders in long, loose waves. She's wearing soft gray shorts and a tank top that reveals about an inch of skin just above that rounded little bump. An oversized beige sweater flares out as she spins in a circle— dancing slow and barefoot on the shiny hardwood floor.

And it's instantaneous—immediate—everything locks into place inside me. The free-falling, freaked-out feeling is gone . . . because . . . okay, I may not know what I'm doing—but I know what I want.

I want to be more than my father and better than my mother. I want to be here for her and for them. I don't want to be a faded fucking picture in the back of an old photo album.

I want to do this, and more than I've ever wanted anything in my life—I want to be good at it.

I rap my knuckles on the oak wood, so she'll hear the knock above the music. When Lainey opens the door, she looks up at me, her pink lips parted, her long, pretty lashes blinking around those big gorgeous eyes in a way that makes me want to kiss the hell out of her.

"Dean, hey…"

The music swells from inside the room—two voices singing about diving into the deep end, leaving the safe shallow far, far behind.

And my tone is clear with the simple, unshakeable truth.

"I'm in. I'm all in."

CHAPTER
Nine

Lainey

'm in trouble.

"This is so weird."

"It is. You're right. Totally weird."

Dean and Jason are on the back porch steps. Sitting beside each other. Looking out over the lake. Talking. Mano a mano, guy to guy, teacher to student, baby-daddy to son.

"It's so . . . disappointing."

"Is it?"

"Yeah."

"How so?"

And I'm in the kitchen peeking out the window and eavesdropping through the crack in the door, like the pregnant creeper I am.

"You're my favorite teacher ever—"

"That means a lot to me."

"And now, I find out you're the guy who . . ." Jay can't

bring himself to say it. Picturing it probably is no picnic either. "That you and my mom—"

"It's better if you don't think about it. Just block it out."

"She's getting bigger by the day—kind of hard not to think about how that happened."

"Fair point."

I think I've handled the whole situation well. I've been calm, mature, strong and dignified. I meant it when I said I'd be fine doing this on my own—I would've been.

"Am I going to be able to stay in your class?"

"I'll talk it over with Miss McCarthy, but I don't see why not."

But I'd be a big, fat liar if I said I wasn't relieved that I don't have to.

Relieved and . . . thrilled. It's the thrilled part that worries me.

"What am I supposed to call you?"

"I dunno. What do you want to call me?"

"Dean would be too weird at school."

"Agreed. You start calling me Dean, the whole class will start calling me Dean . . . it'll be anarchy."

When Dean showed up on my porch, flashing those stormy blue eyes and swore that he was all in—like it was the most solemn, important thing he'd ever done—I almost swooned right on the spot. My knees actually got weak. For. Real.

"But calling you Coach Walker around the house . . ."

Dean shakes his head. "Way awkward. It's like calling someone Grandfather or The Colonel. It'd be like living in a game of Clue—Coach Walker in the bedroom with the turkey baster."

Jason chokes on a snort.

"Too soon?" Dean asks with a laugh in his voice.

And now he's having a heart-to-heart with my Jaybird and it's the most adorable thing I've ever heard. The care in his voice as he talks to my son. The interest.

Having a conversation with a teenage boy about the more complicated situations of life isn't easy. Not many men would know how to handle that, and listening to one who does is a heady thing. An alluring, attractive thing that speaks to a deep, primal part of me.

The part that wants to rip Dean Walker's clothes off.

"All right, so you call me Dean around the house and Coach Walker at school. How's that sound?"

"That works for me."

I can already feel my emotions getting away from me— like a balloon getting caught in the wind, rising higher and higher until it's so far gone you can't even see it.

It's better to keep your feet on the ground.

Hope is scary. Attachment is risky. Disappointment can be crippling.

I've learned that the hard way. It's easier not to expect things from people—not to want or dream about a future that may never happen.

"Are you gonna, like, *be* around the house? A lot?"

"As long as it's cool with your mom, yeah. That's my plan."

But now there's a giddy, gushy sensation in my chest. The smile pulling at my lips is silly and permanent and it's all because Dean has decided to do this with me. To be a part of our lives.

"Just so you know, I don't need a dad or anything.

There've been guys who tried to play the father card—and I'm over it. That ship has sailed."

There was *one* guy that I dated for a few weeks who tried to play the father card. He was a hunter-gatherer type who wanted to share his outdoor-sportsman love with Jay—but gutting a deer in front of a six-year-old is a dealbreaker for me.

"Just so *you* know, I don't think I'm qualified to be anyone's dad, at least not yet. I've got a few months to whip my ass into shape for that. But for now, for you, I just . . . I want to be your friend, Jason."

That soft confession melts my heart into a gooey mess of sweet, tender desire. From the jump, I thought that Dean was a good man—and he confirms it with every word out of his mouth. He's smart and talented and funny—and let's not forget the hot. So very, very hot.

Those glasses—holy hell—goodbye wild-boy drummer, hello sexy professor. The fantasies are instant and numerous. I want to lick every inch of him while he's wearing those glasses.

"Would that be okay with you?"

"Yeah, friends would be good."

"Cool."

"Cool."

How do you stop yourself from wanting a man who's so damn wantable? And wanting Dean is just asking for trouble. It could make things messy and awkward between us. Simple is better. Easy. Keep the focus on the baby. Co-parenting and friendship.

That is all.

I need to keep my thoughts away from Dean's gorgeous mouth, his sexy smile, his hands, his firm, oh-so-grabbable ass and especially—his cock. The beautiful dick that made me light up brighter than the Rockefeller Center Christmas tree. I'm pretty sure it's ruined me for all other penises—including my best vibrator, Charles. Charles and I have had a few encounters since the summer—but it's just not the same.

"The thing is . . ." Jason pauses, glancing around and lowering his voice like he's telling a secret. "My mom's used to doing things on her own. She says it's easier that way. She's never really had anyone to help her—nobody but me. But she deserves that. She deserves someone who'll take care of her." Jason turns to look at Dean. "As long as you do that—you and I will be A-okay."

Dean puts his hand on my son's shoulder and that soft, solemn tone comes back.

"Yeah, Jay—I can definitely do that."

I'm in so, so, *so* much trouble.

After Dean and Jaybird come in from outside, I show Dean around the house—the kitchen, the projects that are halfway finished, the bedroom where the nursery will be. An hour or so later, we end up in the den that's still jam-packed with mismatched furniture and raw materials.

He sits in a taupe loveseat I salvaged from an estate sale that I plan to reupholster, his knees spread, one arm draped casually across the back. And he's watching me. Tracking my every move as I flit around the room.

I unroll a bolt of plush silver faux fur fabric. "I'm going to use this for accent pillows in the living room. Maybe a throw rug or a beanbag chair. I like texture—it adds individuality to the space without overcomplicating it."

I'm babbling—unnerved by the fluttery feeling in my stomach, brought on by the intensity of those ocean-blue eyes.

I take a breath and set the fabric down. "You're not really interested in any of this, are you?"

His mouth curls at the corner—a decadent, dirty kind of smile.

"Oh, I'm interested. No doubt about that."

Then he turns his head toward the boxes and stacks of paint cans.

"I think what you've done with the house is amazing, Lainey." He gestures to a few long-necked, teal wine bottles that I've filled with solar twinkle lights. "I think what you do, how you can make something special out of nothing, is incredible. I've never met anybody like you—and that's not a bullshit line."

Dean rises from the couch and moves closer, looking into my eyes and pressing his hand against my stomach. The feel of his palm is warm and soothing—the kind of touch you want to sink into.

"Between your creativity and my brain and superior athletic skills, our kid is going to be all kinds of outstanding."

Our kid.

It's not a phrase I'm used to hearing, but I like the sound of it. And for the first time in ever, I let myself imagine how it could be to not do this alone. To have someone to share it all with.

The thought is really, really nice.

When you get used to carrying a weight around on your shoulders for so long, you don't realize how heavy it actually is until it's been lifted off.

I put my hand over Dean's and smile. "Yeah."

"Moooom!" Jason's dragged-out voice cuts through the intimacy of the moment. "What's for dinner?"

The question of teenage boys around the world.

Dean glances at his watch. "How about you and Jay come to my house for dinner? You can meet Grams. I have to pick her up from movie night at the senior center."

That fluttery feeling plummets like an inner-tube on a waterslide—straight down.

"Grams?"

"My grandmother. My parents aren't in the picture, I don't have brothers or sisters. Grams raised me. She's the only family I have."

"Oh." I tap my fingers on my stomach. "Does she know about the baby?"

"Not yet."

"Don't you think you should tell her first?"

He seems confused. "That's what we'd be doing—telling her."

Apparently, once Dean is on board with something, it's full steam ahead. It must be the football coach in him—gotta move that ball down the field. Go, team, go.

His eyes search mine. "What's the problem, Lainey?"

"Is it a good idea to just spring it on her like that? I'm going to show up at her house pregnant and with my teenage son—two children, with two different fathers. Your grandmother is from a whole other generation . . . won't she think I'm, like . . . a whore?"

Dean throws his head back and laughs, deep and rumbly. And that Adam's apple is there—taunting me again with its sexiness.

Maybe I *am* a whore.

Dean's laughter fades as he looks down at me. "Back in the day, Grams was an attorney. She had my mom later in life and worked a lot when she was growing up—her office was in the city. Her main area of expertise was women's rights—sexual harassment claims, fighting for equal pay, abortion rights. She's burned her bra on the steps of the capital and argued before the Supreme Court. Though not on the same day."

"That's amazing."

"Yeah." Dean nods. "But the moral of the story is you could have seven kids by eight different fathers and she wouldn't give a rat's ass. You're having her first great-grandchild and I'm happy when I'm around you—that's all that's going to matter to her."

His words trip around in my head. "I . . . make you happy?"

Seems a little early to make that call.

But that playboy smile drags across his lips and his voice goes low.

"You make me hard."

Like a magnet to metal, my eyes make a beeline for Dean's crotch. And—oh my—he *is* hard. The long, thick outline of him strains against the zipper of his jeans. My mouth waters, remembering the taste of him and the hot, smooth feel of his flesh against my tongue.

"The happy tends to follow close after the hard, so yeah—I think happy qualifies in this situation."

Deans leans in and presses a quick kiss to my cheek.

"Don't be nervous, Lainey. I've got you."

Mr. Giles, Lakeside's local carpenter, has a few scrap pieces he said I could pick up tonight, so I suggest taking my truck to pick up Dean's Gram and the wood along the way.

Dean stands in the driveway. "Sure. I'm confident enough in my manhood to ride bitch."

Beside him, Jason strikes a similar stance, nodding.

"Me too. I don't mind riding bitch."

And I wonder if Dean knows he's got a burgeoning mini-me who already idolizes him.

He opens the truck door and shuts it closed behind me after I climb aboard. I don't get out of the truck when we get to Mr. Giles's place, but instead watch in the rearview mirror, with a strange swirly tenderness swooping through my belly, as Dean and Jay load the long boards of oak into the bed for me.

Then Dean directs me across town, and we pull up in front of the school-size brick building of the senior center. He hops out and a few minutes later, exits the building with a petite, gray-haired woman—literally half his size—shuffling along beside him.

Dean opens the passenger side door. From behind round, violet glasses that take up more than half her face, his grandmother peers bewilderedly at the distance between the ground and the seat.

"Going to need an assist with this one, Deany."

He lifts her up into the truck, then buckles the seatbelt around her as he introduces us.

"Grams, this is Lainey Burrows and her son, Jason."

I hold my hand straight out and a bit too eagerly—I don't have a lot of experience meeting the parents. "It's a pleasure to meet you, Mrs. Walker."

She puts her frail hand in mine and smiles. And I notice, Dean gets his eyes from his grandmother.

"Call me Grams—everyone does."

Jason waves from the backseat and Grams waves back.

"How was movie night?" Dean asks as he climbs in.

She clucks her tongue like an annoyed hen. "Just terrible. It was Driving Miss Daisy. Why would I enjoy watching a film like that—I'm practically living it."

Grams runs her hand over the dashboard.

"I like this vehicle, Lainey. Very muscular. I bet no one messes with you in this bad boy."

I smile. "That's true. And it comes in handy with my work."

"Lainey's a decorator, Grams." Dean tells her. "She makes furniture, artwork. She's redoing the old house on Miller Street."

"Oh, that's a lovely home—it's nice to know a young family is living there again."

And it's all going so well.

Until Dean says, "Hang a left up ahead, Lainey—onto 2nd Street."

But when I make the turn, and my wrist brushes the button on the steering wheel that activates the bluetooth. The speakers come alive inside the cab, and the truck automatically syncs to my phone—playing the audiobook of *A Brand New Ending* by Jennifer Probst—a fabulous romance I started listening to when I was doing the backsplash work in the kitchen.

The narrator's voice comes through loud and clear.

"She dragged her teeth over his flat stomach, blowing her breath over his hardened shaft until he jerked with need."

I press button after button, but I can't find the right one.

"Where's the button? Where's the fucking button?" I think I say it out loud, but it's hard to hear myself over the blood pounding in my eardrums.

"*She closed her hands around his erection, squeezed, sent her tongue darting out to taste his essence—*"

And . . . got it! The sound cuts off—though I'm definitely going back to listen to the rest of that scene when I'm alone.

An awkward silence is shrouded over the cab—as my eyes dart to Dean's grandmother. "Sorry. It's an audiobook I was listening to."

Her thin, penciled eyebrows rise. "I'll have to borrow it from you when you're finished." And then she winks. "Can't wait to hear what happens next."

The anxiety that was squeezing my chest, loosens. Dean and Jason's muffled laughter comes from the backseat, and a second later I join them.

I pull into the driveway of a modest home. We all lumber out of the truck and head inside. In the foyer, a small black cat comes padding around the corner, curling itself around Jason's leg. He crouches down and scoops the fluffy ball up into his arms.

"Careful with the cat, Jay," Deans warns, "She's not—"

The cat loves on Jason hard—rubbing its head along his collarbone, purring loudly like a happy mini-lion, planting a string of adoring, licking kisses along his jaw.

"Son of a bitch," Dean mutters.

"What?" I ask.

He shakes his head, pouting. "Tell you later."

And when I glance at the cat—I swear she's wearing a gloating, smirking expression—aimed right at Dean.

"That's my Lucy," Grams says, scratching her head. "It's

good to have a pet around the house. It teaches boys to be re-sponsible and nurturing."

"Except when the pet is trying to kill you," Dean mur-murs under his breath.

I swapped my cotton shorts for a pair of navy yoga pants before we left the house. They're comfy, but snug around my middle, putting the bump on full display. My sweater shifts as we all move into the living room, and Grams suddenly stops short.

She puts her hand on my shoulder, and speaks like she's breaking the news to me—in case I didn't know.

"Lainey, you're pregnant, dear."

Over her shoulder, Dean chuckles soundlessly.

"Uh, yeah." I fidget. "I know."

Dean moves around his grandmother to stand beside me, and takes my hand in his.

"Lainey and I met over the summer, Grams. We're having a baby. Together."

I wait for her reaction—this woman who raised Dean, who obviously means the world to him. I brace myself for sus-picion or disapproval to creep into her aged eyes. But her gaze just shifts back and forth between me and her grandson. And then she covers her mouth with a slightly trembling hand.

"Oh, how wonderful!"

Then she hugs me—wrapping me in an embrace that's warm and welcoming and surprisingly strong. Then she gives Dean the same treatment.

"What a beautiful child you two will have. This calls for champagne—life is short, drink champagne whenever you can. Jason," she calls with an easy familiarity. "That liquor cabinet there. The key is beneath the elephant on top. Open it up and get the bottle of champagne. Dean—get the crystal glasses from the dining room."

I opt for apple juice, but once Dean, Grams and even Jason have a glass of champagne—Grams holds up her sparkling flute.

"Welcome to the family, Lainey and Jason. The best days are when babies come—to the best days coming our way soon."

We all click glasses and my son drains his in one gulp.

Then he makes a face. "It doesn't taste anything like stars. John Green is full of shit."

We sit on the couch and Grams pats my knee. "How far along are you?"

"About four and a half months."

"That's when things start to get interesting." Grams pats Dean's leg with her other hand. "And if the baby grows up to be a hellion like you—you'll know all the tricks they'll try before they do."

"Dean was a hellion?" I ask.

"Oh, yes. But mark my words—they grow up to be the best fathers."

Grams pours herself another glass of champagne and Dean rubs his hands together. "What are we doing for dinner?"

"You could make your spaghetti sauce," Grams replies.

I meet Dean's eyes. "You cook?

"I do. I cook spaghetti sauce. That's the only thing."

"But it's delicious," Grams adds, proudly.

"It is delicious. She's not lying. But I can't cook spaghetti Grams—Lainey has heartburn."

He remembered. Is it weird that that turns me on? Cause it does. A lot.

"You still jonesing for Boston Market?" he asks me. "I can go pick it up and we can eat back here."

"Sounds good."

After we get our orders straight, Grams rises from the couch to the bureau, then hobbles back with a stack of photo albums in her arms.

"Let me show you some pictures of Deany—he was such a precious baby."

Dean stands, lifting his chin at me. "Lainey—keys?" I take the keyring out of my purse and Dean catches them one-handed. "Hey, Jaybird—you coming or are you going to hang with the girls and look at my bareass bathtub baby pictures?"

Jay scrunches his face. "I'm with you, dude."

"Good choice."

And it all feels so effortless. Comfortable. Like we're just sliding forward into this new, uncharted, crazy stage in life . . . sliding into a family.

No sooner does the front door close behind Dean and Jason than my stomach lurches like an anchorless boat—the apple juice I swallowed bubbling like battery acid.

It happens sometimes, the "morning" sickness comes out of nowhere, hits me hard and fast, and then after I get sick, I feel totally fine. Like my schizophrenic body's saying—*okay, we puked, now what's for dinner?*

Grams must see the look on my face, because she leans in and in her wispy granny voice asks, "Are you going to blow chunks, dear?"

I squint back at her. "I'm sorry?"

"Blow chunks, spew, hurl? They showed *Wayne's World* at the center last week—now, that's a movie. That Garth is an adorable boy."

I would laugh, but my palms are moist and a cold sheen of sweat breaks out all over my body. Pregnancy sucks so much ass.

Grams gestures down the hall. "The bathroom is just over there."

I stand on wobbly legs and make it to the bathroom just in time before the apple juice that was swirling in my stomach isn't in my stomach anymore. I rinse my mouth at the bathroom sink and splash cold water on my pale cheeks.

When I step back into the living room, Grams is waiting with a chilled glass of water.

"Thank you. Sorry about that."

She shakes her head and tucks a pillow behind me on the couch.

"Don't apologize. They used to tell us the sicker you were, the healthier the pregnancy was. But I think that was a load of crap—something they just say to make you feel better, like rain being good luck on a wedding day."

Grams drags a photo album onto her lap—and I get a glimpse of Dean Walker: the younger years.

He *was* a gorgeous baby, and from the look of the pictures, a rambunctious boy, a handsome high schooler. There are photos of Dean playing the drums, scoring touchdowns, being admitted to the National Honors Society, graduating from college summa cum laude. And scattered through all those accomplishments, are photos of Dean with girls.

And then more girls.

Girls to the left of him, girls to the right—at prom, in a car, on a couch, at the lake, in front of a bonfire. There are blondes, redheads, and brunettes—all of them are pretty—but with each turn of the page, none of them are the same. None of them seem to have stuck around for long.

I clear my throat. "Dean had a lot of girlfriends."

"Oh yes, he was very popular. Quite the ladies man."

I don't know what to say about that—how to feel. I don't know if I'm supposed to feel anything at all, so I say nothing.

Grams pats my knee again.

"Cake batter."

I search my mind for a Wayne's World quote involving cake batter.

"What do you mean?"

"My grandson is like a bowl of cake batter, Lainey. All the ingredients are there, just waiting for the right flame to come along. Once he's done cooking, he's going to be an exquisite piece of cake. I'm old—I know these things. You just wait and see."

It's after nine when we get home. Dean drives back with us to get his car, but comes inside after we pull into the driveway. Jason heads straight up the stairs without being told.

"I have to shower and hit the hay—it's a school night."

I hit the jackpot in the good kid department with him. Though, I guess that means I should be prepared for karma to even things out with baby number two. It's probably going to be a demon.

"Hey—how was that calculus homework?" Dean calls after him. "Did it kick your ass?"

"Nah, I didn't even break a sweat."

"I'll have to up my game."

Jason waves. "I'll see you in school tomorrow . . ." he

pauses awkwardly ". . . *Dean.*" Then he shakes his head. "Still weird."

"You'll get used to it. See you tomorrow, Jay."

After Jason's bedroom door closes, I move to the kitchen with Dean following close behind. I get a glass of water from the refrigerator.

"Do you want something to drink? Tea or water or lemonade?"

"I'm good."

The pitch-black night outside the window makes the dimly lit kitchen feel cozy and safe. Being here with Dean, just the two of us alone, fills the air with a close, familiar intimacy. He leans against the counter, arms crossed, and my eyes roam over the toned, rugged forearms beneath the pushed-up sleeves of his black sweater. I take a long drink of water as I look at his hands next—those big, sure hands. The remembered feel of them on my body brushes across my skin, and my breasts tingle with an achy need.

A ghost of a smile teases Dean's lips, as if he can sense where my mind is wandering.

"There's something I've wanted to ask you," he says.

"Go ahead."

"Am I really the only person you had sex with in five years?"

I laugh. "Yep."

A growly sort of sound comes from his throat.

"That's a goddamn sin. I could cry." He drops his hands, leaning closer, his chin dipping, and his voice rough. "How is that even possible?"

"I was . . . busy."

"No one is *that* busy."

I was working two jobs, trying to save up for a place I could afford on my own. My parents never gave me a hard time about living with them, but I knew it wasn't how they wanted to spend their retirement years. They'd raised their kids and when I had Jason, they had to start all over again. And babies are bossy. You'll see."

Dean takes his glasses off and sets them on the counter. Then he gazes down at the bump between us—but there's nothing tender or paternal in his expression now.

His eyes are heated. Possessive.

I know that look, I remember that look. I saw it above me, behind me—it's the expression he wore when he couldn't wait another second to push inside me. To have me, take me, make me his.

He scrapes his teeth across his bottom lip and my own lips part in answer. His eyes drag up over my breasts, my neck, settling on my mouth.

"What are your plans the rest of the night?"

I try to play it cool even though my muscles are strung tight and every cell in my body is reaching towards him.

"I'm going to get changed, get into bed . . ."

"I like where this is going . . ."

I smile. "And then I have some videos to edit. Sketches for the nursery to finish."

Dean inches even closer. So close I can feel the heat of his chest, sense the ripped muscles hiding beneath his shirt, smell the seductive scent of his skin.

If I lift my chin and lean just a bit—I could kiss him right here, right now.

He touches me with the tip of his finger—just the tip—dragging it along my collarbone, and that soft brush of a touch is almost enough to make me moan.

"Want some company, Lainey?"

Yes. God yes. Please, please, yes.

The words are right there on my lips, waiting for breath. Because I want his company—in my bed, in the shower, here on the kitchen counter—I know firsthand how blissful Dean Walker's company can be.

"I . . ."

My heart thrums quick and hard, and I lick my lips . . . but then I shake my head.

Because I have to be smart about this. *We* have to be smart. Adult. Responsible.

No matter how much it sucks.

"Dean, I think it would be a mistake for us to get involved romantically."

His brow furrows. "Again, I'm going to go with 'a little late for that, don't you think' for $500, Alex."

"*Jeopardy?*" I raise my eyebrows. "Cute."

"I can be adorable when I want to be."

"I'll rephrase—I think it would be a mistake for us to get involved romantically *now*."

"Ah, I see." He mulls that over. And he shrugs. "We can just fuck, then."

My pelvic muscles clench—and my vagina thinks this is an amazing idea.

The last inches between us disappear as Dean presses his forehead to mine, stroking his thumb along my chin and across my bottom lip. His voice is a plea and a promise.

"I'll make it good, Lainey. It'll be so fucking good."

And I know it will be.

I close my eyes. "You could do that? Stay unattached.

Just make it physical?"

I feel his nod. "I could do that. You won't regret it, I'm an awesome fuck buddy."

I open my eyes—and stare into the scalding blue waters of Dean's gaze.

"I'm not. A fuck buddy, I mean. I was telling the truth when I told you I don't do one-night stands. I've had sex with four people in my life and you're number four. I'm a relationship kind of girl. I get emotional when it comes to sex."

"Would that be such a bad thing?"

"I don't know. And that's the problem. You literally just decided to do this with me, Dean. We're going to be involved in each other's lives forever—and we're just starting out. To bring sex into that mix now is . . . not smart." I press my hand between us, on my stomach—the feel of the firm bulge helping me focus on the right things. "It could end up being a disaster for all of us."

Dean closes his eyes a moment, then he straightens up and steps back, tilting his head to the ceiling and blowing out a deep, frustrated breath. He scrubs his hand over his face, like he's trying to wake himself up.

"Okay, I see what you're saying. You're right."

He turns toward the door—but then changes course and spins back around to face me.

"But I'm putting this on the table . . . anytime you feel like being not smart, I'm your guy. You change your mind and want to hook up, for one night . . . or ten . . . I am up for that." He gestures to his groin. "Literally, up for it. Just say the words."

A giggle tickles my throat. "What words?"

"Yes, Dean. Please, Dean. Now, Dean. Supercalifragilisticexpiali-fuck me, Dean. Any combination of those will work. Don't be shy—I'm a sure thing. Okay?"

And now I laugh—not just because it's funny, but because being around Dean already makes me happy too.

"Okay."

"Good." His movements are tense and quick—horny—as he takes his glasses off the counter and slides them back on his face.

Then, smoothly he reaches over and kisses my cheek. I savor the feel of his firm, full lips—and he seems to linger there just a second longer, breathing me in.

Then he's backing up toward the door.

"Don't stay up too late editing. You're percolating our kid—that requires energy. You need your sleep."

I smile. "Okay. Bye, Dean."

"Goodnight, Lainey."

And then my wild drummer boy, sexy professor, baby daddy slips out the door.

CHAPTER
Ten

Dean

ainey's killing me.

As sure as a gorgeous, incurable, stage-four disease.

After I left her house last night, her scent followed me, haunted me. I had to jerk off three times before I could finally lay on my stomach and fall asleep without my hard-on poking me in the gut. It's a new record—and not one I'm particularly proud of.

It was bad enough when she was just a memory, but now, with her real and close and in-person, I'm going to be a walking, talking pair of blue balls and a serious case of raw dick by the time our kid makes an appearance on the world stage.

Each time I came, it was more intense than the last, and every time was with Lainey's name poised on my lips—and the picture of her full, perfect tits, that pouty mouth and pretty pussy in my head. Sometimes all three at once. Then there were the images of her eyes, her smile—making her smile yesterday, that was a rush—the scent of her hair and the sound of her voice. It's all so damn good.

Too good.

Motherfucking addictive.

Being this close to her and not being able to have her—possibly ever—I'm toast. No way I'm making it out alive. And it's all because Baby Mama is into relationships. Can't say I'm surprised—though she gives outstanding dirty-girl in bed, out of it, she definitely gives off the good-girl vibe.

It's not like I haven't had girlfriends before. I've had plenty. I've done relationships.

I just suck at them. Screw them up. Every time.

It became a pattern, in high school and into my twenties. The first few days, I was golden—life was good—the bloom was on the rose. But then I'd start to get that itch, start to get bored.

The pussy would start to look pinker on the other side of the street.

And then I'd fuck around. I didn't set out be a jerkoff, hurting a woman's feelings was never the goal. The drama, tears, and headaches that always followed weren't fun either. Which is why when I was older, wiser and more mature, I swore off relationships all together. I went legit—became a straight shooter. I discovered being direct with a woman, putting my not-interested-in-a-relationship cards on the table was even easier than screwing around and inevitably getting caught.

And now here we are boys and girls.

A hellish situation of my own making where a sex-only, no strings attached arrangement isn't going to cut it.

Even if Lainey would consider giving a relationship with

me a shot, I'm not sure that's a route we should take. I don't trust myself not to fall back into old habits—and that's not an option with Lainey. I won't risk starting something with her that I'm not certain I can finish. It's like she said, we're going to be involved in each other's lives *forever*—if I'm going to do the dad-thing right, hers is a heart I can't afford to break.

And I don't want to. The thought alone makes my stomach twist painfully in my gut. I'll punch myself in the nuts before I hurt Lainey.

The rub is—I want her. Badly. More than I've ever wanted any woman. I've waited for her—gone cold turkey for months, and that's unheard of for me.

But it's still too risky. Building a solid foundation with Lainey, for our kid, is bigger than my boner and more important than my sex drive. So, until I get my head on straight or my dick decides he's willing to play nice with others—it's going to be me and my hand for the foreseeable future.

Goddamn it.

The next day, after school, I give Garrett the heads-up that I'll be late to football practice. Then I swing by the grocery store to pick up a few things and head to Lainey's house. Jason lets me in and I find her in the living room—with those long, toned legs peeking out from itty bitty cotton black shorts and a power drill in her hand, standing on a ladder, and Bruce Springsteen singing "I'm Goin' Down" from a speaker in the corner.

And, dear God—the things I could do to her on that ladder. Wonderful, filthy things that instantly make my heart pound and my cock throb. She's the perfect height for me to

just walk over there and put my mouth between her legs. I picture it, see it in my mind—the way she'd grip my hair and pant
my name, arch her back and writhe against my face . . .

But then I catch sight of the small bump of her stomach,
and reality smacks me in the head. I think about the baby—and
how making Lainey lose her mind three feet off the ground
wouldn't be the safest option. My protective instinct overrides
the desire to get freaky on the ladder.

"Hey, Dean." She sets the drill on the ledge and picks up
a beeping light green rectangle, running it along the wall.

"What are you doing up there?" I ask.

"I'm getting ready to record—to show The Lifers the fin-
ishing touches in the living room."

I don't have a decorative bone in my body, but the room
looks good—with light gray walls and navy corduroy covered
couches, reclaimed wood tables and a dozen different-sized
candles filling the white-washed brick fireplace. It's clean and
simple but warm, the kind of place you'd look forward to coming back to every day.

"I'm going to hang up those boards." Lainey gestures to
three square planks, with ornamental arrows burned black into
the wood. "I just want to make sure this stud-finder works."

"If you're looking for a stud," I wink, "I'm standing right
in front of you."

"Ha-ha. I'll keep that in mind."

She turns back to the wall, reaching up over her head and
stretching onto her tippy toes on the narrow step. I move under
the ladder to catch her if she goes ass over end, and a stab of
terror slices through me at the thought that Lainey would still
be doing this if I wasn't here. Alone. Without Jason even in the
room in case something went terribly wrong.

What the hell is up with that?

"I read that you're not supposed to reach above your head when you're pregnant."

"That's just an old wives' tale."

I wrap my hands around her hips, holding her steady.

"Maybe the old wives knew what they were talking about. Come on, come down."

Slowly, Lainey lowers her arms and turns in my hands. I lift her off the ladder by her hips, tilting my head back and holding her above me for a moment, before sliding her slowly down. And the feel of her softness rubbing against me, the friction—it's fantastic.

When her feet are on the ground, I dip my head and our faces are just millimeters apart. Close enough to count the sprinkle of cute, light freckles that dust the bridge of her nose.

"That's better," I say softly, taking the stud-finder out of her hands. "I'll do it."

"Okay." Lainey's tongue peeks out, wetting her bottom lip. "Thanks."

Like I said . . . *fucking killing me.*

Self-preservation sends me climbing up the ladder and Lainey points to the grocery bag I walked in with.

"What's this?"

"Grams told me that you were sick last night, so I did a survey of all the teachers who've had kids about what helped them with the morning sickness." I mark the studs with a pencil, then drill the screws into the wall, so she won't have to. "There's ginger ale and coke, there's crackers and chamomile tea and peppermint tea, and these tablets that you're supposed to let dissolve on your tongue. Somebody said chocolate-covered Oreos settled their stomach and I don't know what that's about, but they're in there too."

"And these?"

I glance over my shoulder and Lainey is smelling the bouquet of wild flowers I picked up. They reminded me of her—vibrant and wild and unique.

"Those are for you."

I step off the ladder and stand in front of her.

"I figured it's the least I could do since you're the one who has to do all the puking."

Lainey's eyes get this shiny, tender look as she smiles. "Thank you. That's sweet."

"Yep, that's me—sweet. But . . . you've had a taste, you already know that."

Lainey cheeks flush the prettiest pink—and I want to spin her around and fuck her over the back of that comfy navy couch.

Jesus, I need to stop thinking shit like that—I'm just torturing us both.

She clears her throat and puts the flowers down.

"Since you're here, I wanted to ask how you felt about being in the *Life with Lainey* videos? No pressure—Jay doesn't show his face on camera. And I've mentioned you, but the Lifers don't know your real name."

"What do you call me?"

She shrugs, fidgeting with her hands.

"Baby-Daddy, Sexy Drummer Guy and once . . . Mr. Fuck-Hot."

I chuckle. "Highly accurate nicknames."

"Yeah."

"But, it's cool—I'll be on camera and you can use my name. I've never been shy."

"Great. Do you . . . want to do a live video with me now? I could introduce you to the Lifers." She grins. "They can be a frisky bunch, but they're fun."

"Sounds like a plan."

"Okay." Lainey runs her hands through her hair, shaking out the spiral curls. Then she positions her laptop on the table, aiming it at us and hits a few buttons, before stepping back next to me. "And we're live."

She smiles into the camera, all warm excitement, and for a minute I forget about the camera and I just watch her. I could make a full-time hobby out of watching this girl.

"Hi, Lifers! I have a special surprise for you today! Mr. Baby Daddy is here with me to meet you guys! And you're not going to believe it—he's actually Jaybird's teacher! Crazy, right?" She gestures to me. "This is Dean Walker. Dean, these are the Lifers."

I salute the camera and give it my best smile.

"Hi, everyone. Nice to meet you."

And the notifications explode. There's smiley faces, thumbs-up, and hearts galore. There's also comments that pop up along the side of the screen.

Jackpot!

Ooooohhhhh, he's pretty.

Lainey, guuuuurrrllll!!

He can be my Baby Daddy any day.

I'm dead. Dead, died, done, just leave me here on the floor.

Lainey looks up at me, laughing. "I think they like you."

I gaze into the camera. "Of course you like me. I mean, you're all into Lainey's show, right? Obviously you have awesome taste."

It turns out, I didn't think the whole "appearing on Lainey's social media show" all the way through. There are some unexpected developments that I didn't anticipate—and one of those developments hit front and center three days later, in the middle of AP Calculus.

I review Hailey's answer on the board to a particularly challenging problem.

"Nice job, Hailey, you got it. You want your question now or later?"

She pushes her hair behind her ear. "I have a question that I want to ask now, but I don't know if I can."

I hold my hands up at my sides. "You can ask anything— that's the whole point. Hit me."

Her eyes dart over to Jason, then back up to me, and my spidey senses start tingling.

"So, my mom watches this webcast—*Life with Lainey*— it's the one Jason's mom does." She smiles at Jay. "She's a big fan."

Jay nods with a chuckle.

"And the other day, she said she saw you on one of the live videos. And she said that you and Lainey are, like, having a baby. Is that true, Coach Walker?"

I scan their faces and can tell right off the bat who Jason confided in and who he didn't. Quinn knew—along with Diego and Louis. Daisy, Min Joon, Martin and Keydon were in the dark.

Then I glance at Jason, to read how he's taking this. And he's not embarrassed, he looks more . . . contemplative. Waiting on me, weighing my words, my reaction—watching to see how I handle this. And more importantly—how I'm going to talk about his mom.

"Yes, it's true. I'm having a baby. Miss Burrows and I are having a baby together."

I'm smiling when I say it. Because every time I do, it feels a little bit cooler—more exciting and amazing.

"So are you guys . . . dating?" Hailey asks. "Like a couple?"

Small towns are awesome in a lot of ways, but they can also be brutal. Because opinions are like assholes—everyone's got one. And this is never more true than in a town where everybody knows everybody, and whispers can be deafening and judgements permanent and labels stick for life.

I'm not going to let anyone have a chance to give Jason shit about his mother, or to think badly of Lainey—not on my watch.

"Yeah, we're dating. In a relationship. We met before Jason and his mom came to Lakeside."

Quinn smiles and passes Jason an "I told you so" look that girls pull off so well.

"We've kept things private for a few months," I say. "But now we're going public. I care about her very much, and . . . she's my vole."

The kids stare at me.

"Your what?" Louis asks.

"My prairie vole—look it up, you'll learn something. But the point is, we're together and I couldn't be happier."

Jason gives me a subtle nod of approval and I feel like I just aced my first Dad-material test. Thank Christ.

"That's so romantic." Daisy sighs.

"It's cool when old people get together," Keydon says.

"Yeah," Min Joon adds, "I read an article about this couple who met in the nursing home and got married a couple months before they both died. They were cute."

"Hopefully, we've got a couple years left before the nursing home comes for us," I reply dryly.

"Hold up, hold up." Louis raises his hand. "Just because you're with Jay's mom, that's not gonna like effect the curve or anything, right?"

They all await my reply with rapt attention, because the curve is right up there with Wi-Fi—one of the most important things in life.

"No guys, it's not going to affect the curve."

There are sighs of relief all around.

And Martin adds, "Good for you, Coach Walker. It's nice to see you settling down. And congratulations on the baby."

I make a mental note to email Mrs. Smegal—to remind her that she's got a great kid.

And I make a bigger note to talk to Lainey—to let her know that as far as Lakeside is concerned, we're a couple.

For the first time in almost a decade, I've got a girlfriend . . . kind of.

This is gonna be interesting.

CHAPTER
Eleven

Lainey

"We have to date."

I look up from the curtains I'm sewing for the nursery—a billowy cream-colored fabric that will have the effect of puffy clouds floating around the windows.

Dean looks young when he says these words— mischievous and playful—the kind of look a boy would wear if he was trying to convince a girl to cut class and make out behind the gym. Totally irresistible.

"Or . . . you know fake-date. Act like a couple. Pretend."

"Fake-date? Sounds like the plot of a rom-com."

Dean fingers the end of the curtain. "Maybe. But the fact remains we have to go out—show our faces around town, to-gether."

"It's not like we're hiding."

"Yeah, but we need to act like a couple. Hit up the diner, the bagel shop, the movies—we have to hold hands, walk with my arm around you . . . kiss."

My traitorous eyes go right to his mouth—that gorgeous, sinful mouth.

"Kiss?" The syllable comes out high pitched and strangled.

Dean grins. "Yeah. I mean, if you're okay with that."

It's terrifying just how okay I am. In fact, I'd be good with practicing right now.

Instead, I clear my throat. "Why do we have to do these things?"

Dean explains the question he got in class from one of his students and how he answered.

"So, you want to like—protect my honor? How old-fashioned." I laugh.

"Yeah, your's and Jay's honor. I have a reputation around town and mother insults are still a thing. 'Your mom is dating Coach Walker' is a lot weaker than 'Coach Walker fucked your mother and knocked her up before she even knew his last name.' That could sting."

He makes a valid point.

Or maybe I'm just deluding myself. Letting myself be swayed by the argument that will lead to holding Dean's hand, going out with him, kissing him wherever, whenever—because that's what I really want to do. Because the more I get to know him, the more I want him, and all the reasons I told myself we shouldn't get physically involved feel thinner by the hour.

Dean moves in closer and slides my hair back from my shoulder, toying with the feather earring hanging from my earlobe. And his voice shifts gears, losing some of that playfulness, dropping low and tantalizing.

"Of course, anytime you want to stop pretending we're

doing the deed and make it a reality, you just need to say the word, beautiful."

My pulse quickens as his tone washes over me, his tempting words—talk about lethal. Dean Walker's voice should be labeled a weapon of mass seduction.

But I don't want my life choices blowing back on Jason—this would preemptively solve that. It would also satisfy my craving, give me a taste of what being in a relationship with Dean would feel like. It's basically all the plus and none of the downside.

None of the risk.

Because it's not real.

"Okay. I'm on board. What should we do first?"

For the next two weeks, Operation Fake Couple goes into effect. We go to the movies, grocery shopping, we look at cribs at the local furniture store, and adorable baby-sized football jerseys at the Lakeside spirit-wear pop-up store on the school lawn. We eat dinner at Dinky's Diner, and on Sunday morning Jason, Dean and I grab warm bagels at The Bagel Shop, just like a real couple—a real family.

Dean's a popular guy—everyone around town knows him—and he introduces me to everybody. As his girlfriend.

This is Lainey, my girlfriend.

Good to see you, have you met my girlfriend, Lainey? We're expecting a baby in the spring.

Stop looking at my girlfriend's ass, Schwartz—she's taken.

Even though I know it's not real, it gives me the warm

and fuzzies inside every single time. It's been a while since I've been anything close to anyone's girlfriend. Since it felt like I belonged to someone. And Dean's a fantastic fake boyfriend. He's attentive and sweet when we're out together, holding my hand and pulling out my chair.

The one thing he doesn't do, besides a few quick pecks on the cheek, is kiss me. It's the only thing Dean doesn't deliver on, and I find myself waiting breathlessly for the moment he'll press his lips against mine. Waiting and wanting it more than I can put into words.

The second week in December is the annual St. Bart's Christmas Bazaar—which apparently is a very big deal around Lakeside. Everyone who's anyone, and even those who aren't, show up. It's an indoor/outdoor event—held on Main Street and in the St. Bart's school cafeteria—with tables of homemade crafts and cakes and goodies for sale.

There's a Santa for lap-sitting and picture-taking in the corner, who Dean whispers is actually the high school guidance counselor, Jerry Dorfman. I haven't met him yet, but Dean finds Jerry decked out in his Santa gear completely hilarious. He takes a picture on his phone for the yearbook.

There are garland and lights and real evergreen Christmas trees decorated in every corner of the cafeteria. There's a little stage on one side of the room where Dean says the school's choir will sing Christmas carols at the end of the night. The streetlamps outside are hung with wreaths and bows, and everywhere I look, people are laughing and chatting.

I knew Lakeside was a beautiful town . . . but this is different. It's picturesque, stunning—something straight out of Norman Rockwell—as if neighborly warmth and holiday cheer suffuse the very air we're breathing. Jason disappears into a group of high schoolers soon after we get there, and Dean holds my hand, leading me along the tables inside.

"You could set up a table here next year," Dean suggests. "Your stuff would sell like crazy."

"I did a whole video series last year about making home-made Christmas gifts. They were good gifts too, nothing chintzy. It might be fun to do something like that—a craft tutorial."

We run into Garrett and Callie Daniels, with little Will bouncing between them. Callie and I compare bellies—she's got a slight lead on me, but I'm catching up. Dean's told me a lot about Garrett—how he's like a brother to him, how growing up his house was a second home.

So it feels nice when Garrett smiles and says, "Good to finally meet you, Lainey. I've heard great things about you."

I meet more people from around town. Most seem curious, in a friendly way, about the woman who's apparently locked down Lakeside's legendary Coach Walker.

Most come right up and introduce themselves.

There's Lara Simmons, who dated Dean their senior year and still has their prom picture framed in her living room.

There's Debbie Christianson who went out with Dean junior year, before catching him having sex with her best friend, in her bed. She can laugh about it now.

There's Peggy Gallow who went out with Dean freshmen year of college and, according to her—she's still not over him.

There's Jenny Dunkin—mother of three—who swore Dean broke her heart into a million pieces.

And there's old Mrs. Jenkins.

She didn't date Dean. But she rubs my belly and wishes us well, before shaking her head with a sweet smile. "Alicia must be so happy. I never thought I'd see the day when her wild grandson finally settled down."

And I'm sensing a theme here.

I take Dean's hand, and pull him into a corner, away from the shifting, bustling crowd. "Question."

He runs his finger along the brim of my gray knit newsboy cap, looking down on me with a tempting, teasing expression.

"Answer."

"Have you had sex with all these women?"

He hesitates, squinting. "*All* is such a strong word."

I laugh. And I'm not jealous, but more . . . curious. And maybe a little intimidated. But I want to know him—the way the people in this town seem to know him. The details and the stories, all the pieces that, added together, have turned him into the man he is today.

"What's a more accurate word?"

Dean looks up, scanning the room—and I think he may be counting. "Half? Two-thirds tops."

"Two-thirds?!" I choke.

He dips his head, and it's the first time I've seen him anywhere close to sheepish. "I got around a lot when I was younger."

"I would say so. At least your ex-girlfriends still seem to like you. That's a good sign."

And Dean sobers right up. "Not all of them." His voice gentles, going delicate. "You might hear things."

"What kinds of things?"

"That I was a player. A dog. A heartbreaker. That I lied, cheated on every girlfriend I had."

My stomach dips with a sinking sort of ache—that sense

that pokes and prods when you worry something bad is about to happen.

"And if I hear those things, would they be true?"

Dean kicks at the ground with the tip of his toe. "Anything you hear about me is probably right on the money."

"Oh." I breathe out a slow breath. "I see."

"But, Lainey," Dean cups my cheek with one hand, resting the other on my rounded stomach, like he's taking an oath. "I'm not like that anymore, okay? I don't do that anymore. Not to anyone—but especially not to you."

A little voice hisses in my head that that's exactly what a player who's still a player would say. But I ignore it.

Because maybe it's the hormones or my own stupid, hopeful heart . . . but I believe him. The sinking, worried feeling is swept far away with the brush of his lips against my forehead and the feel of his arms pulling me in close. His wool coat is warm and smells like him—a manly, delicious, sandalwood scent that I remember in my dreams.

I tilt my head back, and lift up on my toes—and press my mouth against his. And god, the feel of his mouth—of him—it's electric and wondrous, every bit as amazing as I remember. My breasts grow heavy and aching for the touch of his hands, and the muscles low in my stomach pull and tighten.

For a moment, Dean doesn't react, like I've surprised him by making the first move. But then he recovers—and I'm treated to the head-spinning sensation of his wet tongue tracing my lips, before plunging inside my mouth, stroking hungrily. He tugs my hat off, cradling my head, fingers tightening, pulling me closer, and a deep groan passes from his throat to mine. Dean spins us around and presses me into the wall, opening his mouth wider to suck at my lips and scrape them with his teeth.

And I feel lightheaded and languid and desperate for more.

Dean's voice pants against my ear.

"Christ, you're making me crazy. The things I want to do to you . . . you have no idea."

I meet his eyes, and touch his jaw—my palm tingling with the feel of that sexy, scraping stubble. "I don't know about that. I have some pretty interesting ideas of my own."

Hello, sending signals . . . meet mixed.

But I want him. Good or bad, smart or stupid—it just *is*. I've wanted him against me, inside me, over me and all around me since the second I laid my eyes on him, and nothing has changed that. I'm starting to suspect nothing ever will.

"Hey now—this is a family event—keep your tongues to yourselves," a deep, joking voice says from behind Dean's back.

He turns, revealing a tall, handsome, dark-haired man in a police uniform with a petite, smiling woman beside him with black curly hair and the most beautiful skin I've ever seen. At her side is a wide-eyed girl, about nine years old with braces, who's the spitting image of her mother.

Dean holds out his hand begrudgingly. "Ryan. Good to see you."

Ryan shakes Dean's hand warmly. "Dean making out with a girl in the corner—this feels familiar."

The curly haired woman smacks him on the chest and speaks in a thick, Brooklyn accent. "Stop it, Ry, don't embarrass her—they're together now." Then she waves at me. "Hi."

"Lainey, this is Ryan Daniels, Garrett's brother," Dean introduces us, "and his wife, Angela—we all grew up together." Dean winks at the little girl. "And that's their daughter, Frankie."

"It's wonderful to meet you, Lainey," Angela says excitedly. "My gawd, you're so cute! It sure took you long enough to pick one, Dean, but when you did, you got a good one. I'm Italian, I can tell."

"It's like they were eating each other's faces!" Frankie exclaims, and heat rushes to my cheeks. Maybe the basement of a church during a holiday festival wasn't the best place to jump Dean's bones . . . and yet I have no regrets. It was a great kiss.

"I'm never gonna let a boy chew on my face like that."

Ryan fist-bumps his daughter.

"That's what I like to hear."

A while later, Callie is in the ladies' room, and Dean lets Will drag him up onto the empty stage to the drum set that sits, unused, in the corner.

"You're good for him, you know."

I turn my head at the sound of Garrett's voice, looking up at him as he watches his little boy sit on his best friend's lap as he puts the sticks in his hands and shows him how to play the drums.

"You think so?"

Garrett nods. "Dean's the kind of guy who was always on the move. He could never sit still, couldn't just . . . be. Even when we were kids, especially when we were kids, he was always the one pushing for more—a bigger party, a bigger play, louder music, girls, drinking—like he was rushing around trying to find something. Trying to fill a void. I don't think he even knew he was doing it. But since he's met you, found out about the baby, these last few weeks, he's been settled. Content. Happy. As his friend, it's really good to see him like that."

I think about the last few weeks—about Dean throwing the football around with Jason out beside the lake. It's not my son's forte, but he had fun. And I think about how nice it's been to have someone to talk to and laugh with, and how I look forward to dusk now, because that's when Dean comes to the house every day.

I remember my doctor's appointment last week, when he came with me and we listened to the swish of our baby's heartbeat, which is just the best sound in the whole world. And it felt different than when I was pregnant with Jason—even more joyful—because I had someone there to share it with.

No, not just someone . . . *him.*

"He's good for us too."

I meet Dean's eyes across the room, as little Will Daniels sits on his lap, smacking the sticks against the drums. Dean smiles at me and winks, and a deep tender warmth suffuses my chest that's bigger than attraction and more intense than lust. It's scary and exhilarating at the same time. It's a piercing, intimate, cherishing kind of emotion—that doesn't feel even a little bit fake.

CHAPTER
Twelve

Dean

The week before Christmas break, a thick, invisible haze settles over a high school that saps motivation and slows down time. Everyone feels it—I embrace it—and assign my students therapeutic coloring assignments at the end of every class. During my free period, on the way back from making copies in the office, I pass the open doors of the auditorium and see Callie working with Rockstetter—the football player who needed hardcore tutoring and an easy theater-A.

Garrett said she's been working overtime with him, one-on-one, to get him prepped for his theater debut in the February musical.

This year, it's *The Little Mermaid*.

I walk down the aisle to where Callie is standing, directing the big lug of a kid onstage in his red, meaty clawed costume.

A few music students in the pit begin to play, and the tinkling notes of a Jamaican steel drum, strings, and flutes, swirl together and float through the air.

I cross my arms. "How's it going?"

Callie rests her hands on her baby-bulging stomach, tilting her head. "Well . . . there's no way for it to get any worse. So there's that."

"Good job looking on the bright side."

"The glass is always half-full."

I cup my hands around my mouth, and give the wide receiver the same direction I give him on the field.

"Dig, Rockstetter, dig deep! You can do it!"

He waves to me with one claw-covered hand.

"Let go of your embarrassment," Callie calls. "Feel the water around you—move with it. Think like a crab, be the crab."

"Wait a second." Rockstetter shakes his head. "I thought I was a lobster."

"No, you're a crab, it's in the script. It's in the name—Sebastian the Crab," Callie replies.

"Ah, shit!" Rockstetter throws his claws up in the air. "I'm so screwed."

Callie hangs her head. And I verbalize what every teacher will experience at some point in their career. "Yeah, you're gonna earn your money with this one."

* * *

The next day—a Saturday—a mid-morning blizzard blows in and parks itself over the tri-state area, dumping about three inches of snow an hour on us. After I clear Gram's driveway and make sure she's good to stay put for the rest of the day, listening to an audiobook with Lucifer curled on her lap, I make my way over to Lainey's.

She's in the kitchen, in a tank top and lacey pajama shorts, shaking her irresistible ass and ever widening stomach to Adele while mixing a bowl of dough with a wooden spoon. There are cookies cooling on metal racks all over the counter, and the air smells delicious and sweet.

Not as delicious as Lainey Burrows—but a close second.

"Let me guess," I say, "Boston Market is out—chocolate chip cookies are in on the craving front?"

She giggles, and just like most everything she does—it goes straight to my dick.

"Snowstorms make me bakey."

"Bakey?"

Too fucking cute. So fucking fuckable.

"Yep—try one." She takes a bite of the cookie and pops the other half in my mouth. And—yes—the fact that it touched her lips before mine actually does make it taste better.

How pathetic am I?

"The roads look pretty bad on the news," Lainey says. "What are you doing here?"

"The roads suck," I confirm. "I was sliding all over the place—thanks, New Jersey. They said it's supposed to keep snowing all day."

I press up behind her, my chest to her back, my crotch nice and snug against her ass, because I just can't frigging help myself.

"I'm here to shovel your drive, baby. Feel free to take that as the pun it's intended to be."

She laughs, leaning back against me—comfortable, warm. That's where our relationship is now. It's a sexually frustrating—but good—place to be. I take a deep, quick sniff of her hair, like a coke addict needing a fast fix to get him through the day.

"Jason still sleeping?" I ask.

"Ah, no. He's actually at my parents' house. He needed a haircut and wanted to go to his regular barber in Bayonne. My dad picked him up early this morning before the snow started."

My reaction to this news is an instant, raging hard-on.

Pretty sick, I know.

But the idea that this is now a kid-free space, that it's just me and Lainey in this big house all alone, that we could do anything—everything—in any room we want, is almost more than I can take.

I swallow hard and breathe deep—and throw myself at the door.

"Sounds good. I'll be outside."

It takes me about an hour and a half to clear the main portion of the driveway, the porch steps and front path. The icy wind whips at my face and the wet snow soaks through my gloves. And despite it being colder than a snowman's cock, I'm every bit as hot for Lainey when I step back in the kitchen as when I left.

She's talking on her cell phone near the sink as I pull off my boots and hat and hang my coat on the hook at the back door.

"No, Dad—it's fine. Stay off the roads, keep Jay with you for the weekend. I'm good. Dean is here."

I don't know what her father says, but she does this cute little eye roll that makes me want to kiss the ever-loving shit out of her.

"Yes, Dad, Dean is the guy. You'll meet him soon. Okay,

bye."

Lainey sets her phone on the counter and slides the last batch of cookies onto the rack.

"Jay's staying in Bayonne for the weekend?" I try to sound casual—to mask the hurricane of pent-up lust swirling inside me.

"Yeah, until tomorrow night." Her eyes slowly drag over me, from my shoulders to my feet and everywhere in between. "Your shirt is wet. You should take it off."

Take my clothes off? Such a great goddamn idea. She should join me.

I reach back between my shoulder blades, tugging the Henley over my head and dropping it on the floor.

And then, we're drifting toward each other—two trains on the same track, who can't wait to crash. We stand just a few inches apart, and Lainey reaches out like she's hypnotized, infatuated, trailing her fingers across my shoulder and down my arm.

The look on her face nearly wrecks me. It's naked heat and hungry fascination as she watches her palm slide across my pec and down the center of my chest.

My heart slams against my ribs and I don't want to say anything that may break the spell—I just want her to keep touching me. But when her hand travels down my abs, resting just above my waistband, so torturously close to where my cock is already so hard it hurts, I groan. "Lainey."

Her eyes dart up to mine and her chest rises and falls in these quick little pants.

For a few seconds we stay just like that, burning each other up with our eyes. Then there's a small shift in her features—her lips part and her chin lifts—like she's on a diving board ready to jump.

"Dean?"

"Yeah?"

"Supercalifragalist—"

I'm on her before she finishes the word. My lips on her lips, my tongue spearing and stroking, my hands on her hips pulling her close—then lifting her up onto the counter. And Lainey matches me move for move—it's almost violent the way we attack each other. Her nails dig into my back and she wraps those long legs around my waist, pulling me in tight, trapping me between her thighs.

Our kiss is all rough desperation—pure need—a pulling, tugging, pleading devouring of each other's mouths. And it's the best fucking kiss I will ever have in my life. I know that, right here right now.

I lick down to her neck and suck on her pulse point—hard enough to leave a bruise. She angles her head to give me better access, even as she gasps out a question.

"Dean, should we be doing this? It could confuse things."

I groan against her neck. "I'm already so fucking confused I don't know if I'm coming or going."

Lainey pulls back just slightly, laughing. And I stare at her swollen pink lips, stroking the velvet softness of the bottom one.

"No, that's not true. I'm not confused at all about this. About how much I want you, Lainey. It's constant and relentless." I press my forehead to hers, panting like I just sprinted sixty yards. "Say yes. I need to hear you say yes. Christ, Lainey, please say yes."

I'm begging and I don't even care. I need to feel her, fuck her, throw her legs over my shoulders and eat her. I want to drown in her, lose myself in her, make her come so many times we lose count and she loses her mind.

And I want to do it all now.

Her fingers trace my jaw and she looks into my eyes.

And she nods.

"Yes."

I'm not a praying kind of guy, but—hallelujah.

I dive back for her mouth, kissing her greedily until she's breathless, until words aren't possible, and it's all needy, high-pitched little whimpers purring from her throat.

The feel of her hands on me—scraping my chest, my back, skimming down my stomach, yanking on the clasp of my pants like they offend her . . .

"So good," I groan. "It's so good."

I tear at her tank top—pulling it over her head and make quick work of her bra.

I'm the motherfucking Houdini of bra clasps.

When it's gone, when she's bare from the waist up, I force myself to take a moment to just look at her. Take her all in. Appreciate the trembling, stunning view of her. And there's so much to appreciate.

The pale globes of her breasts are larger than they were this past summer, the dusty pink, quarter-size nipples a shade darker. I cup her in my hand, almost reverently, and I groan from the bottom of my throat. She watches with heavy-lidded eyes as I bend my knees to take her in my mouth—slowly clasping my lips around her nipple and sucking until she whimpers. I flick the pointy, tasty little nub with my tongue and scrape her soft flesh with my teeth.

And it's beautiful. So fucking hot it's almost too much to take.

"Dean, Dean, Dean, Dean..." Lainey chants, pulling at my shoulders.

"That's me, baby. I'm right here." I knead her breasts in my palm, blowing on the pointed peak. "I've got you."

"Please," she keens. Her hips lift off the counter, rubbing against my thigh that's wedged between her legs—reaching for sweet friction where she needs it most. "Please, Dean, I need . . . so much."

Hell, yes.

She incoherent, but I know—I understand—because I need too.

I grip the waist of her shorts and yank at the same time Lainey lifts up, leaving her totally bare. So much beautiful skin to touch and lick, and I'm going to worship every inch of her.

I straighten up and step back, opening my pants and stepping out of them—leaving them in a puddle on the floor. Lainey consumes me with her eyes, then she wraps her pretty hand around my cock, pumping the shaft with firm, confident strokes.

"I've missed you," she sighs.

I pull back enough to chuckle.

"Are you talking to me or my dick?"

Her hazel eyes are darker with heat—a gorgeous golden green. She looks up at me innocently and I want to tear her apart.

"Both of you."

Yep, works for me.

She sighs into my mouth when I press my lips against hers, stroking the hot cavern of her mouth with my tongue. And there's a blissful relief in having her in my arms again— after all this time—feeling her against me. Good and right and mine. It's a perfect space of bliss and pleasure carved out for just the two of us that I never ever want to leave.

She slides closer to the edge of the counter and spreads her legs wider as my hips nudge back in between them. It's the hottest thing—her openness, confidence, shamelessness and trust.

I give my cock a long stroke, then tease her slick seam, up and down, with the weeping, broad head. She's so wet, she coats me, and her heat makes me lose my fucking mind. I slide the tip inside her, biting my lip hard to keep from just ramming all the way home.

Lainey's rolls back as I push slowly all the way in—her sweet pussy gripping me snug and beautiful.

"Oh, yeah," I moan into her hair.

I grip her upper thighs, holding tight, pulling my hips back—just to push back in.

"Yes, oh, yes," she keens.

I hold her waist, pumping deep inside her. My hips withdraw, circle and plunge over and over, until she's quivering against me—clawing at my back and chanting my name.

I thrust faster, harder, as the pleasure rises and builds, our breaths mingling, our hearts pounding in the same rhythm, cresting to a frenzied peak.

Christ, I feel it when she comes. When she shatters in my arms, and her wet heat grips and spasms around my cock. And I follow her there, thrusting one last time—jerking inside her, filling her, groaning her name—as the heated carnal joy spikes through me, like my orgasm is torn from my goddamn soul.

We don't move for a while. We stay just like that—trading lingering kisses and tender touches—wrapped close and snug around each other. And then, when I can feel my knees again, I pull out of her, lift Lainey up and carry her into the living room.

Because we have a lot of time to make up for, and I'm just getting started.

It's a full-on fuck-fest from there. We've deprived ourselves for too long, so now we get to indulge—gorge ourselves on every sexual activity we can come up with—no matter how mundane or deviant. I don't plan on stopping until I've screwed her in every room in the house, on every available surface.

I might not survive—banging Lainey may be the last thing I ever do on this earth—and I'm really okay with that.

I lean back on the couch, my feet on the floor, legs spread. Lainey's knees straddle my waist as she rides me—her rounded stomach tapping against my chest with every buck and sway of her hips.

I gather the gorgeous strands of her hair in my hand, and tug—just hard enough for her to feel it, as I thrust up into her.

"You like that, baby?"

She gives a jerky nod and a long, sweet moan. Her hips quicken when I lick at her nipple slowly at first, then flicking at the tight bud relentlessly with my tongue. She bites her lip and loses her breath in a gasp, as her pussy contracts like a tight wet fist and she comes hard all around me.

When Lainey collapses against my shoulder, breathing hard, I slide my hands up and down her spine.

And I chuckle. "Oh yeah, you definitely liked it."

In the late afternoon, with the snow still pounding away out-side, I build a fire in the fireplace and Lainey and I eat sand-wiches and cookies for sustenance—wrapped naked in blan-kets on the floor.

Her eyes roll back in her head as she licks a line of gooey melted chocolate off her finger. "Mmmmm, it's so gooood."

It takes every ounce of control I have not to pounce on her, but I manage it. She's a human incubator—she needs to eat.

We cuddle and we talk. About our parents—and my lack thereof. I tell her about the time I came home sloppy, stum-bling drunk and Grams tugged on my ear so hard she tore the skin—and then had to drive me to the hospital to get two stitches. And she felt absolutely no guilt about it whatsoever.

Lainey tells me about the time her parents left her at the beach—and made it all the way back to Bayonne before realiz-ing they were one daughter short.

She tells me stories about when Jason was a baby, the joys and the terrors. I rest my hand on her stomach and we talk about our baby—if it'll be a boy or a girl—we decided not to find out the sex because Lainey said that's one of the greatest surprises ever and she wanted to wait until the delivery to find out. We talk about what we think the baby will look like, whether it'll have her eyes or mine and what it'll be like to hold it and have it with us on the outside.

And the crazy thing is, these hushed words and quiet, in-timate moments are every bit as awesome as the sex.

In the evening, after the sun has gone down, I force myself to put on clothes and head back out for a second round of snow shoveling. I don't want ice to form that Lainey could slip on in the days ahead.

When I come back in, I find her painting the walls of the upstairs bedroom. She's back in her pajamas, filling in the vertical lines that have been drawn in pencil on the wall—thick navy and white alternating stripes that look like wallpaper. It's part of the video she'll be posting this week for the Lifers on different painting techniques and faux finishes.

I strip back down to my black briefs and as Lainey paints I sit propped against the wall, staring at her ass. Now *that* is a Saturday night well spent.

"I could watch you do this all day."

She smiles back over her shoulder. "You could watch me paint lines all day?"

"Fuck yeah."

"That sounds about as interesting as watching paint dry. Would you watch that too?"

"If you're wearing those shorts, bent over just like that? Bet your sweet ass I would."

Lainey makes her way over to the corner—and my dick gets the best idea. We're back on good terms again—he's a genius.

I lift up on my knees and shuffle toward her. "How about you paint while I'm going down on you?"

Her brush freezes mid-stroke.

"I don't know if I can keep the brush straight if you do that."

"Only one way to find out."

I slide between her legs, push those shorts aside—and my tongue gets to work.

She's not able to keep the brush straight.

Behind the door, there's an indelible stutter in one of the navy lines. And it's like visual Viagra—every time I look at it, from this night on, I get an instant hard-on.

Later, when the sky is midnight-black and the lake is a glassy pool, and the mounds of snow shimmer beneath the silver cast of the moon, Lainey and I kiss our way into the master bedroom. David Gray sings "The Year's Love" softly from the house speakers, and Lainey lets go of my hand, stepping her slippered feet back through double doors, onto the snow-covered balcony that overlooks the rear of the property. Tiny flakes float down around her and her hair frames her face in golden waves as she spins slowly, dancing to the song.

And there's this punch of emotion that hits me right in the gut as I watch her. Because her smile, her long-lashed, innocent eyes, her laugh, her mind, her heart—they're all so beautiful—precious, to me. And it's not until this moment that I realize I can't remember what my life looked like before her. And now, I can't imagine my life without her in it. I don't even want to try.

I walk out onto the balcony and take her in my arms and spin and sway and dance with my girl, because that's what she loves to do.

I've suspected for a while that Lainey owned me, but now I'm sure of it.

I'm done. This is it for me—*she*'s it for me.

The next morning, my balls ache from all the action the night before, but my dick is wide-awake with morning wood—which is kind of a miracle when you think about it.

I spoon up against Lainey, and she wriggles her ass, reaching back, cupping the back of my head—letting me know she's up for it. I kiss her shoulder, her neck, scraping my words against her ear.

"I can't decide what I want to do first. I didn't get to come in your mouth last night—that would be fun. But you look so hot riding me . . . and so pretty on your knees with your ass in air."

I cup her breast and feel her heart pounding against my hand.

"Decisions, decisions . . ."

I end up taking her sweet and easy from behind, clasped together on our sides. After, when we're both a little sticky and sweaty, that same bone-deep sureness wracks through me. It says that what Lainey and I have, who we are together, is a good thing—the best kind of thing—something that should be held on to and protected and cherished. And once again I'm steady, solid—I know exactly what I want.

"I want to be with you," I whisper against her neck.

"You are with me."

"I want a relationship with you, Lainey."

These words have been said to me a hundred—maybe a thousand times. But I never wanted it, needed it, like I do now.

"We're already there. I don't want anyone else, you don't

want anyone else. We're having a baby . . . why are we overthinking it?"

She's quiet for a minute, then she rolls onto her back and looks up at me, morning-mussed and beautiful.

"You said you're not good with relationships."

"I can be good at it with you," I swear.

She runs her hand tenderly through my hair.

"I want that. It's a little scary how much I want that with you, Dean."

A jolt of happiness surges through me—the same feeling as scoring a touchdown—but so much better.

I lean down over her, my lips hovering.

"Okay, then."

"Okay," she smiles back.

Then I'm kissing her long and languid—losing myself in all that she is, all that she means to me, all over again. And I swear to God and to myself that I'll never, ever do anything to screw this up.

But there's a reason some last words are famous.

Because . . . P.S. . . . I screw it up.

CHAPTER
Thirteen

Lainey

Since we decided to give a real relationship a shot, things between Dean and me are amazing. Better than amazing—more than I'd ever let myself dream. After having Jason, being with Dean is the second best decision I've ever made. My body certainly thinks so, since he's kept her thoroughly, exhaustedly satisfied. And as corny as it sounds—my heart thinks so too.

Dean and Grams come with me and Jason to my parents on Christmas Day. I look at it like the final boss battle in a video game, or the last obstacle on *American Gladiators*. If my whole family in one small house doesn't send Dean running for the hills, I can start getting used to the idea that maybe nothing will.

They converge on us in the foyer—taking our coats, enveloping us in hugs and kissing our cheeks. Jason gets swallowed up in a sea of my nieces and nephew.

"Lainey!" My sister Linda squawks, looking at Dean. "You didn't tell me he was hot! He's like a life-size Ken doll!" Her gaze drops appraisingly to his crotch. "An anatomically blessed Ken doll."

Oh boy.

I wedge myself between them. "Yes, Linda, he's hot."

"I like this sister," Dean says, his lips close to my ear, making me shiver. "She seems like the smart one."

"I'm the gay one," Linda volunteers with a wink. "But that doesn't mean I can't appreciate a fine-looking specimen such as yourself." She lifts her glass of my mother's home-made eggnog. "Cheers!"

Next, Judith approaches. "That's what you two should've been for Halloween—Baby Daddy Ken and knocked-up Barbie." Judith snaps her fingers. "Missed opportunity for a great costume."

"I'll make a note for next year."

Judith shakes Dean's hand, her eyes reserved and slightly judgmental.

Brooke steps forward and introduces her brood—perfectly polite as always.

Then Erin appears, bracing her shoulder against the doorway and waving standoffishly. "Good to see you again, drummer-guy."

Dean nods—calm, cool, and devastatingly sexy.

"Nice to see you too, Erin."

My mother gives Dean a hug—the only member of my family to accept him fully, right off the bat—unless he gives her a reason not to. It's just how she is.

Unlike my dad.

He introduces himself to Grams, being all old-school

sweet and Jimmy Stewart charming. My mom leads Grams into the kitchen, asking if she wants a glass of sherry.

Grams replies, "That would be lovely, Desiree. I always like to get drunk on Christmas."

Then Dean introduces himself to my father, holding out his hand and delivering the perfect "meeting the parents for the first time" greeting.

"Mr. Burrows, sir, it's a pleasure to meet you."

And my dad looks at his hand the same way he looked at the stinkbug infestation he found last year in an antique hatbox I had stored in the basement.

"Is this the guy?" he asks, turning to me.

"Yes, Dad, this is Dean—he just told you that. Be nice please."

My dad kisses my cheek and pats my head, and chooses to completely ignore my new boyfriend. "How are you feeling, pumpkin?"

"I'm good." I rub my belly. "We're both good."

"I'm glad."

Then he rakes his gaze over Dean one last time. And a "hmph" is all he gives, before he walks away.

I stroke my hand down Dean's arm. "Don't mind him. He's just mad that you had sex with me."

"Okay, great." Dean smacks his lips together. "Gonna be a fun day."

Jack walks into the foyer and taps Dean's back. This time, when Dean holds out his hand, it gets shaken.

"Jack, right?" Dean greets. "Good to see you again."

"Same, dude. Congrats on the baby—hit the bullseye on the first night, huh?"

"I always had good aim."

Jack greets me with a kiss on the cheek, then says to Dean, "And don't worry about the old man—he's hated me for years too—on account of me and Erin living in sin and everything. But now you're here, so at least my life is about to get easier. Welcome to the Burrows jungle. Want a beer?"

My mom makes roast beef for dinner and we all eat together in the long, extended table in the dining room. Jay doesn't complain, but I can tell he's bummed that once again he's relegated to the kiddie table in the basement—and I promise him this will be the last year. After dessert, we all squeeze into the living room to open presents.

My sisters seem happy with their gifts—mosaic glass picture frames and knit hats. And I get some great maternity clothes and a few baby items—a memory book and an antique rocking horse for the nursery, and a bib that says, "My mom is hotter than your mom."

While the room is loud with family chatter, Jack approaches Dean, wiping his hands on the front of his pants nervously. "Hey. If this goes to shit, do me a favor and just punch me in the face, okay? Knock me out cold."

"If what goes to shit?" Dean asks.

"You'll see," is all Jack replies.

Then he moves back beside Erin and taps on his beer bottle with a butter knife to get everyone's attention.

Jack clears his throat. "I know I've asked before, but it was half-assed and partly just screwing around." Jack's face goes soft as he looks my sister in the eyes and lowers down to one knee. "I'm not screwing around anymore."

Out of his gray suit jacket, he pulls a ring. It's a huge round diamond that shines as bright as a star in a platinum band.

"I love you, Erin. I'm never going to love anyone as much as I love you—and I'd be a mess without you. Will you marry me?"

Erin covers her mouth with her hand, and tears well in her eyes. For a few seconds, she doesn't say anything—and you can feel the collective anxiety in the room that she may actually say no.

But then she pulls in a shuddering breath. "I love you too, Jack. You make me happy and you make me laugh, and I want to spend the rest of my life making you happy too. So . . . yes, I'll marry you."

Everyone claps, and "awwws" and hugs—and Jack slides the ring on my sister's finger. Then he stands and plants a massive kiss on her, lifting Erin right off her feet.

Without even thinking about it, I reach for Dean, twining my arm around his and resting my head against his bicep. I feel his kiss against my hair, and when I glance up, he's gazing at me with a sexy smile and tender eyes.

"Holy shit—I said yes!!" Erin bounces up and down. "We're getting married!"

Grams lifts her glass of sherry, like the geriatric version of Tiny Tim and his crutch. "Congratulations, every one."

Then she hiccups.

As we're still basking in Jack and Erin's post-engagement glow, a horn honks outside. And honks, and honks, and honks again—blaring and obnoxious. I look out the front window and see Chet, the neighborhood guy from hell, standing on our lawn on drunk, unsteady feet, with his lime-green muscle car vibrating in the middle of the street.

"Burrows! Get one of these cars out of my fucking spot!"

Parking spaces are tough to come by in Bayonne— fighting for them is a pretty common thing—especially around the holidays.

My dad steps out the front door onto the stoop—and the whole family squeezes out with him.

"That's not your spot, jackass!" He points at the line of my family's cars parked at the curb in front of my parent's place. "It's on my side of the property line."

I feel it when Chet's attention shifts to me. It's like a snake slithering over your grave.

"Are you kidding me, Lainey, you're pregnant again? You gotta learn to keep those legs closed once in a while, babe. Learn to just say no."

I hate that my neck goes hot with embarrassment. I have nothing to be ashamed of—I know that and the people I love most know it too. But to hear him say those things in front of my son, my parents—to know that's what he thinks of me, even if I don't care what he thinks—is pretty awful.

My sisters react faster than I do, flipping Chet off, cursing him out—even Brooke, who hardly ever curses tells him to eat shit and die. My own "screw you" is locked and loaded on my lips, but before the words are out, another voice cuts through the clatter of outrage.

"What the fuck did you just say?"

Everyone goes quiet. Because there's both fury and authority in Dean's voice—like he owns the right to defend me.

That tone snaps in the air like a whip and demands to be listened to.

I follow behind him as he heads down the steps to the walkway.

"Dean, it's fine."

"Nope, not fine. Not even a little."

I grab his arm.

"He's not worth it."

Dean stops and turns around, his eyes blazing. Then he holds my chin.

"No, he's not. But you are."

And I'm pretty sure my heart faints.

My sisters, up on the porch, concur.

"Ooh, I'm starting to like him," Brooke says softly.

"He's slowly winning me over. Like salt and vinegar chips," Judith adds.

"It was a good line." Erin shrugs. "We'll see."

Linda takes a pencil out of her hair. "I'm gonna use that."

A moment later Dean is right up in Chet's face, pushing the douchebag back with the force of his presence alone.

"I asked you a question, asshole. What did you say and what makes you think for a fucking second that you can say it?"

"Are you with her, dude? Sorry to break it to you, but Lainey's a total slut. In high school she—"

And that's all she wrote. That's all Chet gets to say—because Dean clocks him square in the face, knocking him on his ass with one punch. Blood spurts from his nose and I swear I hear the crunch from here.

"Yes!" Judith jumps up—she was always the bloodthirsty one. "Nice shot."

Dean crouches down and lifts Chet up by the front of his shirt. "Talk about her again and I'll break every bone in your body. Do not make me come back here—you'll fucking regret it."

I'm not usually into violence, but I'm not going to lie—the way Dean Walker does it is nothing short of magnificent.

After the front lawn fight, Dean and Jason are out on the back porch, having another mano a mano chat. And I'm in the kitchen, peeking out the window—watching and listening—again. But this time I'm not alone. Eavesdropping is strong in my family, and my sisters and mother are all gathered round.

"That was freaking awesome!" Jay exclaims.

"No, Jay. It was not awesome."

"What are you talking about? He said—"

"I know what he said. And it was messed up and wrong . . . but they were just words. Adults shouldn't solve their problems with fighting, I want you to understand that. I could get arrested for assault. I could lose my teaching license."

Jason scoffs. "That's not going to happen. He's too much of a chump to ever admit to anyone you kicked his ass."

"That's not the point, kid."

"So what are you saying? You regret it?"

Dean snorts. "Not even a little."

Jaybird starts to laugh.

"Your mom deserves someone who's going to kick anyone's ass who talks about her like that—and I'm happy I get to be that guy. But I don't want *you* doing anything like that. Ever. You use your words. Are we clear?"

I can almost hear my son rolling his eyes.

"So basically, you're saying do what you say, not what you do?"

"Yes. That's what I'm saying."

"Wow, Dean. I think that officially makes you a dad. Congratulations."

"I think that officially makes you a smartass." Dean laughs, nudging Jay's shoulder. "But thanks."

My father steps out onto the porch next and hands Dean a beer and a bag of frozen peas.

"For your hand," he says gruffly.

Dean takes a drag from the beer and lays the peas on his knuckles.

"My daughters tell me you're a drummer," my dad says as he lowers himself into the folding chair.

"Yes, that's right."

"He's the offensive football coach too, Pops. And the Mathlete's advisor," Jason volunteers. Then he asks Dean, "Can I have some of your beer?"

Dean hands the bottle over. "A couple sips. Don't chug it."

The smell of my father's cigar wafts through the window. "I was a guitar man, back in the day. When Fender was new."

"No kidding?" Dean asks.

Listening to the three most important men in my life talk, and knowing my dad approves of Dean—he doesn't tell his guitar stories to just anyone—is the best Christmas present I could've gotten.

Dean

I don't know what wakes me—but something does. We knew we'd be getting back late from Lainey's parents' place, so Grams packed a bag and we all decided to spend Christmas night at Lainey's house. But everyone's been asleep for hours now, and the house is still and quiet. The weight of Lainey's head rests against my arm. I run my hand down her side, over her stomach where the baby lays.

That's when it happens. The boop, the bump, the nudge, the kick—I feel the baby moving under my palm.

And it's the wildest fucking thing, a miraculous thing. My vision goes blurry as I watch, wait, to feel it again.

"Hey, in there," I whisper. "Merry Christmas. We all really can't wait to meet you."

As if it's answering me back, another little jolt kicks up against my hand.

So incredibly cool.

I lay there, waiting for more movement, but after a half an hour, I figure the baby's gone back to sleep. So I slip out of bed, pull on a pair of sweats and head downstairs to check everything out, to make sure all is as it's supposed to be.

Lainey's made some good progress decorating the past few weeks. The kitchen, the living room, Jay's room and two other upstairs bedrooms are finished. And Christmas is her favorite holiday, so the house is a veritable wonderland of wreaths and bows and soft glowing lights. She's got real evergreen garland along the fireplace mantle and an eight-foot spruce in the corner of the living room, decked out in silver and gold stars and popcorn garland.

I do a lap around the first floor, looking out the back window at the shadowed trees, double checking the locks on the doors and windows. I walk back upstairs and peek into Jason's room—where he sleeps in a burrito of blankets. Then I check on Grams, where she's snoring away in the queen-sized bed of one of the finished spare rooms.

I close the door and go back to our room, stripping out of my sweats and slipping back into bed. Lainey shifts, turns, I wrap my arm around her and she curls against me.

"Dean?"

Her skin is soft and warm and she smells so good.

"Yeah, baby, it's me." I kiss her forehead. "Go back to sleep."

CHAPTER
Fourteen

Dean

January

On Sunday night, I leave Lainey editing a video in the living room and Jason reading in his bedroom, and head home. Grams will be the first to tell anyone that she's self-sufficient—and these days, her social life is more active than mine—but I don't like to leave her alone too many nights in a row with only Lucifer for company. And I stayed over Lainey's Friday and Saturday night—fucking her in all kinds of creative ways to accommodate her ever-expanding midsection. God bless Mother Nature.

We did it with Lainey riding me fast and dirty while I teased and toyed with those highly sensitive pink nipples. We screwed standing up in the shower with my knees bent low and Lainey's hands gripping my ass—there are few things in life hotter than the sight of a slicked, soapy Lainey Burrows. Our last round was over the side of the bed, with her hands braced on the mattress, while I pounded into her from behind—that was a particular favorite for us both.

We had to be quiet, because of the teenager in the house, but not too quiet—because Jason was awesome enough to pick the bedroom farthest from the master suite. I think I'm going to buy him a present for that.

Anyway, Monday morning I get to the school an hour early to catch up on some paperwork that Lainey's sweet pussy distracted me from doing over the weekend. I grade papers at my desk for a while, then stand up and start writing out the problems I'll go over with the class today on the board.

I hear the door open and glance over my shoulder to see Kelly coming through it, closing it behind her.

"Hey, Kel, what's up?" I ask, my eyes back on the board.

"I want you to fuck me until I feel better."

My hand freezes mid-pi symbol. Cause there's no way I heard her right.

"What?"

And then I turn around. Kelly's black turtleneck dress is already on the floor, and she's standing in front of me in a very sheer black bra and matching panties.

"Whoa!" I hold up my hand. "What the hell are you doing?"

Her big blue eyes meet mine, and that's when I see hers are wet—swimming with tears and pain.

"Richard left me."

"What?"

A tear streaks down her pale cheek. I've known Kelly since we were fourteen and this is the first time I've seen her cry about anything ever.

"He was cheating on me. With his secretary. How clichéd

is that?" Her face crumples. "And she's not even pretty."

"Ah, shit."

"Can you believe it? He cheated on me! On *me*!" She runs her hand across her body. "I mean, look at me! I could've done so much better than him. I could've married a CFO or an NFL player—or all kinds of other letters! But I married down so I wouldn't have to deal with this bullshit and now he wants a divorce."

"I'm sorry, Kelly."

And I am.

On the outside, Kelly may not seem like the best person, but when you've known someone as long as I've known her, you see what's underneath and deep down. You feel it, not always in what they say or do, but in who they are. Anyone who spends five minutes in Kelly's class—watches her with her students—will have no doubt that she's a good person. Certainly good enough to not deserve getting fucked around on.

"I'm so sorry."

"I don't want your sorry, Dean . . . I want your dick. In the good old days, it always made me feel better."

"Kelly—"

But she's already on the move—springing forward, faster than Lucifer ever moved—wrapping her arms around my neck, cementing her body to mine, kissing my jaw frantically, heading straight for my lips.

I grip her arms, peeling her back gently.

"Kel, Kelly—stop."

She rolls her eyes, like she thinks I'm playing—teasing her.

"Come on, Dean. This room used to be Miss Everstein's

English class—you always said you used to daydream about banging me on her desk. Now's your chance to make that dream come true." She lifts up on her toes, going for my lips again. "No one has to know—it's just us."

I jerk my head to the side, out of range.

"*I'll* know. And I can't. It's different now. I'm different—everything's different."

There was a time I thought Kelly Simmons was the perfect girl—and she's beautiful don't get me wrong. But there's only one woman who's perfect to me now.

She happens to have a stomach the size of a basketball at the moment, and that's perfect too. She's got a smile that owns me and a laugh that takes my breath away and everything about her makes me happy and horny and so fucking content.

Lainey's the only girl I want to screw on Miss Everstein's desk. The only woman I want, period.

I straighten my arms and step back out of Kelly's reach. Her eyes dim with confusion and her mouth puffs into a pouty bow. This is the first time I've turned her down . . . and it's not even hard.

"It's because of that girl you're with?"

"Lainey. Yeah."

Kelly wraps her arms across her bare stomach.

"You're really into her, huh?"

I tell her the truth—and that's easy too.

"I really am. I won't screw it up, not for anything."

She nods, jerkily, looking toward the windows and tucking her hair behind her ear. "I'm happy for you, Dean. It's like the end of an era, but I'm happy for you. She's a lucky girl."

She covers her face with her hand, sobbing into it. "I thought Richard was into me like that."

I open my arms. "Fuck, c'mere."

Kelly steps into my arms, wailing, "I have to start all over again . . . and I'm so old now!"

She soaks my shirt with tears and snot, but it's okay—that's what friends are for.

"You're not old now." I pat her back. "You're gorgeous and smart and in no time at all, you're going to have some Chris Evans lookalike kissing your ass—literally. And Richard's gonna be punching himself in the nuts for letting you go."

She sniffles, looking up at me. "You really think so?"

"I know so."

Her breath shudders. "The thought of Richard punching himself in the nuts does make me feel a little better."

I wipe a tear from her cheek with my thumb. Then I scoop her dress up from the floor. "Let's get you dressed. And we'll go find Merkle and Jerry, and Alison, and Garrett and Callie, and we'll make plans for Chubby's tonight. We'll get you trashed and talk about what a douchebag Richard is—that'll make you feel even better."

She takes the dress from my hands.

"Okay."

It turns out, I'm a baller when it comes to being in a relationship. I can't remember why I ever thought this shit would be hard. I keep my dick in my pants, except with Lainey, I hang out with her, make sure her and Jay are happy. And it's all awesome. Piece of cake.

When you're ready, and when it's right—relationships are the easiest thing in the world.

After the Kelly incident, the morning moves fast and before I know it the first period bell is ringing. The kids work at their desk for a few minutes, on the problems I've written on the board.

Then I clap my hands. "Okay, pencils down—let's see how you brainiacs did. Jason, how about you tackle the first problem?"

First red flag: Jason doesn't lift his head, doesn't look at me, but stares hard at his desk.

Second red flag: "How about you go fuck yourself?"

The air goes thick, like the molecules have frozen in place and a sudden, shocked silence cloaks the room. Every wide eye in the class is on Jason, because these kids—my kids— they don't talk to teachers like that.

"What?"

He lifts his head and meets my eyes, and he doesn't even look like himself. His face is tight and his mouth is twisted— like a furious parasitic alien has taken control of his features.

"I said, go fuck yourself, *Dean*."

I look around the room.

"Is this a joke?"

Jason shakes his head. "Just leave me alone."

I stand up from my desk. "Let's go in the hallway and talk, Jay. You and me."

"Are you deaf? Fuck off."

"Jason!" Quinn calls, her voice bordering on panic.

But Jay keeps his furious right eyes on me.

I know how I'm supposed to deal with a student like this. It's textbook attention-seeking behavior. I should clear the room, send the rest of the class to the auditorium, take the audience away.

But that's not what I do.

Because I'm an idiot.

And because Jason Burrows is so much more to me than just a student.

"Hallway, now," I bark in my coaching voice—the one that says do what you're told and don't even think of arguing. "I'm not asking."

Jason sits back in his chair and folds his arms.

"And yet I'm still saying no. Funny how that works. And there's nothing you can do about it."

"I can have you escorted to McCarthy's office by security. You don't want to talk to me—you can explain this temper tantrum to her. Is that how you want to play this?"

His mouth clamps shut and his chin juts out.

Goddamn it.

I move toward the phone on the wall, but even as I do, I don't know if I'll actually make the call. Because once I bring the administration into this, it's out of my hands—I can't protect him, I can't fix this for him. A whole host of bad shit could happen and there'd be nothing I could do to stop it.

Jason's chair scrapes across the floor as he pushes it back.

"You know what?" He stands beside his desk, looking like he wants to pop my head like a grape with the force of his eyes alone. "Fine. Let's go in the hallway."

The vise that was crushing my chest loosens.

"Okay, good."

"Just one more thing."

"What's that?"

But it loosened too soon.

Because this good, smart, amazing kid—who's never had so much as a tardy on his record—picks up his chair and hurls it straight at the windows. The glass shatters—cracks and spiderwebs—as sharp shards of window pane fall in clattering chunks to the floor.

I stare at those broken pieces.

"Fuck."

We all end up in McCarthy's office. Me, Lainey and Jason sit in the chairs across from her desk.

"What do you have to say for yourself, young man?"

Jason slouches in his chair. "My teacher's a douchebag—how about them apples?"

"Jason!" Lainey gasps.

McCarthy turns to Lainey. "Has he always been this much of a shithead?"

"No! No, he's never acted out before."

"Well, he's certainly making up for lost time." McCarthy shuffles some papers on her desk. "Coach Walker's douchebaggery notwithstanding—you destroyed school property."

He shrugs. "Seemed like a good thing to do at the time."

Miss McCarthy is a hardass and a little bit crazy, but she cares about every student in this building. Hell, David Burke—an epic-level screw-up from a few years back—became her foster kid, and is currently in his second year at a top-notch college because of McCarthy. But every administrator has a point of bullshit no return, where they'll bring the hammer down hard. And because I've personally pushed her to that point more than once, back in the day, I know for a fact, she's there now.

"You could have injured the other students in your class.

That doesn't fly with me."

I try to throw myself on the grenade.

"This is on me, Miss McCarthy."

"Oh? Did you use his arm to pick up the chair and throw it through my window?"

"No, but I could've handled the situation differently. If I had just—"

She turns back to Jay. "You're going to be expelled if you don't start explaining yourself right now."

"Expelled?" Lainey chokes. "But he's never—"

"Dean kissed Miss Simmons."

My blood goes cold and the tips of my fingers tingle. And every drop of color drains out of my face.

No, no, no, no, no . . . this is not fucking happening.

"What?" Lainey's voice is breathless, like she got punched in the stomach, like the wind has been knocked from her lungs.

She turns her head to me, so fast her golden hair swings out behind her. "What is he talking about?"

"I saw him." Jason leans across his mother toward me—his face twisted with hurt and fury. "I saw you."

I shake my head. "That's not what you saw, Jay, I swear to God."

I put my hand on Lainey's shoulder, bringing her eyes to mine.

"I can explain."

Wrong answer, asshole.

I'm batting a thousand today. Because explanations are for cheaters—she doesn't want to hear an explanation, she wants to hear it never happened, it wasn't me, some kind of mistaken identity.

212 | EMMA CHASE

But I can't tell her that. Not really. Not now.

"Mom." Jason's tone is suddenly soft. Tired and sad. "I *saw* them. They were in class and they were all over each other. I wish I didn't see it, but I did."

"That is not what happened," I try, but it's already like talking to the wall.

She's going to believe him.

Of course she's going to believe him. Lainey's a good mother. And Jason's a great kid.

And I am truly and completely fucked.

Lainey gazes down at her hands for a moment. Then she lifts her head and hardens her jaw, and meets McCarthy's gaze head-on.

"I think Jason should be taken out of Coach Walker's class."

Coach Walker? *Son of a bitch.*

Miss McCarthy nods.

"Agreed. It's a personal issue, a personality conflict. We can't fix it overnight so it's best for everyone involved that Jason be put in another class."

"Hold on." I lean forward, practically falling out of my chair. "You can't do that. I'm the only one who teaches AP Calc—he could be taking college-level courses. Where are you going to put him—Algebra 2? His brain will atrophy."

"Then I'll get him a tutor." Lainey's voice is subzero and she barely looks at me. "It's not your concern."

"What the hell does that mean? Of course it's my concern!"

Miss McCarthy snaps the papers on her desk again.

"Six-day suspension. Three out, three in-school. If you stay out of trouble, Jason, this won't go on your record. You step an inch out of line again, and you are done here. Is that understood?"

He nods. "Yes, Miss McCarthy."

McCarthy turns to me, and her tone is dripping with the disappointment I remember so well. She's known me a long time, so she believes Jay too.

"As for your personal issues, it's not my business. Take it outside, Dean."

I walk Lainey and Jason out to the parking lot. I have to get back to class, but I can't let her leave like this. And there's no way I'm letting them pull Jason from my class. Which means I have three days to get him to understand that what he saw, was not what he thinks he saw. No time like the present.

"Kelly stopped by my classroom. She was upset. Her husband—"

Lainey stops beside her truck.

"Kelly? That's the woman you used to hook up with on and off, even when you were with someone else?"

Her eyes are guarded, like she's looking at a stranger—a stranger who may have just slashed her tires and kicked her dog. A stranger she wants to kick in the balls.

"In high school, yes, but—"

"Do you know what they say about you?" Jason asks from behind Lainey's shoulder. "The stories the other kids tell about the different girlfriends you've screwed around on, and crazy hookups and how you're like this legendary player around town?"

Karma sucks. If I had a time machine, I would go back

and kick my younger self's ass. It's all his fault, the little fucker.

"But it didn't bother me. Because I believed you cared about us. No way he's like that now, I thought—he's into my mom—he'd never hurt her like that."

The words scrape raw up my throat.

"I didn't, Jason. I wouldn't."

But he just shakes his head and jabs his finger at me. "Screw you for making me believe you."

There's a special kind of peace, especially for a boy, in knowing your mom is safe. If no one's around to ensure that, the responsibility falls on your shoulders, even if it's not supposed to—that's how it feels. It must've been a relief for Jay to know, for the first time in his whole life, that his mom wasn't alone. That she had someone to take care of her, protect her . . . love her.

That's blown to hell now, but I swear on my life, I'm going to give that back to him. To both of them.

Lainey holds up her arms between us, like she's afraid the kid is going to take a swing at me—and at this point, he might.

"Jason, get in the truck. Now."

With a final glare my way, he climbs in, slamming the door behind him.

Lainey stands stiff and distant, her hands cradling her stomach, her shoulders and back strung tight with distrust and hurt. She can't hide it and doesn't try to, it radiates off her like the vibration of a bass drum. And I just want to take it away, make it better. I want to rewind to last night when she kissed me with soft, pliant, laughing lips and every part of her body and her heart was mine for the taking.

I reach out, kneading the tension in her shoulders. I press

my forehead against hers, whispering, "I know this looks bad, baby. But I swear, it was nothing. It's just a misunderstanding."

For a moment, she leans into me and I soak up her scent and closeness greedily. But then she takes a deep breath and backs away on the exhale, lifting her chin and hardening her eyes.

"I have to get Jason home—he has to be my priority right now."

"I know."

"I have to talk to him, calm him down, figure out . . . I have a lot of things to figure out, Dean."

"All right. I'll come to the house after school and we'll straighten everything out."

For a second, Lainey looks like she's going to tell me not to come, which would really suck because there's no way that's happening.

But then her eyes drop and she nods. "Okay."

Okay. Good. I can salvage this. I may be down but the game's not over. Not even close.

I move my hand to the back of her neck, pulling her near and kissing her cheek. "Don't give up on me, Lainey. Not yet."

Henry the janitor cleans up the glass in my classroom and boards up the window, but it's still a major distraction. I assign busy work across the board and the kids complete it without commentary or complaint. Because high school is a petri dish of rumor and innuendo, so the stories of the shattered window in the Dork Squad class, the drama between me and Jay, and me and Lainey—and hell—probably some whispers about me and Kelly, spread like a contagion through the halls.

Garrett swings by my class on his lunch break, but I'm too strung out to talk about it. It's like my lungs are filled with concrete. The only person I want to talk to is Lainey, and if I let myself contemplate what she must be thinking right now, I'll lose my shit.

Garrett pats my shoulder.

"I'm here if you need me, man. If there's anything I can do, just let me know."

Finally, after what seems like a week, the clock ticks to three o'clock. I weave my way through the mass exodus of students, and I'm out the door while the echo of the last bell is still ringing in the hallway. Then I'm in my car, driving straight to Lainey's house.

When I pull in the driveway, I see that she's called in the reserves. Three of her sisters are waiting for me on the front porch, and I just bet number four is inside.

That was fast. I wonder if they all took a bus together or something.

I walk up the steps to the door.

"She doesn't want to see you yet," Judith says.

"Then she can tell me that herself."

I open the door and walk inside. Lainey is in the kitchen, sitting at the breakfast bar. And it's not good. She looks down, beaten—so frigging sad.

Linda, the writer-sister, steps between us and gives me the stink-eye above her tea cup. "You done messed up, cowboy. She's not stupid—you only break a Burrows girl's heart once."

"I didn't do anything to break anyone's heart."

"That's not what I heard."

From the corner of my eye, I see the other three peek around the corner—like a blond totem pole.

"Look—you're Lainey's sisters and I get that—but can you all kindly fuck off for two minutes?"

Slowly Linda sets her tea cup down on the counter, smiling ruefully. "I do like you, Ken-doll. I really hope you don't turn out to be an asshole, because that would just be a damn shame."

Then she steps out of the room, taking the other Three Amigos with her.

I hold out my hand to Lainey. "Come on."

She lets me lead her outside to the back patio. I grab her coat, the pink Sherpa one, off the hook because it's cold.

Lainey crosses her arms and looks out across the lake as the breeze tousles her hair.

"I talked to Jason. He told me what he saw."

"Kelly's husband was screwing around on her. He left her. She came to me, she wanted to hook up and I turned her down. *That's* what Jason saw."

Lainey fidgets and twists her fingers together—it's what she does when she's nervous or uncomfortable or upset—and I hate that I've made her that way.

"I think we should take a step back, Dean. Slow things down between us. Focus on the baby."

I laugh and it sounds bitter. Because "take a step back" is just woman-code for break up.

"You don't believe me?"

"I've thought about it, I've processed it . . ."

My words come out clipped and colder than the breeze off the lake.

"Oh, you've *processed* it? That makes me feel so much

better."

"It's fine, Dean. I understand. I get it.

"What do you get, exactly?"

"We can be friends."

"Fuck friends. I don't want to be your friend."

I want to be her everything. Because somewhere along the line—Lainey, Jason, our baby—that's what they've become to me. Everything.

Her stance changes, she leans forward breaking out of whatever shell of passive acceptance she's retreated to. Her eyes heat up—sparking with anger.

"You're a player. Self-admitted."

"I've never played with you."

"You've lied. Cheated. That's what you told me."

"I was trying to be honest." Boy, was that a fucking mistake. "I've never lied to you, or cheated."

"This wasn't ever supposed to be anything."

"But now it is. And it's so good, Lainey. Christ, it's so good between us and I want it so bad, sometimes I can't stand it."

She pokes my chest, fully fired up now—and I'm glad. I want her to get it out—the hurt, the doubt—so we can fight it out and then move on. Move past this.

"You kissed Kelly Simmons! While she was in her underwear!"

"*She* kissed *me*!"

Lainey's eyes dart between mine, and then she laughs—and now she sounds bitter too.

"Do you hear yourself? Are you serious right now?"

I step closer, standing over her. "It's the truth. You want to hear another truth? You're just scared. That's what all this is about."

"I'm not scared."

"Bullshit! You're so scared you can't see straight. So you go through life, telling yourself you're easygoing and a free spirit and it's fine—everything's fucking fine. I want to walk away, I don't want to be in the baby's life—that's fine. I'm screwing around on you, you can't trust me—that's fine too—we'll just be friends. And it's all because you're too fucking scared to take a chance. Jesus, Lainey—you'll pull an ugly, broken table out of the garbage because you can see how beautiful it could be . . . but you're so goddamn eager to throw us away. And it's because you've convinced yourself it won't hurt if you're the one who walks away first."

I move forward, lean in toward her, close enough I can feel her panting breath against my throat. And my voice turns aching and desperate.

"But I'm not going anywhere. I'm not walking away from you, *ever*—why can't you see that? I'm a chance worth taking, I swear to God."

When I open my eyes and look down at her, her skin is bleach-white and she's stone-still—like she's about to pass out.

"Lainey?"

I brace my hands on her hips.

"What's wrong?"

She takes a step back, holding her stomach with one hand and lifting the hem of her floral maternity dress with the other—high enough to expose her thighs.

"Dean?"

And my heart, my stomach, my whole being plummets. Because she's bleeding.

CHAPTER Fifteen

Dean

T here's a special kind of hell when your child is hurt or in danger—even if they're not born yet. I didn't know that, didn't understand it—one of the many things I didn't know until I met Lainey Burrows.

But I know it now.

There's a four-alarm fire burning in my brain as I get Lainey in my car and tell her sisters I'm not waiting for an ambulance, that it'll be faster to take her to Lakeside Memorial myself.

I'm not panicking. That won't do dick. Lainey needs me to step up—help her, save her . . . help our baby. And that's exactly what I'm going to do.

Garrett's brother, Connor, is a doctor in the ER and I ask for him when they take us in. They whisk us into a curtained area, get her in a gown and take her vitals, a nurse hooks her up to a monitor that measures contractions, and another runs a

Doppler, which detects the fetal heart rate, across her abdomen.

The strong, steady, swooshing sound that fills the room calms me more than I ever thought any sound could. A few minutes later, Connor Daniels walks into the room in full-out doctor mode—white coat, solid demeanor, warm and confident.

He meets my eyes. "How's it going, Dean?"

I swallow hard. "I've been better."

He gives me a nod that says he understands. Then he turns to Lainey.

"Hi, Lainey, I'm Dr. Daniels."

She smiles weakly, her face streaked with quiet tears.

"You're Garrett's brother."

"His older, smarter, better-looking brother, yeah."

The smile that rises on Lainey's lips is less forced.

"You have the same eyes."

Connor glances down at Lainey's swollen abdomen.

"So it seems this one is already giving you trouble, huh? Have you been having contractions?"

"Um, yes, there's been pressure. I thought I was just sore—" she looks at me, like she thinks she owes me an explanation "—from working around the house. Muscle spasms. But now, yeah, they were contractions."

Connor nods. "I'm going to take a look—see what's going on, okay?"

"Okay," Lainey answers, looking scared out of her mind.

I take her hand in mine, holding it tight.

Connor sits on a stool and a young dark-haired nurse in glasses gives him a pair of latex gloves, then spreads gel on his fingers.

And maybe it should feel weird that the guy who's like a brother to me has his hands between my girl's legs—but it doesn't, not even a little. There's no one else in the world I'd rather have taking care of Lainey and our kid.

Lainey flinches as he examines her.

"Sorry," he says in a kind voice.

Lainey shakes her head. "It's okay."

"How many weeks along are you?"

"Um . . . twenty-five. It's early." And then she starts to lose it—her eyes swell with tears and her face crumples. "Dean, it's really early."

I brush back her hair, and make a promise I know I can't keep—but I do it anyway. "It's going to be okay, Lainey. The baby's going to be fine, I swear."

Connor stands and removes the gloves, then moves to the sink to wash his hands.

"Okay, Lainey—you're about two centimeters dilated, and it looks like you're in preterm labor. But we're going to give you something to stop that."

Connor writes on a clipboard and tells the nurse to administer medication. She nods eagerly, looking up at Connor with idol worship in her eyes, hanging on his every word, like he's a doctor god. But Connor doesn't notice.

If was in my right mind, I'd tell him he should give the pretty young nurse a second look. But at the moment, my only focus is on the woman next to me, so Connor's on his own.

"Then we're going to send you up to OB and they're going to take really good care of both of you there. All right, Lainey?" Connor smiles reassuringly.

And Lainey's head bobs in a jerky nod.

"We're going to get the IV started with the medication

and I'll be back to check on you in a little bit," Connor says.

"Okay," Lainey answers. "Thank you."

When Connor steps out through the curtain, I kiss Lainey's hand.

"I'll be right back."

Then I leave her with the nurse, following him out.

"Connor."

He's already waiting for me. My voice is raw and hushed, because I don't want Lainey to hear.

"They're going to be okay, right? I need you to tell me they're going to be okay." A lump swells in my throat, threatening to strangle me. And my eyes burn hot behind my eyelids. "But if they're not—I need you to tell me that too."

Out of all Garrett's brothers, Connor was the one we went to when things got serious—when we *really* screwed up. When we were all in my car, when we were seventeen, and I hit a curb and blew out the tire because I'd had a few beers before getting behind the wheel—we called Connor. He reamed my ass out, and then he helped us fix it. When Garrett, Callie, me and Debs missed the last train home from New York City—when we weren't supposed to be anywhere near New York City—it was Connor who came to pick us up.

He's a rock—more than a big brother, the closest thing I've ever had to a hero. So if he tells me Lainey and the baby will be okay, I'll believe him.

He puts his hand on my shoulder. "The contractions aren't ideal, but she's healthy and her water hasn't broken and the baby is good—there's no signs of distress. Those are all positives."

I let out a relieved breath. "Okay. Good, good."

"I've seen early labor before, even a few weeks earlier

than Lainey. With medication and bed rest, those pregnancies were carried to term—baby and mom both came out of it healthy." He smacks my shoulder. "Are you going to be able to hold it together?"

There's not even a speck of question in my mind, not a shred of uncertainty. There was a time when I thought being completely whipped over someone put you at their mercy. Made you weak.

Boy, for a guy who's so smart I was a real moron.

Caring with every piece of your being makes you strong, makes you capable of doing things you never imagined you could.

"Yeah, I'm good. I'm here. Anything she needs, it's already done."

They admit Lainey to the OB ward, put her in a private room and give her terbutaline to stop her contractions. Lainey calls her parents and sisters to let them know what's going on. I call Grams and fill her in, and she calls Garrett and asks him to drive her over to Lainey's so she can check on Jason, even though Lainey's sisters are staying at the house with him.

As the clock creeps toward midnight, the hospital halls settle down and go still except for the occasional nurse walking past or coming in to check Lainey's vitals. It's after visiting hours, but no one gives me a hard time from my perch on the vinyl chair beside her hospital bed—which is good—because they'd have to knock me unconscious and drag my ass out, if they want me to leave her.

The lights are low and the room is dim except for the gray

glow of the television on the wall that neither of us are watching.

"You don't have to stay, Dean."

Her voice is soft and sniffley, her eyes still leaking worried tears. And I would give anything to take them away.

"I'm good here." I tap the arms of the chair. "Super comfy."

I may never be able to stand up straight again after this.

But it's worth it.

"This is a really bad one," Lainey whispers and I hate the flatness of her tone. Defeated. It doesn't sound anything like her, like she's supposed to sound.

"A bad what?"

She shakes her head and dabs at her puffy eyes with the tissue clenched in her hand.

"I have this theory, it's stupid. Life is full of surprises— good and bad. And this one . . ." Her words choke off in a sob, and it's like I can feel my heart breaking in my chest—like the sound of her sadness is tearing it in two.

I slide into the bed beside her, wrapping her up in my arms and rocking her slowly as she shudders and hiccups against me.

"Dean, if the baby's born too early, it may not—"

"The baby's going to be fine, Lainey. You're both going to be fine."

"You don't know that."

"Yes, I do."

I put my heart and soul into those words, swearing them with my lips pressed to her damp cheek.

"How do you know?"

"I just do."

I know, because it has to be. Because I can't fucking fathom any other outcome. Because I want this baby with her, so much.

And even more than that—I want more babies with her after this. It's a realization that kind of sneaks up on you. Not one you give long hours of contemplation to—but that you accept immediately and whole-heartedly anyway, simply because it's true.

I never wanted a family—never dreamed of having kids—but I'll dream it now. Because I want what Garrett and Callie have. I want what their parents had. A house full of rambunctious feet and laughing voices, long nights and early - dawn mornings. I want to teach Jason to drive, and talk to him about girls and work and life. And I want to be the guy holding Lainey in my arms when she cries on the day he leaves for college.

I want the whole package, and I want it with her.

Only ever with her.

"I don't expect you to stay if the baby doesn't—"

"Shhh . . . stop, don't finish that sentence." I run my hands through her hair and down her back, soft and gentle. "Why do you keep trying to get rid of me? It's hell on the ego. Good thing mine is larger than most and can sustain the blow."

She snorts out a tiny laugh.

"I'm not going anywhere, Lainey," I whisper against her hair. "I'm in this, I'm here, I'm not leaving. There's only you. I promise, I swear, it's only you."

I don't tell her that I love her—even though I do.

It's a soul-searing kind of love that brands itself on you, that changes you. I've never felt this before and I know I'll never feel it again with anyone else. But it's the wrong time to tell her. The first time I give her that, I want it to be beautiful for her—and without a single shred of lingering doubt that the words come straight from my heart, and that they're true.

She doesn't say anything back, just breathes softly. But then her arm tightens across my chest, and she wiggles in closer, tucking herself right against me, not leaving a wisp of air between us. And there's solace in holding each other. Comfort in whispered words and gentle touches.

I'm giving her that and she's letting me. And for now, that's enough.

"I know we still have a lot to talk about, Lainey, and we will. After we get through this, we'll finish that conversation. But right now, I just want to hold you. Okay?"

A moment passes, and then Lainey rests her hand on my stomach and nods against my chest. I press my lips to the top of her head, and keep her safe and warm in the circle of my arms.

"Try and sleep, baby. I'll be right here when you wake up."

CHAPTER
Sixteen

Lainey

They send me home from the hospital two days later on super-duper strict bed rest—that's my term, not the doctor's. It basically means I'm allowed to get up to pee and go to the OBGYN. But that's it. No long walks around the lake for me, no walking—period. Not for ten weeks.

And I'm okay with that—I would stand on my head for the next ten weeks if it means our baby will be okay. That first night in the hospital, while Dean was asleep, I wrapped my arms around my stomach and talked softly to the baby. I told him or her how much I loved them, how much their daddy and I wanted them, and I asked them to try and stay inside for just a little bit longer.

My parents brought Jason to visit me the next day, and I heard the relief in his voice when he was able to see that the contractions had stopped and I was okay. My sisters visited that afternoon too and it was bustling and busy and distracting.

But now that I'm home, it's all really hitting me. What the next ten weeks are actually going to be like. And so I lay on my back, propped up on pillows on the mattress in the unfinished master suite, with my phone in my hand, and no makeup on my face—crying—as I record a live video.

"Good news and bad news, Lifers. We're home. The contractions have stopped and the watermelon and I are okay. But I'm on bed rest for the rest of the pregnancy. And I don't know what I'm going to do. I mean, the baby is good—and I know that's all that matters. And I feel so damn guilty for even worrying about anything else, but there's so much to do. I don't know how I'm going to take care of Jaybird, and the house is barely half-finished. I can't decorate from bed and I can't—"

Dean walks in the room, the muscles in his short-sleeved T-shirt straining under the weight of a giant duffel bag thrown over his back. He drops it on the floor with a plop.

"Hey."

"Hi," I sniff. "I'm doing a live video."

I turn the camera Dean's way. He waves.

"Hey, Lifers." Then he looks at me. "You need anything? Tea, something to eat?"

"No, I'm good."

"Okay."

Then he turns and walks back out the door.

I look into the camera. "When I have more details, I'll let you know. Worst case scenario is—"

Dean comes back into the room, this time with a stuffed black garbage bag—like a poor man's Santa Claus. He drops it beside the duffel without a word, and walks out again.

Seconds later, he's back—carrying two drums from a set that he puts in the corner.

I sit up straighter in bed. "Dean?"

"Yeah?"

"What are you doing?"

His tone is Captain Obvious—like I should already know. "I'm moving in."

"You're moving in?"

"Shit, yeah. The house is only half-finished and you can't decorate from bed. Then there's Jay—someone has to make sure he eats something besides Pop-Tarts and doesn't study too much. You're going to need rides to OB appointments, and you might need something in the middle of the night. So . . . I'm moving in."

He leans over me on the bed and plants a firm, hot kiss on my lips that will tolerate no arguments. Then he's striding out the door again—a drive-by kissing.

I stare into the camera, and I shrug.

"He's moving in."

And the Lifers flood my screen with hearts.

Dean

After I finish moving my stuff in, and Lainey is settled upstairs, I head into the kitchen to see how Jay's doing. When he came to visit Lainey in the hospital, he wouldn't even look at me. But he wasn't openly hostile and all nearby chairs stayed out of the windows. Today around the house, he's been civil but cold—trying his damnedest not to interact with me and pretend I don't exist.

He sits now on one of the kitchen stools, with a glass of juice on the counter and a book in his hand.

I open the conversation with food—teenagers are big on food.

"Are you hungry?"

"No."

"I was going to make my spaghetti sauce for dinner."

His eyes don't move from the pages of *The Crucible*.

"I'll make myself a sandwich."

I try the easy charm that's never let me down before.

"Come on, dude—you have to try my spaghetti sauce. It'll change your life."

Jason stands and pushes his stool in under the counter.

"No thanks. I'm good."

When he goes to leave the room, I call his name, putting a little more force behind it.

"Jason—wait up."

He stops and turns around, and even though his eyes are on my face, it's like I'm a ghost—like he's looking through me.

"Listen, Jay, I wanted to—"

"You need to be here," he cuts me off. "For Mom. She needs you here—I understand that. And the baby is half yours." He motions from his chest to mine. "But you and me? We're not friends."

Ouch.

I saw a Viking show on the history channel once. A guy got sliced open across the middle, his guts spilling out. That's how Jason's words feel to me.

Eviscerating.

And I can't even argue my case. Because he's a teenager

and he's pissed off, and he's been burned before, and even worse—he's watched his mom get burned. So even if I make him sit down and listen, he's not going to hear me.

The only thing that's going to convince Jay that I'm the man he used to think I was . . . is time. The proof is in the pudding—shit like that. Nothing else is going to move this stubborn needle. So, I let it go for now.

Because time will tell—and I'm going to make sure my time tells it loud and clear.

Lainey

T wo days later, when Dean goes back to work and Jason goes back to school, my parents come down early in the morning to be with me and help out where they can with the house projects. My dad is uncomfortable being recorded, but he knows it's part of my job, so he doesn't complain while he sands an old dresser that will go in the master bedroom, with the eye of my computer camera watching his every move. My mom hangs curtains in the dining room while I'm laid out on the couch, painting a tall ceramic vase that will be the table's centerpiece.

There's a knock at the front door, and I hear my mom's footsteps move to the window to see who it is.

"Lainey—there's a bus outside."

I clean my paintbrush in the cup of water and set it on the tray across my lap.

"A bus? What kind of bus?"

"From the looks of the crowd getting off it—it's some type of senior citizen class trip."

The knock comes at the door again, and my mother answers it.

A chorus of bustling voices reverberates from the foyer, and then Grams comes into the living room, with her squad behind her.

"Hi, Grams."

She shuffles over and pets my head. "Hello, honey. How are you and the little bumpkin?"

"We're okay. What . . ." The energetic group of seniors behind her ooh and aww as they take in what I've done with the house. "What are you all doing here?"

"I've called up the Gray Army."

"The Gray Army?"

I wonder what movie they showed at the senior center this week.

"We're here to help you finish decorating the house, for your show—Dean told me all about it. The bus will bring us here twice a week. Florence Reynolds over there was a seamstress for Broadway musicals. And old Dirk Despacio used to be a plumber."

A hunched bald man scoots up beside Grams. "I was a handyman in my day. You just tell me what needs fixin', and I'll get her done."

A smiling wrinkly-faced little woman moves forward next. "When I was a girl, I built planes in the factory during World War II."

Another man, this one with thick gray hair rubs his hands together. "I was a roofer—where's your ladder?"

Grams grins. "We're old, but we're not dead yet."

She gestures to an adorable gentleman in a tool belt and flannel shirt. "This is my boyfriend, the Widower Anderson."

The widower pulls the trigger on the drill in his hand. "I brought my power tools—drill, baby, drill."

Grams and the Gray Army aren't the only surprise visitors I get. After the senior bus leaves around 1pm—to take them to the early bird dinner special at Dinky's Diner—Debbie Christianson, Dean's old friend, stops by with her little girl.

Debbie is sweet and friendly and about my age. She does a great job of recording a video of her and my mom hanging a chandelier and helping my dad finish the dresser project. On her way out, she tells me she'll come by again on Monday for a few hours.

A little while after that, Angela Daniels, Garrett's sister-in-law who I met at the Christmas Bazaar comes over—with a huge tray of lasagna and spaghetti sauce and chicken cacciatore that she puts in the freezer for us to eat next week.

My mom makes coffee and the three of us sit in the living room.

"Thank you for the food, Angela," I tell her. "It's so sweet of you."

She waves her hand. "It's nothin'. You're Dean's girl, you're family now. And that's how it is around Lakeside—we take care of our own." She gazes at the swell of my stomach. "Can I touch it?"

"Oh, sure."

She moves closer and gives the bump a rub—sighing with a mixture of longing and relief. "Frigging kids, am I right?

Miracles that turn your hair gray. The worry starts now, and it never ends."

I'm settled in bed, editing a video that I'll post tomorrow when Dean and Jason get home, at about nine-thirty, from a Mathletes competition. Jason comes in to talk for a few minutes before giving me a hug and heading to bed. I know things between him and Dean are strained, but he's going with the flow and he's been on his best behavior—and he's doing it for me. So I won't worry. And for the thousandth time, I wonder what I did to be blessed with such a great kid.

I hear Dean lock up downstairs and he turns down the hallway lights before coming in the room.

Sex and orgasms and any below the waist action are off-limits while I'm on bed rest. We still haven't fully discussed the Kelly incident, and I know we have to—but I've made a conscious decision not to think about it right now.

Dean loosens the green tie around his neck as he walks in. The only thing more stunning than Dean Walker in a suit that shows off those broad shoulders, tapered waist, and perfect ass . . . is watching him take said suit off.

And I do—watch him. I set my laptop aside and stare unabashedly as he opens the line of buttons down his torso and peels the shirt off his arms, revealing tan, taut skin and ripped muscles, and lickable abs. Then the pants go—unzipped and stripped off with sure, confident moves, leaving Dean in snug black boxer briefs that don't leave anything to the imagination.

He hops onto the bed with a lion's grace, making me bounce beside him. Then he rests his head on one hand and runs the other up my arm, toying with a curl of my hair and teasing with his tone.

"How was your day, dear?"

Dean lays his big hand on my stomach, rubbing.

"Both of your days."

"Surprisingly eventful. We had lots of visitors."

The amused twinkle in his eye calls to me.

"No kidding?"

"But you already knew that."

"I did know that." He nods. "Did you make any progress?"

"Yeah—we finished bedroom number three, and the dining room is starting to come together—and I recorded enough footage for two videos that I'm editing now."

"Good." The corner of Dean's mouth hooks into the smile that I love. "The football team will be by tomorrow after school, so if you want any pieces moved from the den, that's the time to do it."

"The football team?"

He leans over and kisses my forehead, humming.

"Mm-hmm, and the Mathletes on the weekend. I have unlimited access to free child labor, so, I don't want you to worry. You can direct from this bed, or a chair, or a couch, and we'll get everything done."

"*We* will, huh?"

He looks into my eyes and brushes his fingertips across my cheek.

"Yeah. We're in this together. Haven't you figured that out yet?"

And everything inside me goes warm and liquid—melty and mushy. Tears spring into my eyes, and clog my throat.

Because I've never let myself depend on someone else—not really. It's always been too risky. Too scary. Too hard.

But Dean's making it easy. To count on him. Believe in him . . . in us.

"I think I'm starting to get that," I tell him softly. "It may take a little time."

He tugs me into his arms, across his chest, and the warm feel of his smooth skin surrounds me.

"If there's anything I can do to help out with that, let me know. Otherwise, I'll wait."

He tilts my chin up and slowly leans down, pressing his mouth against mine, tracing my lips with the tip of his tongue, making me tingle everywhere. And the taste of him—Dean tastes like hope and home.

"We're worth waiting for, Lainey."

CHAPTER
Seventeen

Dean

I've never lived with a woman before—I mean, not counting Grams. It's a surprisingly easy transition. And because it's Lainey, it's awesome. The intimacy of it, the little things like watching her brush her teeth, sliding into bed beside her, holding her against me through the night, seeing her sleepy-eyed sexy first thing in the morning—can't be described as anything less than really fucking awesome.

We talk, laugh, she lets me kiss her, touch her—and sometimes when she thinks I can't see, she gets this eager, hungry look in her pretty eyes, like she wants to rip my clothes off and screw me stupid.

And that works for me.

The downside is, she's worried about the baby, she's stressed about her show, she's grateful for the help everyone is giving but feels bad that she can't return the favor, and sometimes she gets this guarded look on her face and I know she still hasn't made up her mind on if she believes me about the "Kelly incident."

Jason definitely doesn't believe me. Our relationship is like a frozen lake—cold and at a standstill. The kid can hold an impressive grudge. But I'm hoping my actions, the things I do every day, will thaw things out between us and he'll see just how much him and his mom mean to me.

I was able to convince McCarthy to give Jay another shot at staying in my class. I used every ounce of charm and intelligence I have. I promised to accept full responsibility if Jason acted out in class again, I got sentimental and reminded her that she's known me since I was fourteen years old—and how I'm so much less of a dumbass now than I was then and I owe it all to her. Turns out, even Miss McCarthy isn't immune to flattery and desperation.

Sometimes it feels like the hard moments are a penance, atonement, for my past selfish, dickheaded deeds. And sometimes I'm glad for it, even when it sucks—because the very best things in life don't come easy. You have to want them, work for them. And if it means in the end I'll be better, stronger, more worthy of Jay and Lainey and our kid—then it'll be more than worth it.

The following week, the faculty throws me a baby shower in the teacher's lounge—also known as The Cave—at school. I've always been a guest at these work party things, never a guest of honor, and they went all out. I'm touched.

There are balloons and streamers and a massive pink and blue cake, because these fiends will do anything for a sugar fix.

And there are presents.

A daddy diaper bag, little Nerf drum sticks, a football chew toy, and about a hundred diapers—which according to everyone with children should get us through the first three days. Maybe.

Garrett and Callie give me a jogging stroller, so I can bring the baby when I go running around the lake.

Alison gives me a huge, gorgeously illustrated book of fairy tales.

"You might want to pre-read," she says. "Some of them are pretty dark."

Jerry gives me a bottle of double-malt scotch.

"For those nights when the baby won't let you sleep—a few glasses of that, you'll be out cold—and so will the baby, from the fumes."

Evan gives me two fluffy, furry stuffed animals—prairie voles—Velcroed together at the paws.

And Merkle—I don't know what the fuck Merkle gives me. It's this weird sling contraption with tubes and . . . nipples.

I hold it up. "Please tell me this is a sex toy."

"It's a male breastfeeding system. So you can bond with the baby through the joys of breastfeeding."

Garrett laughs so hard he almost falls out of his chair.

"Dude, I am begging you for pictures. *Please.*"

I give him the finger.

That's not happening. I'll do diaper duty all day long, I'll take night shifts, I'll sing to my kid and tap out every goddamn song I know on their diaper-covered ass.

But I'm not strapping on a pair of tits. That's my line in the sand.

The next day, I'm in The Cave, eating leftover cake for lunch.

"What's that?" Kelly points to the paper in front of me.

"I'm making a list of all the girls I've screwed over through the years."

"Like one of the steps in AA except you're not an alcoholic?" Mark asks.

"Exactly." I nod.

"Why?" Kelly asks.

"I've been thinking about . . . karma. I mean, what if I have a daughter? What if some little douchebag breaks her heart because I was a jerkoff back in the day? And, I just . . . I want to be a better man, you know? Do something tangible to show Lainey that I can be." I raise my voice and announce to the other teachers in the room, who were listening anyway, "So if anyone has any suggestions on how I can make up for doing these girls dirty—feel free to toss them out there."

"How about chocolates?" Peter Duval suggests.

I shake my head. "Pathetic."

"Belgian chocolates? Teddy Bears?" he adds.

"Still amateur."

Across the table, Merkle smiles smugly at me. "I always knew this day would come."

"All right, Wonder Woman—I'm asking. How do I make up for all those years that I messed with self-esteem and damaged trust? How do I apologize for something like that?"

She flicks me on the side of the head.

"You just say you're sorry. Say you're sorry and mean it. That's all any of those women will need from you. Tell them you were a selfish little shithead."

"I was." I nod.

"And you couldn't see past the end of your own dick."

"Jesus, it's like you're in my brain right now."

"I know men." She shrugs.

Jerry wiggles his eyebrows and nods. "She knows us well."

I move my finger between them. "I finally get you two now."

Then I go back to working on my list.

At the end of the third week of bedrest, Lainey hits a rough patch. The house is coming along and she seemed okay earlier today when she recorded me putting bookshelves together for the nursery.

But later, when I come out of the shower and slip on a pair of briefs and get into bed—she's quiet. Sad. Not like herself.

I bet she's sexually frustrated—I know I would be. Hell, I'm jerking off at least twice a day and I'm *still* sexually frustrated.

Beside some G-rated cuddling and kissing, things haven't been real physical between us. She's banned from any orgasm action, so while a guy can dream, I don't expect her to help me out in that department. That's why God gave me a hand. Two, actually, because he really wanted us to use them.

"Hey." I wiggle her leg. "How are you doing?"

Her voice is listless. "I'm fine."

"You wanna watch TV?"

"No."

"Wanna . . . play cards? I'm up for strip poker if you are."

"No, thanks." She sighs.

"You want me to play you a song?"

Lainey likes it when I play the drums for her, sing for her—the other night I sang and played the soft beat of "Wonderful Tonight" by Eric Clapton for her. The baby likes the drums too—the little guy or girl in there kicks and stretches when I play, and they get really crazy when I slam out a long, loud solo—so I suspect we may have a future metal-head on our hands here.

Lainey shakes her head, and pushes her hands into her hair, tugging.

"I want to get up, Dean. I can't stand this—I'm going crazy! I want to move, run, skip—God I miss skipping! Why didn't I skip more when I had the chance?"

And she looks so cute and miserable, a laugh rumbles in my chest, but I keep it locked down.

"I'm so tired of *laying* here, and I know that doesn't make sense. I'm just . . . so bored I could cry."

I could think of a few ways to keep her occupied. For hours and hours. But—nope—banned, banned, banned.

She needs a distraction. Something she's not expecting. Spontaneous.

A surprise.

Out of nowhere, I ask, "Why doesn't anyone play poker in the jungle?"

Lainey looks at me like I've lost my mind. "What?"

"You heard me—why doesn't anyone play poker in the jungle?"

"Why?"

"Too many cheetahs."

She looks deeply confused, but less dejected than she did a minute ago, so I push on.

"How did Darth Vader know what Luke got him for Christmas?"

"How?" Lainey asks hesitantly.

"He felt his presents."

Her pretty, pouty mouth twitches. We're getting warmer.

"What's the difference between a tire and 365 used condoms?" I ask.

A genuine smiles spreads across her lips. "What?"

"One's a Goodyear. The other's a *great* year."

And that gets a laugh out of her. That beautiful fucking laugh—definitely my favorite sound.

"Want more? I can do this all night. I can do lots of things all night."

She cuddles in close, resting her head on my chest, and, thankfully, it seems like the great skipping craving has passed.

"Okay."

"What do you call a herd of cows masturbating?"

"What?"

"Beef strokin' off."

Lainey groans, laughing, because that was pretty bad.

"Let me try one," she says.

I nod. "Go for it. Hit me."

"Why shouldn't you write with a broken pencil?"

"Why?"

"Because it's pointless."

I chuckle, running my fingers through the silken curls of her hair. And that's what we do, the rest of the night—crack each other up with terrible jokes. It's silly and stupid and by the time we turn off the lights to go to sleep, it's a night I'll remember for the rest of my life.

In the dark of the bedroom, Lainey's whispered voice finds me.

"Dean?"

"Yeah?"

"When is your door not actually a door?"

I'm almost afraid to ask.

"When?"

"When it's ajar."

CHAPTER
Eighteen

Lainey

After six weeks, I'm still not used to bed rest. I don't think it's something you're supposed to get used to.

I have become accustomed to how hard it is—that's not surprising anymore—the yearning to run and jump and dance is a constant hum, like background noise. That steady familiarity makes it seem like it's a little bit easier.

And then there's the joy—that helps too. Every day that I stayed pregnant was a day closer to my baby being born healthy and strong. And now I'm just four little weeks away from the finish line—there's a lot of joy in that.

The nursery is almost done. I sit on the floor, propped against pillows, recording Erin as she arranges things at my direction. Dean painted this room—the cream walls and chocolate-brown accents. He bolted the bookshelves to the wall and set up the rocking chair and changing table just where I wanted them. He's held off putting the crib together, so as not to jinx us. I'm not usually a superstitious person, but with our little guy or girl so eager to make an appearance, I figured staving off any bad luck where we could wouldn't hurt.

Erin hung a framed needle point that I stitched and some pretty black-and-white photos of the lake and the clouds on the wall. And I like that it's my sister putting these final touches on when I can't.

"Those go on the top shelf," I tell her.

She gazes down at two white sock-bunnies. "You really made these—from socks?"

"Yeah, it's easy. I'll text you the video."

She sets the furry friends on the shelf and then comes and sits beside me.

"So how are you feeling?"

"Like Jabba the Hut. No—like if Jabba the Hut and a whale had a baby—it would be me. That's how I feel."

Erin laughs. "You're a lot prettier than Jabba."

"Kind of a low bar, but thanks."

Our laughs die down and then, quietly, I tell her what's really been on my mind.

"I miss Dean."

"Miss him? You're living with him, Lainey."

"I know." I pick at the fibers of the dark beige throw rug. "But we haven't been . . ."

"Getting any? Giving any? Doing it?"

I chuckle and point to my stomach. "Doing it isn't an option for me. But no, I haven't been with Dean like that since the Kelly thing, and I miss it. I miss him."

It's a deep, yearning, painful need. I ache for him. To feel the way his muscles ripple beneath my touch, the way his fingers dig into my flesh because it feels so good and he just can't help himself, the way he goes hot and hard in my hand, the way he groans my name.

"I believe him, Erin. Even if he wasn't doing all the things he's been doing the last few weeks—I would still believe him. Because I trust him. I've trusted him with everything since the moment I met him. It just is. And I'm done being worried about if that makes me stupid."

"You could never be stupid." Erin plays with my hair. "Trust yourself to trust him. And then tell him, and put the guy out of his misery."

Once Erin goes home, I'm on the couch in the living room with Jason. He's watching TV and I'm planning tomorrow's projects. I look over at him and I can't not smile, because he's growing up so good—strong and handsome and smart. And the move here to Lakeside and everything that's come after has been wonderful for him—for both of us.

And that's when I know we need to have a conversation.

"Can I talk to you a second?"

He pauses the television. "Sure. What's up?"

I look at my son, and I give it to him straight—like the adult he almost is.

"I love Dean, Jaybird. I'm in love with him."

Jason glances down at his hands and for the first time in his life, I can't tell what he's thinking. I'm not sure if he even knows. The anger that was so prominent all those weeks ago has faded. And now what seems to remain is a cool, cautious, distrust.

I cover Jason's hand with mine, and his eyes rise back to

my face.

"There's so much about Dean to love. He's smart and funny and talented—and he's good, and real, and he cares about us, Jay. You have to see that—he's doing everything he can to show us, to take care of us . . . all of us. And I think you love him too, and that's why it hurt so much when it seemed like he'd cheated. But I don't think he did. I believe him, Jay—I believe that it happened like he said it did. And I think if you take a step back and let go of some of that hurt and really look at everything, you'll believe it too."

I squeeze his hand. "I'm not going to tell you what to do. You have every right to feel what you feel and think what you think. But I don't want you to go through life afraid to trust yourself or someone else. Afraid to take a chance. I don't want you to talk yourself out of taking the risk of letting yourself love someone, and of letting them love you." My voice goes soft and a little choked. "Because love, Jay, real love—the kind of love that slams into you and holds on even when you don't expect it—it's so worth it. It's worth everything."

Before he can say anything, the front doorbell rings. Jason goes to answer the door and a few moments later comes back with the last person I thought I'd ever see—it's Kelly Simmons.

Surprise, surprise.

I'd looked up her picture on the school website, but she's even prettier in person—perfect shape, flawless skin.

"Hi." She tucks a blond hair behind her ear and clears her throat. "I'll make this quick. I don't do nice. It's not who I am. When I was younger, nice never got me anywhere, and now my students don't need nice. They need someone who's going to push them and fight for them, so that's what I do."

Her eyes move between me and Jason and her voice is firm and distinct as she says, "Nothing happened between me and Dean, you need to know that. I kissed him when he wasn't expecting it . . . and then he turned me down flat. I'm not telling you this to be nice, I'm telling you because it's true."

Kelly folds her arms. "He's a good friend and a good guy. Every woman in this town has suspected for a long time that if Dean Walker ever really fell for someone, he would be so much better than good—he'd be incredible at it. And he's fallen for you—for both of you. If you can't see that, you're idiots. And you don't deserve him."

She takes a deep breath, blowing it out as she shrugs. "That's it—that's all I came to say. I'm out."

And with that, Kelly Simmons turns around and walks out the door.

It's almost ten when Dean gets back from Grams's. He stopped over to have dinner with her, do some maintenance around the house, make sure she can read all the bills clear enough to pay them.

"How was your night?" he asks, walking into the bathroom to brush his teeth, wearing navy boxer briefs that make my mouth water, because he looks so hot, and big and already semi-hard—and tonight's the night I do something about it.

When he emerges a minute later, I rise up on my knees and move toward the edge of the bed. I feel ungainly and awkward but the heat that spikes in Dean's eyes and the hunger that tightens his jaw makes me think I must look pretty damn seductive.

I can feel how much he wants me. I always could. And just like every time before—Dean wants me a hell of a lot.

I rest my arms on his shoulders and look into his ocean-blue eyes.

"Kelly Simmons stopped by the house today. She told me and Jason that she kissed you and you turned her down." I run my fingers through the silky hair at the nape of his neck. "But I'd already decided that I believed you, before she came. I was going to tell you when you got home. It's important to me that you know I believed you. Do you?"

He breathes out a sigh and tugs me closer. "Yeah, I do, Lainey."

"And I've missed you."

Dean runs his hands along my arms, up my neck, through my hair—just touching me.

"I've missed you too. So goddamn much."

He holds my face and kisses my lips and it's like my entire body goes slack with the relief of being close to him again. The stroke of his tongue makes my hips swivel and my muscles clench. And though there's nothing to be done about it on my end—I'm going to take care of him. I want to show him—with my hands, my mouth, my tongue—how much I want him, how much he means to me.

I trail kisses along his collar bone and down his chest. I lick the water droplets from his skin and moan at the taste of him.

I maneuver my body so I'm on all fours and trace Dean's abs with the tip of my tongue. His hand slides through my hair, occasionally clenching like he just can't help himself and that shaky control turns me on even more.

Dean's cock is a hard, thick outline beneath the navy cotton of his briefs. I mouth him over the thin fabric, letting him feel the heat of my mouth and the stroke of my tongue.

His head lolls back on his neck as I slip the boxers down his hips. His voice sounds strangled, like he may have swallowed his tongue.

And swallowing is my job.

"Lainey . . ."

"I want this, Dean. I want to touch you—taste you—I want it so much." I look up at him, meeting his eyes. "Do you want me to?"

His hand fists in my hair again, tugging harsher.

"Christ, yes."

And I smile—right before I pump him in my hand, and lick around the smooth, hot head of his dick. I don't tease him—he's waited long enough. I take the hard shaft between my lips and slide on the way down—until he's balls-deep in my mouth.

And it's so good. He tastes so fucking good—I moan around him. I withdraw slowly, stroking the underside of his shaft, then push back down until I feel his thickness nudge the back of my throat. Then I do it again and again—faster, wetter—sucking hard.

And it's not just for Dean—this is for both of us. Because he makes me so happy and I love making him feel good.

My hands grasp his hips and I urge him forward and back—giving him permission to pump into my mouth.

"Jesus fuck."

His breaths are gasping and his voice is a growl. He holds my shoulders and thrusts in quick, shallow strokes.

"Lainey," he groans. "Coming…"

And then he does—hot and thick in my mouth—and it is

glorious. I swallow him down and a simmer of naughty satisfaction races through me when Dean collapses, face-first, like
dead weight on the bed beside me.

I pepper kisses all over his back, his arms—then I lean
over and sink my teeth into his fabulous, firm ass.

He rolls over, laughing, and reaching up to nip at my
neck.

"I'm keeping track—and you can bet your bitable ass I'm
going to pay you back orgasm for orgasm and bite for bite, just
as soon as the doctor gives us the okay."

He shifts up to the pillows and tucks me in against him.

"Is that a promise?" I ask, going in for another kiss.

He smiles against my lips.

"Baby, it's a guarantee."

Dean

The morning after Lainey tells me she believes me about
what went down with Kelly, that we can put it behind
us—and then gave me the blow job of a lifetime—I wake
up with this new, different sense of confidence settled in my
chest. It's invigorating and peaceful at the same time. The
closest I can come to describing it is when you're just steps
from the end-zone, inches from the finish line—when the peak
of the mountain is right there in your sight.

And you know—*you know*—you're going to make it.
That everything is going to be all right. Better than all right.
That life is about to get real joyous, real quick and chock-

fucking-full of amazing.

Just around the time I'm thinking the day can't get much better, it does. While I'm in the nursery, putting the crib together. And Jason walks in the room, looking at me in a way he hasn't looked at me in weeks—like I'm not an asshole, not an enemy. His hazel eyes, the same shade as his Mom's, are soft and open and a little hesitant.

"Hey." He lifts his chin, hands shoved in his pockets.

"Hey." I greet him back from the floor, with a wrench in my hand.

"What's going on?" Jay asks.

"Nothing. What's going on with you?"

He shrugs. "Nothing much."

He points at the pieces of cream, wooden crib sprawled across the floor. "Do you, um, want some help with that? We could do it together . . . if you want."

My throat squeezes and the backs of my eyes go hot. Because it's a simple question—but it means so much more than what the words say. We're guys—we don't need to talk and analyze every detail and emotion. Shit happened, and it sucked, but now Jason wants to move on. Let it go. He wants us to be friends again.

"I, ah . . ." I clear my throat. "I'd love that, Jay."

"Cool."

He sits down next to me and reads over the instruction manual. After a few minutes of tightening bolts, Jason says, "So, I was thinking about asking Quinn to junior prom. Do you think it's too early?"

"It's never too early to lock down a date for prom."

Jay nods thoughtfully.

"Are you asking her as a friend or more than a friend?" I

ask, though I'm pretty sure I already know the answer.

"The latter," Jay confirms. "But I'm not sure if I should tell her that part. I don't want to lose her as a friend, you know?"

It feels every bit as cool as I imagined talking to Jason like this. Passing on my vast knowledge and skills to such a worthy pupil.

"Would you not want to be friends with her anymore if she's not into you?" I ask.

"No—I'd still want to be Quinn's friend."

I stand and line up the last side of the crib as Jason holds the other piece.

"Quinn doesn't seem like the type to ditch you because you have feelings for her," I point out. "Even if she doesn't return them."

Jason's forehead crinkles as he takes this in. "No, she wouldn't do that."

I tighten the last bolt, and put my hand on Jay's shoulder.

"Then go for it. Be bold." I wink. "Girls dig bravery."

Jason smiles, happy and sure, and that mixture of contentment and exhilaration slams into me again, even stronger than before. And I know without a doubt, we're going to be okay.

CHAPTER
Nineteen

Lainey

Spring comes early to Lakeside. I film and post videos on spring cleaning tricks and Dean carries me outside, where I sit in my overalls, in the dirt of the flower beds, and with him and Jaybird plant tulips and hyacinths, daffodils and peonies that are bursting with color all around the house. The cherry blossom trees bloom and scatter the backyard in a shower of soft pink petals every time the wind blows. Grams and the Gray Army refinish the dock—making for some hilarious videos that the Lifers absolutely love. Dean and Garrett build a brick firepit off the back patio—working shirtless—which the Lifers love even more. By the end of March, I have double the subscribers to *Life with Lainey* than I did when I first signed the contracts with Facebook.

It's a magical time for me and Dean and Jason—for our family. A peaceful, beautiful time.

At the thirty-eight week mark in my pregnancy, I have an

appointment with my OBGYN, and—blessed be—she takes me off bed rest! Off all restrictions. It feels like Christmas and my birthday and the 4th of July all rolled into one. Not that I plan on doing anything too wild and crazy—because I'm gigantic—but just knowing I'll be able to stand and walk, dance and yes, skip again is more exciting than I can describe.

There's also another fantastic benefit . . . one that Dean and I put to immediate use the minute we walk into the kitchen and see a note from Jason that he'll be out for the rest of the day with Quinn.

I look up into Dean's turbulent, hungry eyes—and I know he sees the same need in mine—because great, and insatiable minds think alike.

He takes the note from my hands, balls it up and throws it over his shoulder.

And then we're kissing—hot and hard, wild and wet. I moan into his mouth as he sweeps me into his arms and carries me up to the bedroom. I suck on his tongue and tug on his hair. My muscles clench and my clothes feel rough on my heated skin—because I want them off and I want him inside me. In the bedroom, Dean plants me on my feet without taking his mouth from mine, and strips my leggings down my legs. I yank his shirt off and lick and nibble the taut, warm skin of his gorgeous chest.

Dean cups my cheek in his palm and breathes out hard.

"Lainey, are you sure you're okay with this? You want this?"

"Why are you asking?" I ask. "Because I'm a thousand weeks pregnant?"

Dean presses a kiss to my temple. "Yeah. I don't want you to be uncomfortable."

"No, I'm good." I nod. "Unless . . ." I look down at the belly-button-popping, immensely round stomach wedged between us. "Unless you don't want to?"

A raspy scoff scrapes up Dean's throat—like I just said something ridiculous.

Gently, slowly and deliberately, he skims my cotton maternity dress up over my head, then he unclasps my bra and peels it down my arms. And then he takes his time looking at me—dragging those ocean-blue eyes across my bare body with the same simmering intensity as the first night we met.

I twist my fingers together. "I know I'm—"

"Beautiful," he whispers, with raw, reverent, sincerity. "You're really fucking beautiful."

And I don't just hear the words—I feel them, under my skin and in my heart.

A smile tugs at my lips as Dean steps in close and takes my mouth in a kiss that makes my head light and my world spin. I slide my hand down his stomach, unbuttoning his jeans, so I can touch him, stroking him where he's so thick and hard.

Then he picks me up in those strong arms and carries me to the bed.

What started off as fevered, desperate, wild sex ended up being intense, slow, deep lovemaking. Dean refused to let go until he gave me my third orgasm—he said he still has dozens to give until we're even—and then with a long groan into my hair and his fingers clasping my thigh, he went over the edge with me.

Now we're laying entwined and boneless in the bed. And I love this—the feel of his chest under my cheek, his arms around me, every inch of him so warm and solid. This spot, in Dean's arms is my most happy place.

My eyes wander around the almost finished master suite—at the texture painted deep blue walls and the romantic faux-fur throw rug over the cherrywood floors, the one of a kind, hand-finished furniture.

And I sigh long and low.

Dean's hand, that was combing through my hair, pauses.

"That's not a happy sigh."

I lift my head, resting my chin on his chest, and smile.

"You know my sighs?"

"I have them all mentally categorized. You have a happy sigh, a frustrated sigh, a horny sigh—incidentally that one's my favorite—and a sad sigh. That last one was a saddy. What's up with that?"

I draw little circles on his chest with my finger.

"I called the bank yesterday to check on the reappraised value of the house . . ."

Technically, the bank still owns this house—the Miller Street house. Facebook only leased it for the year, at a low rate, with the agreement that they would cover the cost of all the repairs and upgrades that were done during the filming of *Life with Lainey*. And in the end, the bank would have a more valuable property than they started with.

And oh boy, do they ever.

"And?" Dean asks.

"And it's ludicrously out of my budget."

A sympathetic hum rumbles through Dean's chest. His fingers slide lazily up and down my spine.

"Well, you always planned to find another place at the end of your contract."

He and I have talked about it—how we'll find a place in town together, or Jay and the baby and I will move in to Grams's house until we do.

"I know. It's just that every project I finish is bittersweet now." I sigh again—and the melancholy weighs down my words. "I love this place so much. Not just because I've put my heart and soul into decorating it, or how half the town has helped us finish it—it's all the memories we've made here. It's so much more than a house now . . . it's our home. Yours and mine and Jason's."

Dean sweeps his fingers tenderly across my cheek.

"We'll make more memories, Lainey—good ones, happy ones . . ." he wiggles his eyebrows ". . . dirty ones."

That pulls a laugh out of me—and I press a kiss to the center of his palm. "I know. I just . . . I can't imagine any other place feeling like home the way this one does."

The next afternoon, Callie Daniels goes into labor, and by that night she and Garrett welcome their newest addition—a sweet baby girl they name Charlotte. A few days later, when they're home from the hospital and settled, we stop by to visit. Little Will bouncily shows off his baby sister like she's the best new toy he's ever gotten, and he kisses her cheek whenever she's in reach.

Dean told me when Will was first born, he was too nervous to hold someone so tiny—but this time around, he needs the practice. So Garrett talks him through the various holding techniques before passing Charlotte to his best friend.

"There's the shoulder hold which allows for burping and

GETTING *Played* | **261**

ass-patting, you just have to be sure the baby can breathe and their head doesn't flop around. The two-arm cradle is always a safe bet—just make sure to support the neck. Then there's the one-handed hold, with the baby tucked against your side, her body along your forearm and her head in your hand."

Dean smiles confidently, as Charlotte sleeps soundly in the one-handed hold. "It's just like holding a football."

Garrett nods. "Yep, exactly."

I finish the last decorating project in the house—the den—the second week in April. Which turns out to be perfect timing, because that night I wake up with the urgent need to pee. I'm four days from my due date—this is not an unusual thing.

The house is dark and still and the clock on the night table says two in the morning. After I take care of business and wash my hands—a surging, building kind of pressure suddenly expands in my lower abdomen, making me hunch over and hold my stomach.

The pressure dissipates as quickly as it came . . . right after my water breaks all over the bathroom floor.

"Huh." I look down at the wet floor, reaching for a towel. And then I look at my stomach. "Okay, kiddo. Message received."

And I open the door.

"Dean!"

A few seconds later, he appears in the doorway, squinting in the bright light and yawning, his thick blond hair sticking up in several directions.

"What's up?"

Then he spots the sopping wet towel between my feet and the water still on the bathroom floor.

"Holy shit. Is that because of this afternoon? Did we pop something loose in there?"

"No." I rub my tightening belly. "My water broke. It's time."

And he's suddenly wide-awake.

"It's time . . . wow . . . okay . . . it's time." Dean grabs a dry towel and wipes up the rest of the floor. Then he guides me back to the bedroom, sits me down on the cushioned corner chair, and helps me change into a dry pair of sweatpants and a t-shirt. He jerks his thumb over his shoulder. "I'm going to wake up Jay. Then I'll call Grams. Tell her we're on the way over."

Jason's old enough to stay here alone—I know—but I'll feel better knowing he's with someone, instead of waking up by himself to a note that we've gone to the hospital to deliver his sibling.

And since I grew a whole new human in the last few months—that's a call I get to make.

"Okay."

Dean takes two steps toward his phone on the nightstand, but then he stops and turns back around. He leans over and presses his lips slowly and softly against mine.

And then the corner of his mouth hooks up into my favorite smile—warming me all over. "We're going to have a baby today, Lainey."

"Yeah, we really are." I laugh. "Are you freaking out?"

He takes a second to think it over.

"Nope, I'm good. You?"

I search my feelings—there's a thrum of excitement, a

pinch of trepidation because labor doesn't tickle . . . and an engulfing sense of centeredness, of being protected and cared for . . . and loved. Because Dean is with me, and he's going to be with me every step of the way.

"I'm good too."

He takes my hand in his, squeezing.

"Let's do this."

I was in labor for twenty-eight hours with Jason, but once again, this baby is determined to be different. The labor moves quickly and the contractions come in brutal, breath-stealing waves, with the reprieve time in between becoming shorter and shorter.

"Motherfucker . . . that hurts," I groan after a particularly intense jab that makes me wonder—for the hundredth time—why the hell I opted for a natural childbirth.

Temporary insanity. It's the only explanation.

Dean rubs my back and breathes with me through each contraction. He feeds me ice chips and pats my forehead with a damp cloth. When I need to walk, he stays right behind me in case I need catching, and when I feel the urge to bend my knees and stretch my arms—it's him I hold on to—clasping my hands behind his neck and hanging off him like he's my personal, hot, monkey bar.

"Music," I pant during a contraction. "Dean, I need my music."

He steps away only long enough to tap the buttons on his phone, and the eclectic playlist we created together of "songs to have a baby to" fills the room. Some are relaxing and mellow, others romantic and emotional, some are just my favorite, and still others are upbeat and rock and roll, and Eye-of-the-Tiger-empowering.

When it's time to push, I opt for the bed, chin down and legs up, my hands hooked behind my knees—grunting and panting—with my doula on one side, my OB down below ready to catch, and Dean half on the bed with me, holding me up as pain claws through me. His whispered words keep me calm and focused and his arms, his scent, make me feel safe and invincible.

At the end of another contraction, I collapse against Dean, gasping for breath. He brushes my hair back from my face and I beg him without asking for a thing.

"I'm so tired, Dean. I've never been this tired."

"One more push, Lainey," my OB says cheerfully. "Just one more. You can do it."

And I fucking hate her. She can take her *just one more* and shove it up her ass.

"Dean . . ." I whimper.

I hear the song "Almost Paradise" playing from his phone as Dean presses his forehead against my temple, whispering, "You're doing so good, Lainey. You're almost there, you're so close."

I shake my head, because I don't know if I can do this.

He kisses my damp cheek, and his warm, rough voice brushes my ear. "I'm right here with you, we'll do it together. I love you. Lainey. I love you so much."

The beautiful surprise of his words and the joy they bring, gives me the last lift I need to keep going. To nod my head for him and let him hold me up.

So when those tendrils of pressure start again in my lower

back, weaving their way around, squeezing and squeezing and tightening until it feels like I'll tear in two—I hold tight to Dean's hand and lean against him and breathe deep.

And then I push with everything I have . . . one more time. And that's how it happens, that's when our beautiful baby comes into the world.

Dean

When I walk out to the waiting room there are more people than I expect, considering it's still a few minutes before 7 am. Grams is here and Jason. Lainey's parents and all four of her sisters, two brothers-in-law and one nephew. I didn't grow up with a big family, but I guess I should get used to it—because that's what I've got now.

I tell Lainey's Mom and Dad, "She's good—Lainey and the baby are both healthy."

Grams shuffles over and gives me a big hug. "I'm so happy for you, Deany."

I kiss her cheek. "Thanks, Grams."

And then it's Jason I walk up to—because he's the one I want to tell first. I put my hand on his shoulder.

"You want to meet your little sister?"

His smile builds until it reaches all the way to his eyes.

"It's a girl?"

"It's a girl." I nod.

He peers closer at my face. "Dude, were you crying?"

"Holy shit—so much crying. Wait until you see her—

she's so cute—you'll cry too."

Jay laughs loud and easy—then he comes in for an elated, back-pounding hug.

"What's her name?" Judith asks.

"Ava." And I laugh for no fucking reason at all. "Ava Burrows Walker."

After Ava gets passed around from family member to family member, like an adorable hot potato, everyone eventually heads home, and that night at the hospital it's just me and Lainey and the baby in our room. When Lainey is done nursing, I carry Ava over to the bassinet and change her diaper. Now that she's warm and dry and her belly is full, her dark round eyes inch closed and her tiny, adorable mouth opens in a wide, precious yawn.

I hold her close against my bare chest, skin to skin, because all the books say it's comforting for babies. Then I rock her and tap her diapered ass gently, singing the same song I'm drumming against her diaper—"Africa" by Toto.

Lainey's awake in the bed and I feel her eyes on me, watching me hold our daughter. *Our daughter.* How wild is that?

"I love you too, you know," she says softly.

Her gaze is shiny and so damn sweet—brimming with emotion, and filled with our future.

"I mean, how can I not love a hot shirtless guy singing the best song ever recorded to a newborn?" She gives a little laugh, then she goes on. "I've loved you for a while, Dean. You were right—I was scared. But I'm good now."

I slip onto the bed, holding Ava in the crook of one arm and wrapping the other around Lainey, tugging her close. That surging feeling of contentment and joy comes back again, tightening in my chest, and I'm pretty sure this is as good as it gets. That everything I didn't know I always wanted, is right here in this moment, in my arms.

I kiss Lainey long and sweet—because she's beautiful and perfect and all fucking mine.

"I love you, Lainey. I think it started that first night. When I woke up and realized I'd let you get away and I was . . . wrecked. Then when I found you again—and that feeling, the love, it was still there—and it grew every day." I kiss her again, promising. "It's going to keep growing, Lainey."

"Yeah." Her pink, pretty lips slide into a smile and she rests her head on my shoulder. Together we gaze down at the miracle we made and we plan the life we'll make from this day on.

EPILOGUE

Lainey

June

I walk through the lake house on Miller Street—our house—recording footage on my phone for a goodbye video I'll put together later on. The Lifers probably would've enjoyed a live post, but I opted out because there would've been an excellent chance I'd be a blubbery mess by the time it was done.

Every room in this house has its moments—its memories. Jason's room, is where I told him about the baby for the first time and the attic is where he and his friends bonded over deghosting the house. Dean and I have made love in the master bedroom more times than I can count—and that's also where he told me we were in this together. I walk through the beautiful nursery, the room that only family helped put together and the first place Ava slept when we brought her home.

I touch the striped navy-and-white walls in one of the spare bedrooms and remember Dean's wicked voice and sexy suggestions. I walk through the room Grams slept in on Christmas, and where she's stayed a few nights since when she's come over to help us with the baby.

Down in the living room, I run my hand along the fireplace mantel and close my eyes and remember fresh-baked cookies and the feel of cuddling with Dean under a blanket while a snowstorm raged outside. There have been so many kisses in the kitchen, so much laughter that as I stand beside the marble-topped center island, the echo of it rings in my ears.

I walk to the sliding glass doors that lead to the backyard, and press my hand against the pane. My eyes dart between the beautiful princess-cut engagement ring on my finger, and out to the patio where last month, Dean dropped down to one knee and popped the question—in the warm glow of the firepit and the view of the lake.

And that's the one that does it—that makes my throat clog and my vision blur with tears. Because I'm going to miss this house so much, every room and lamp and curtain . . . and every memory we made here.

Strong arms wrap around me from behind, pulling me back against his solid chest, pressing his face into my neck, kissing the skin there.

"Time to go, Lainey."

Facebook offered to renew my contract for *Life with Lainey* and I accepted. Now that the house is done, we'll be branching out—decorating rooms in other people's houses—and my first project in the fall is Callie's Mom, Mrs. Carpenter's kitchen. But for the summer, we're taking *Life with Lainey* on the road, and I'm doing a six-week series of videos on the best places—bars, beaches, family spots—along the Jersey shore, as Ava and I go on tour with Dean's band, Amber Sound. It's going to be an adventure, but Ava's a mellow baby, easygoing, and she loves music—Dean's drums in particular—so I think we'll survive.

Jason didn't want to leave his friends to come on tour, plus he got a job at the Bagel Shop for the summer, and is taking a math class at the local college to challenge himself. So for the weeks when Dean, Ava and I will be down the shore, Jason's going to live with Grams. Though she says having the house to herself since Dean moved in with me has done wonders for her social life—she's excited to have Jay staying with her and Lucy for a bit.

Dean turns me around to face him and presses a firm, hot, kiss to my lips that's meant to distract me—and it does the job.

"Don't be sad." He brushes the back of his hand along my cheek. "It's going to be all good, I promise. But come on—we've got to go. We're going to be late."

Dean takes my hand and tugs me toward the door. Because while we still have a week before we leave with the band and we don't have to clear out of the Miller Street house just yet—he's found a house that he wants me to look at. A place he thinks will be a perfect home for us, where we'll be able to stay forever.

Dean lifts Ava from the travel crib and talks to her in a way that makes my bones go gooey.

"Right, Ava-baby? Tell Mommy—don't be sad."

He hands her off to me, and I cuddle her close—smiling as I kiss her cheek and smell her soft skin and touch the baby-silk of her blond hair. She's got her daddy's eyes—cerulean with flecks of gold and beautiful.

We walk out to the car where Jay is already waiting. I buckle Ava into the car seat where she'll be asleep in five minutes—a car ride is like chloroform to her. Jay climbs into the back beside her and I slide into the front passenger seat.

Behind the wheel, Dean gives me one of his dirty-boy, player smirks—and then pulls a satin scarf out of his pocket, shaking it out with the hands that I love.

I roll my eyes. "Are you serious?"

"Absolutely. It's a surprise. You love surprises—and this is going to be a good one, because you're going to love this place. Humor me."

I let him tie it over my eyes, and then his breath is brushing my ear as he whispers, "You look hot tied up in a scarf. We should use it again tonight."

"Jesus, I'm right here," Jason groans. "I can hear you."

There's a flinch in Dean's voice. "Sorry, dude."

The car starts and I feel us drive off. Dean holds my hand and my stomach swirls—because this is another new beginning. After about ten minutes, the feel of the car changes from smooth road to rocky gravel, and we come to a stop. Dean turns the car off.

"I'll come around and get you," Dean tells me. "Don't take off the scarf."

A few seconds later, he guides me out of the car . . . and then sweeps me off my feet, carrying me. I hold tight around his neck, laughing.

We move up a few steps, maybe two, and he sets me down.

"Ready, Lainey?"

I take a deep breath and nod.

"I'm ready."

Then he unties the scarf and slips it off. I open my eyes and look around at butter-yellow siding, a big oak door, a wraparound porch and a calm, stunning lake, teaming with geese in the back. We're back in front of the Miller Street house.

And I'm completely confused.

Dean kisses me, soft and sweet, like he thinks I know what's happening.

"Welcome home, baby."

I look up into his eyes. "I don't . . . understand."

His mouth hooks into that cocky smile that stole my heart from the start.

"I bought it."

"You . . . bought it? The house—you bought *this* house?"

He nods. "I bought this house."

Curls of burgeoning excitement swirl like smoke in my stomach.

Oh, my God!

"Can you afford it?"

Dean snorts. "Of course I can. I've been living with my grandmother for the last twenty frigging years—what do you think I've been doing with my money? Investing it. We're all good."

His eyes drift over my face and his voice goes low. "I want to live here with you, Lainey. I want to love you and fuck you and laugh with you . . . and build a life with you. You and me and Jay and Ava and any kids that may come along after— and I want to do it right here, in *this* house."

I cover my mouth with my hand. And I bounce up and down. "Oh, my God!"

I call over to Jason who's standing outside the car with Ava in his arms.

"Did you know about this?"

"Yep, totally knew," he calls back, grinning. Then he makes a silly face at Ava. "That's right, isn't it? We totally knew." He taps Ava's palm with his own. "Baby high-five."

Dean wraps his arm around my waist, tugging me close.

"What do you say?"

And I'm crying again—big, wet, the happiest moment of my life, kind of tears.

I jump into Dean's arms—wrapping my hands across his shoulders and my legs around his waist. I press my forehead to his and tell him fervently. "I say, I love you, Dean. And I'd be perfectly content loving you and building a life with you anywhere . . . but I'm so, *so* happy it gets to be here."

Then I press my lips to his and kiss him with everything I've got.

And that's the story, years later, that Dean and I tell our kids about. The story of how we found it—how neither of us were looking for it—but it was a surprise that we found together just the same. Our forever home, our forever family, our forever love.

The End

ABOUT THE
Author

New York Times and *USA Today* bestselling author, Emma Chase, writes contemporary romance filled with heat, heart and laugh-out-loud humor. Her stories are known for their clever banter, sexy, swoon-worthy moments, and hilariously authentic male POV's.

Emma lives in New Jersey with her amazing husband, two awesome children, and two adorable but badly behaved dogs. She has a long-standing love/hate relationship with caffeine.

Follow me online:

Twitter: @EmmaChse
Facebook: @AuthorEmmaChase
Instagram: @AuthorEmmaChase
Website: EmmaChase.net

Follow me on Bookbub to get new release alerts
& find out when a title goes on sale!

BookBub: bookbub.com/authors/emma-chase

Also by Emma Chase

THE GETTING SOME SERIES
Getting Schooled
Getting Played

THE ROYALLY SERIES
Royally Screwed
Royally Matched
Royally Endowed
Royally Raised
Royally Yours

Royally Series Collection

THE LEGAL BRIEFS SERIES
Overruled
Sustained
Appealed
Sidebarred

THE TANGLED SERIES
Tangled
Twisted
Tamed
Tied
Holy Frigging Matrimony
It's a Wonderful Tangled Christmas Carol

Coming next from Emma Chase,

DIRTY CHARMER

a sexy new standalone romance!

Coming soon in ebook, print and audiobook.

To receive updates and details on this new release,
sign up for Emma's newsletter:

http://authoremmachase.com/newsletter/

PROLOGUE

Tommy

When I was a boy, there was a spindly old woman who lived down by the docks. Some said she was a witch. Others claimed she'd had "the sight" since she was a girl. Still others believed she had simply been around long enough to know things. Despite the whispers, and fire and brimstone warnings from the local priest, all the new young mums would make their way over to her rickety shack with their newborns in tow.

To have their futures told.

The story goes she took one look at me and said to my mum, "Drown this one in the river, Maggie."

She wasn't a particularly nice woman.

"He'll be handsome as the devil and twice as charming," she'd said. "But he'll be wild, stubborn and foolhardy—and he'll break your poor dear heart because he won't be livin' long."

My mother never went back to see the old woman after

that. *Absolute rubbish,* she'd say. Because if anyone is stubborn, it's my mum—and as far as she was concerned, her darling boy was going to live forever.

The kick of it is . . . I'm beginning to think that old woman may've been onto something. Because. . . well . . . there's a good chance I might dead.

I don't feel dead, though I'm not entirely sure what dead is supposed to feel like.

I remember the fire at the Horny Goat Pub. The charring walls, the smoke, thick as black wool, scratching at my eyes and stuffing up my lungs. There's no smoke now, only the sharp scent of disinfectant, a crisp, cool, softness beneath my head and a bottomless darkness—like outer space if the stars blinked out.

I was looking for Ellie in the pub—I remember that too. Because little Ellie Hammond is the sister of our Duchess Olivia, wife of Prince Nicholas. Because it was my shift, and it was my job to guard her, to keep her safe. Because my duty to the crown is one of the few things in this world I take seriously and even if I didn't, my best mate Logan—he's sick in love with Ellie though he won't let himself admit it.

And Ellie's a good lass. She brightens a room the way a jewel takes in sunlight and throws out rainbows over anyone close by. Lo deserves a light like that in his life.

Are you there God? It's me, Tommy.

I know we haven't spoken since my last confession . . . when the blond with the perfect arse was kneeling in the pew ahead of me. I had to say three Hail Mary's and she had to say three Hail Mary's, and before we knew it, we were breaking all sorts of Commandments and a few deadly sins at her flat for the rest of the afternoon.

But I'm hoping you'll look past all that, Lord, because I have a favor to ask.
Please ... let Ellie have made it out alive, even if I didn't.
Logan needs her. They need each other.
That's all for now—perhaps I'll be seeing you soon.
Cheers. Nanu-nanu. Amen.
As I sign off with the Almighty, a rush of air dusts over my skin, shifting and moving—like an incoming answer to my prayer. That stinging sanitized smell dissipates and is replaced by something infinitely sweeter.
Apples.
A whole orchard of round, red, ripened apples suddenly surrounds me. I breathe in deeper, hungry for more of the delicious scent.
"God, look at him," a voice sighs from my left. "Tell me you wouldn't boff his brains out if you had the chance."
The tone that responds is smooth, refined and distinctly feminine.
"Inappropriate, Henrietta."
"Yeah, yeah, I know . . . but still. I would ride him like a shiny new bicycle from here to Scotland and back again."
The silky voice groans, "Etta . . ."
"I bet he knows how to ring a girl's bell too. He's got that look about him. *Ding-ding.*"
I like Henrietta. She seems like my type of girl. Or angel or demon, depending on what the hell is actually going on. It's probably time I find out.
The polished tone takes a turn toward authoritative. "Hush now, I have to record his vitals for Doctor Milkerson."
It's the kind of voice I wouldn't mind taking orders from—the best kind—*lower Tommy, more Tommy, harder*

Tommy. The imaginings cause a pleasant, stirring sensation in my groin and apparently, even if I'm dead, my cock is still in full working order.

That's comforting.

"Speaking of Milkerson, have you noticed the way he looks at you? I bet he'd give his cutting hand to take a peek at *your* vitals. Maybe you'd have a clue about that if you ever bothered coming out for drinks with us after shift."

"I don't have time for drinks. There's too much to do— too much to learn."

"Oh, for Saint Arnulf's sake, Abby," Henrietta gripes. "Why do you have to be so stuffy all the time?"

"Saint Arnulf?" she asks.

"He's the patron saint of beer, everyone knows that. Heathen."

"All right, that's it—out. You're distracting me," Abby returns crisply. "If you're not going to focus, you need to go."

Henrietta's voice retreats, "You know what does wonders for focus? Letting your hair down once in a while—and your knickers!"

The air around me rustles again, before settling back into a quiet stillness. Then, slowly, the scent of apples returns. But it's even better now. More intense. Closer.

A gentle little sigh floats just beside my ear and the satiny, lilting voice goes low—as sweet and soft as the stroke of petal blossom along my skin.

"I'd never tell Etta this, but she wasn't even a little bit wrong. You are a beautiful man, aren't you?"

And I have to know. I have to see.

I hadn't realized my eyes were closed, until I'm able to drag them open. The light is bright, blinding at first—I squint against the glowing white halo that frames her.

"Mr. Sullivan? You're awake."

She has the face of an angel—high cheekbones, luminous skin, and wide, round, dark green eyes. But her mouth is full and lush, and her hair shines like a golden fire, a mass of deep red, honey and chestnut hues.

There's just something about a redhead. A passion, a spirit, a strength, that sets them apart. That makes them unforgettable. Irresistible.

She's too tempting to be angelic.

But still I ask, "Is this heaven?"

If it is, my littlest sister Fiona, who's been contemplating becoming a nun, would be thrilled to know it smells like apples.

"No, you're not in heaven."

I shrug. "I always figured the other spot would be more my scene anyway."

Her rosy lips curve into a smile, and that's blinding too.

"You're not there either."

I shake my head to clear the fog and hoist myself up, coming fully awake. And I look around. It's a hospital room— white walls, sterile chairs, wires connected to a bleeping machine behind me. I touch my chest, my arms to make sure they're still there. I wiggle my toes beneath the sheet because while my cock is definitely at the top of the list, it's good to know the rest of me still works too.

"I'm alive?"

She's still close, still smiling.

"Very much so."

Relief floods through me, making my chest feel near to bursting. And without another thought or a second's hesitation,

I lean forward and crush my lips against this sinfully stunning girl's mouth.

It's an impulse—a reflex—like that photograph of the American sailor and nurse at the end of WWII. Because when you almost died but didn't, all you want to do is feel alive. And I've never felt more alive than I do in this moment, kissing this lovely lass.

I sweep my mouth across hers, sucking gently, luring her to follow. She's stiff at first, surprised, but she doesn't struggle or pull away. And then after a moment, something glorious happens—her muscles yield and her lips go soft and pliant beneath my own. She melts against me, molds our upper bodies together with a breathy, needy moan. My hands delve into the satin of her hair, holding on, tugging her closer, feeling the swell of her breasts tight against my chest. Her hands grasp for my shoulders, digging in, as our heads move and angle together. And our kiss turns hotter. Wetter.

I stroke the tip of my tongue across the seam of her lips, teasing them apart. When they do, I sink right inside the tight, warm cavern. And the taste of her, *Christ*, she tastes like fruit in the Garden of Eden, succulent and forbidden. The desire to suck and lick at more of her, all of her, pumps through me—to see if the rest is every bit as sweet as her mouth.

I lean back, dragging her with me, over me—fucking those pretty, delicate lips roughly with my tongue—and I groan deep and long when her tongue brushes against mine, mouth-fucking me right back.

It's good—so bloody good—I may not have been dead before, but this kiss just might kill me. My pulse pounds in my ears and the machine is fairly screeching behind me with my wild, racing heart.

I think it's the machine that does it, that breaks the spell. Because as soon as the sound penetrates my own awareness, the woman in my arms tears her mouth away and freezes above me, a look akin to horror sweeping across her face.

Breathing harshly, she scrambles away, off the bed, like it's swarming with red ants and I'm their king.

"That . . . you . . . that . . ." her tits rise and fall beneath the buttons of her dark blue blouse with each quick, panting breath. It's lovely. "That was completely inappropriate!"

"It really was," I nod, pushing a hand through my dark hair. "Want to do it again?"

Her eyes flair, gaping.

"Absolutely not. Never again."

I click my tongue. "Careful. Never's a very long time, pet."

A dainty line appears between her auburn brows as she frowns, lifting her perky nose, crossing her lithe arms—the very picture of prim and proper and posh. My cock twitches at the sight and something else awakens inside me. The primal part of a man that craves the challenge, the chase, and even more—the conquering.

"Come on now," I coax her, "it was a kiss. There's no reason to get all flustered just because you enjoyed it."

"I am not your *pet*, Mr. Sullivan. And I don't get *flustered*. And I certainly did not enjoy . . ." she wags her hand in my general direction—in a flustered sort of way, "*that*."

A grin tugs my lips. "I beg to differ. And your tongue's been in my mouth—I think it's all right to call me Tommy now."

Her eyes darken to a shade near to black with passion or fury—with feeling. And I know that Henrietta was wrong. Apple blossom isn't stuffy—she just hasn't met a man who knows how to bring out her reckless side.

Not until now—not until me.

She tugs on the lapel of her white coat, straightening her spine.

"I'm leaving."

"Funny. Typically the girls I kiss like to tell me when they're coming." I wink.

Her cheeks flush a deep, dusky pink, and I just bet those pretty petals between her legs flush the same shade when she's really hot for it.

Saying that out loud isn't one of my better choices.

Because right after I do, she slaps me. Hard and fast. With enough force to jerk my head to the side and leave my left cheek pulsing with the sting. It's impressive.

"Ow."

And it's not like I didn't deserve it.

But looking back now, that's really when I should've known.

In that perfect, indelible, moment as we stare at each other—my eyes lapping her up and her jade gaze swallowing me whole, as each shiny copper strand on her head calls to my hands to stroke and twist and tug.

As we take each other in. Just a few dozen inches apart—taking and taking each other, and already craving more.

I should've known it then.

That she was going to wreck me, and I would happily let her.

That I would ruin her, and she'd make me swear to never stop.

That this . . . one splendid kiss and a spectacular slap . . .

this was just our beginning.

CPSIA information can be obtained
at www.ICGtesting.com
Printed in the USA
LVHW041536241019
635237LV00002B/178/P